THE MEMORY HIT

Also by Carla Spradbery

The 100 Society

THE MEMORY HIT

CARLA SPRADBERY

Hodder
Children's
Books

A division of Hachette Children's Group

Typeset in Berkeley by Avon DataSet Ltd, Bidford-on-Avon, Warwickshire

Printed and bound in Great Britain by Clays Ltd, St Ives plc

MIX
Paper from
responsible sources
FSC® C104740

The paper and board used in this book are made from wood
from responsible sources.

Hodder Children's Books
An imprint of Hachette Children's Group
Part of Hodder & Stoughton
Carmelite House
50 Victoria Embankment
London EC4Y 0DZ

An Hachette UK Company
www.hachette.co.uk

For Sophy

The memory came in much the same way as a dream.

Barely detectable at first, it curled into existence like smoke, growing denser until there was nothing but the vision, as if it were all happening for the first time.

The man stood in front of the barbecue pit, clenching and unclenching his bloodied fist. Ice clinked against glass as he lifted a tumbler to his lips, the glow of the fire reflected in the cut crystal.

For a moment, the image was clouded by a stream of foggy breath. When it cleared, there was someone else in the picture. A boy, walking silently across the lawn to where the man still stood, watching the flames as they danced over the pit. There was something beautiful about the fire, a beauty that had since been impossible to recreate. But that was what Nostalgex did – it enhanced every image and every feeling. It made colours so bright, you could almost feel them in your bones.

Nostalgex. The ultimate memory hit.

The man turned and said something to the boy, something that was never clear enough to hear, no matter how many times the memory was revisited.

But that was OK. This memory wasn't a favourite because of what was said.

It was a favourite because of what the boy did next.

Without seeing that there was someone watching from behind the pagoda, the boy wiped a hand across his bloody mouth and said something in reply.

Then he lifted the gun, pulled the trigger and shot the man in the face.

JESS

The windscreen cracked under the weight of Jess Gordon's foot, the glass fracturing beneath the pointed heel of her stiletto.

'Tell me that didn't just happen,' she groaned. She pulled herself up on to the roof of the car and peered down at the web-like pattern that had etched its way across the windscreen. Freezing drizzle sparkled as it hit the glass, flickering orange under the light from the streetlamp above.

'OK,' Luke replied in a whisper as he glanced around them. 'That didn't just happen.'

'How did you get me into this?' Jess grabbed the PIZZA GO-GO sign that was bolted on to the top of the delivery car, and pulled herself closer to the plastic snowman that sat on the other side of the roof, secured to the pizza sign with a zip-tie. The snowman grinned as its head, grimy and blackened from the London traffic, turned slowly to face

3

her. For a moment, she stared it in the eye, trying to ignore the accusatory expression on its face. The neon light inside pulsed intermittently as it stared back.

'It's called truth or dare, Jess,' Luke whispered, his rubber Frankenstein's monster mask perched on his head like a hat. 'And you'd better hurry; he's going to figure out he's been set up in a minute.'

Jess looked up to see the pizza delivery guy at the house down the street. The front door was open, framing a man who was holding his hands up in denial. The delivery driver was waving a receipt and pointing at his bag, which Jess knew contained a large pepperoni. A piece of mistletoe hung above them, swaying in the breeze as they argued over the pizza.

'Sorry,' she muttered, half to the delivery driver and half to the snowman, as she plucked the plastic monstrosity from its zip-tie seatbelt and tossed it to Luke. She slid across the wet car roof and grimaced as the rain soaked through her tights and into the fabric of her black dress. 'This is ridiculous.'

Luke laughed and tucked the still-flashing snowman under one arm. 'You were the one who made a New Year's resolution to start living more dangerously.'

'Yeah, well, the new year hasn't officially started.'

She slid down to the pavement beside him.

Luke's face glistened from the rain as he smiled at her. 'I've never been more proud.' His rubber mask bobbed grotesquely on his head.

4

'I've never been more ashamed,' she replied, but her expression softened as he leaned in to kiss her. 'You taste like beer,' she muttered against his mouth and he pulled away, laughing.

'That's probably the closest you've ever come to drinking alcohol. What *would* your father say?'

'You think it's bad that I don't want to upset my dad?'

Luke kissed her again and she could feel him grinning against her lips. 'You don't need him any more. You've got me now.'

Jess twisted his shirt in her fingers. 'He'll always be my dad. Besides, I expect he'd have more to say about me kissing you in the middle of the street than about me drinking alcohol.'

'Then how about we give him something to really talk about?' Luke leaned towards her again, his lips curling in a smile just as the pizza guy began to shout.

'Hey! Hey, what are you doing? You put that back right now!'

Jess turned to see the pizza guy jogging towards them, his shouts interspersed by great puffs of air as he wheezed his way towards them. In his red cap and matching puffy jacket he looked like an angry bouncing tomato, but there was nothing funny about the expletives and the threats that were spilling from his mouth.

'Uh-oh.'

'Uh-oh is right.' Luke pulled his mask down to cover his face, grabbed Jess by the hand and ran. She trailed behind,

5

but her heels were high and the pavement uneven. Overhead, a solitary firework popped loudly, spraying green sparks into the dull night sky.

'Is it midnight?' Jess called, scanning the sky.

Luke checked his watch. 'Forty minutes to go,' he replied. 'Don't worry, we'll be back in time for Auld Lang Syne.' He pulled her round the corner and they ran together until they reached a house with a large wreath hanging on the front door. They skipped up the steps, the wreath swinging wildly as Luke burst through, dragging Jess behind him. With a final glance outside into the empty street, he slammed it closed and thrust the snowman into Jess's hands.

'You didn't?'

Jess looked up to see a girl staring at her from behind an emerald green mask perched above a button nose that held a stud in one nostril and a silver hoop in the other. The girl's long black-and-purple streaked hair tumbled around her shoulders as she shook her head disapprovingly.

'She absolutely did, Hannah,' Luke said, pulling the Frankenstein's monster mask from his head to reveal a crop of messy black hair and a huge grin. While he was handsome in a boy-next-door kind of way, it was his smile that really melted Jess.

Hannah lifted her mask to reveal a splash of freckles and eyes lined with thick black pencil, a look that Jess would never be able to pull off. She frowned, but her eyes, as green as the mask she wore, shone. 'I've been at uni for

6

less than six months and this is what happens?'

Jess shrugged and bit her lip, trying to stifle a laugh.

'You were supposed to tame my little brother,' Hannah said, flicking Luke's ear as he tried to duck out of the way. 'And you were doing such a fine job; applying to uni, getting straight As . . .'

'Hey,' Luke said with mock hurt in his eyes, 'don't act like I haven't always been a genius.' He placed an arm round Jess's shoulder. 'It just took me until now to realize what I wanted to do.'

'Uh-huh. And it just so happens that you want to be a doctor? Like Jess? At the same university that Jess is going to?' Typical Hannah. Always sceptical, always one to speak her mind.

Jess couldn't help but smile. 'You don't think it's romantic that he wants to come with me? My mum and dad got together when they were our age and didn't spend a day apart until she died.'

'Hey, it's your decision. As long as you make the right choice for yourselves.' She glanced at Jess, one eyebrow raised. 'Because you never know what's going to happen in the future, right?'

'I'll tell you what's going to happen.' Luke's voice was beginning to slur as the beers he'd downed through the night finally took hold. 'What's going to happen is that we're going to have the most awesome life together.' His arm tightened around Jess's shoulders. 'Isn't that right?'

Jess's smile widened. There was a reason why her

friends referred to them as Juke, as if they were one person. Jess never went anywhere without him, so why would it seem strange that he'd want to go to the same uni as her? It was true love, just like her parents.

'Right,' Hannah said. 'That all sounds great.' She pointed at the snowman tucked under Jess's arm. 'And I'm happy for you, I really am, but he wasn't supposed to corrupt you. And if he did, it certainly should have taken him longer than six months.'

'The best six months of her life.' He grinned at Jess. 'Come on,' he said, aiming a kick at his sister's shin and missing, 'let's go and find someone who appreciates us.'

He led her through the crowded hallway and Jess glanced back to see Hannah shaking her head as she pulled her mask back down.

'We're back,' Luke announced, 'and we have a new friend.'

A cheer erupted from the crowd gathered in the kitchen and Luke grabbed Jess's wrist, lifting it like a referee announcing the winner of a boxing match. 'She did it,' he called over the thumping bass music.

Jess half-heartedly lifted the flashing snowman into the air, waving it in reluctant triumph.

A tall girl in a white dress and matching butterfly mask ran towards Jess, shrieking with laughter and clapping her hands. 'You got it? Oh my god, I can't believe you actually did it.'

'Don't tell anyone,' Jess said, leaning in close to whisper

in her ear, 'but I'm going to take it back tomorrow. I don't think I can stand the guilt, Scarlett.'

Scarlett laughed and pulled off her mask. She was almost impossibly beautiful, with long blonde hair and huge blue eyes that gave her a permanent look of owlish surprise. 'Of course you can't. That's why we love you.'

Jess shook her head. 'You guys are going to get me arrested.'

'It wouldn't be the first time one of us got someone arrested on New Year's,' Luke said with a laugh.

A pang of guilt stabbed at Jess's chest and she glared at Luke. 'That's not funny.'

Scarlett looked from Luke to Jess as she chewed on her lower lip. 'Come on guys. That's all in the past.'

'I'd like to think it is,' Luke said, turning to Jess.

'Of course it's in the past.' A familiar sinking feeling stirred in Jess's stomach. 'You know I haven't spoken to him in months.'

'Hey,' Scarlett said, a little too loudly. 'We're here to party, right? No time to think about the past.' She threw her arms around Jess, then pulled back, her nose wrinkling in disgust. 'You're soaking.'

Jess pulled the wet fabric of her dress away from her body. 'Oh, really?' she said, smiling through her sarcasm. 'I hadn't noticed.'

Scarlett took the snowman and placed it on the kitchen table beside the discarded paper cups and empty beer bottles. She leaned in close to Jess, raising her voice over the music. 'You want to get cleaned up?'

'Yes please,' Jess called back. 'And have you got anything I can change into?'

'Please. Like we don't already share wardrobes.' Scarlett looked at Luke. 'You need something too?' she asked with a grin. 'I've got a slinky sequinned number that would look just *divine* on you.'

'Well,' Luke said, following behind, 'I've been told that sequins do make my eyes pop.'

Laughing, Scarlett grabbed Jess's hand and led her and Luke through the crowded hallway. All around them, masked partygoers danced, kissed and shouted to each other over the music. There were shrieks as a skinny guy in a Guy Fawkes mask streaked through the corridor, covering his modesty with nothing but a beer can, his shoulder hitting Jess's as he ran past.

'Hey,' Luke called, grabbing the masked guy's arm. 'Take it easy, mate.'

Guy Fawkes stared back for a moment before he was off again, whooping loudly as he ran through the open front door, this time almost colliding with someone in a white mask and black hooded top who was making their way up the front steps. Not the most inspired of outfits to wear to a masquerade, but Jess supposed it was better than a naked Guy Fawkes.

'And I thought this was going to be a small, sophisticated New Year's party,' Jess called over the music.

'We're seventeen,' Scarlett shouted back with a laugh.

'We've got the rest of our lives to be sophisticated. And do you really think my parents are ever going to let me have another unsupervised party after tonight?'

Stepping over a questionable stain on the carpet, Jess nodded in agreement. 'Good luck clearing this all up before they're back tomorrow morning.'

'It'll be fine,' Scarlett called over the music. 'Stop worrying so much.' She untied the rope that had been secured to the bannisters at the beginning of the evening, to prevent the party from spreading up through the next three floors of her parents' townhouse.

They stepped over the legs of a girl who was slumped against the bottom of the staircase clutching a bottle of black vodka. A tiger mask was pulled down around her neck, her face covered with smudged makeup. She mumbled something as they passed, before shrieking with laughter as she lifted the near-empty bottle to her lips.

'Easy there,' Scarlett said, rolling her eyes at Jess. 'And remember, any puking is to happen in a bathroom, not on the carpet, OK?'

The girl muttered again before lurching to her feet and stumbling away.

Jess turned to Luke while Scarlett retied the rope. 'And people wonder why I don't drink.'

Scarlett led them upstairs to the first floor, but Jess didn't need directions to the bathroom. It was next to Scarlett's bedroom, a place Jess knew almost as well as her own home.

'I'll find you something to wear,' Scarlett said, disappearing into her bedroom. A fluffy white towel flew out on to the landing. 'And you can use this to get dry.'

Jess picked up the towel and turned to Luke, the bass music punching at the floorboards beneath her feet. 'Thanks,' she said quietly.

Luke frowned. 'What for?'

'For making me do something stupid.' Jess laughed as she ran the towel over her dripping hair. 'I know I'm a bit boring compared to some other girls, but—'

Luke cut her off. 'You're not boring,' he said, looking genuinely confused. He took her hand and kissed her palm. 'You're talented and smart and funny.' He sighed. 'Don't try to be more like me. I'm a mess.'

'You're not a mess.'

Luke rubbed at the knuckles of his right hand and Jess looked away, not wanting to see the scars there. Not wanting to remember the night the cuts first made their indelible mark. She leaned towards him instead, catching his scent as her lips met his. Soft, warm and familiar. Still enough to make her stomach drop and her heart beat in double-time.

'I've got this yellow one . . .' Scarlett barrelled out of her bedroom, but stopped when she saw the exchange between Luke and Jess. 'Oops, sorry.' She tucked a strand of long blonde hair behind her ear and looked away.

Luke wrinkled his nose. 'Not that one,' he said. 'Yellow's not her colour.'

Scarlett's eyes narrowed. 'OK,' she said slowly, before disappearing back into her bedroom.

'Since when is yellow not my colour?' Jess asked.

He cupped her chin. 'It doesn't do anything for your eyes.'

'This better?' Scarlett called from the doorway, holding a red dress up first to Jess, then to Luke, her eyebrow raised.

'It's fine.' Jess laughed and took the dress from Scarlett. 'I'll be out in a second, OK?' She slipped into the bathroom and the music dulled a little further as she closed the door and reached to lock it. Her fingers brushed thin air. The key that was usually in the lock was missing. She frowned for a moment; then figured that as the upstairs was out of bounds anyway, it didn't really matter.

The wet dress needed a little encouragement to come off, as it seemed to have shrunk in the rain. Jess tossed it on to the tiled floor where it landed with a wet splat, before peeling the tights from her legs. A rash of goosebumps had broken out across her dark skin and she quickly wrapped the towel around her body, shivering. She glanced in the mirror and groaned. Her mask was soggy and misshapen, the eye-hole on the left sagging and deformed. She pulled it from her face, but the elastic caught in the tight curls of her hair and she giggled, a hiccup of a laugh that could quite easily turn to tears of frustration if she let it.

'Scarlett,' she called, the mask dangling from her hair as she pulled the bathroom door open, 'I think I need . . .'

The landing was empty.

Luke's zip-up jacket hung on the bannister, dripping

13

water on to the carpet. But he and Scarlett were nowhere to be seen.

'Luke?' Jess stepped out on to the landing towards the stairs, but stopped when she noticed that Scarlett's door was closed. For a moment she paused, waiting for the obvious explanation she must be missing out on.

'Luke?' she called again, walking to Scarlett's door.

Downstairs, the music thumped, the vibrations of each beat tingling the soles of Jess's feet and the deeper bass tones whomping in her chest as though her heart itself were the source of the music.

She lifted her hand to knock, then paused. Voices were coming from inside the room. It was definitely Luke and Scarlett, but there was something in the way they were speaking to each other . . .

Arguing with each other.

Jess stepped back. Whatever they were arguing about, it wasn't her business, was it?

She bit her lip.

What would they have to argue about?

Trying to ignore the sick feeling that was gnawing at the pit of her stomach, Jess stepped back. But the gnawing continued, like something was alive inside her guts and needed to get out.

She leaned forwards again, placing her ear flat against the wooden door.

'—do you think is going to happen? Nothing good will come of telling her.'

'You don't think I know that? But I don't know what else to do, especially now it's got this far. She'll understand.'

'Understand?' Scarlett snapped. 'That we've been cheating? She'll never talk to either of us again, Luke. You know what she's like.'

Jess shot back from the door like it had given her an electric shock.

Downstairs, something smashed and a cheer rose up, the sound snaking up the stairs to where Jess stood with the towel still wrapped around her body, the mask hanging from her tangled hair.

She stepped back into the bathroom and picked up her dress, then slowly pulled it back on. It was still wet, but her skin felt hot, prickly, and the cool material was a welcome distraction.

Jess stepped over Scarlett's discarded dress and, barefooted, she left the bathroom. She wasn't going to wear it, not now. The gnawing had moved from the pit of her guts to her belly, filling her stomach with a burning nausea.

Inside the bedroom, the voices had lowered, but the tone told Jess that they were still arguing.

She reached for the handle, preparing to fling the door open, totally clueless as to what she was going to say or do.

Cheating.

The heat in her belly blossomed as she turned the handle, but the door didn't move.

It was locked.

A vice seemed to tighten around her chest and Jess stepped back from the door. She had to get out of there, get some air before something inside her exploded. Her heels lay overturned by the bathroom door, the straps trailing from them like dead snakes. Her feet burned and she couldn't bear the thought of wearing them again. She grabbed a pair of trainers that were lying outside Scarlett's room and pulled them on.

Jess turned and took Luke's jacket from the bannister. She hadn't brought a coat of her own, so his would have to do. It didn't matter what she looked like; the night was over for her now. She pulled the jacket tightly around her and paused, noting something bulging from each pocket.

With a shaking hand, Jess pulled out Luke's phone and stared at the screen. For a moment she considered putting it back, because looking would be a breach of trust. Then the conversation she'd overheard began replaying in her mind, as though her brain had somehow managed to tune into the world's worst radio station.

She had to check.

Without another thought, she found Luke's text messages. Sure enough, there was a message from Scarlett. Just one, sent earlier that day. But it was enough.

Hey, I need to see you. Can we meet up before the party?

Tears stung Jess's eyes, but she blinked them back. The next message was from someone called Leon. She didn't know anyone called Leon, had never heard Luke mention him.

16

You have until 6 tonight. Last chance. Whiteface wants his money.

There were other messages from unsaved numbers that Jess didn't recognize.

Want to make a deal. Call me.

Ten reds, got cash ready

you still dealing? i need a hit

Frowning, Jess placed her hand into the other pocket and her fingers touched something bulky, wrapped in plastic. She pulled it out and found herself looking at two bags of red pills. She looked back at the text messages.

Ten reds, got cash ready

For a moment there seemed to be nothing but silence and Jess realized the music had stopped. The floor-shaking bass had been replaced with shouting, a roar of voices that seemed to grow louder with every second.

Was it midnight already?

She didn't really care any more; she had to get out of there, get outside into the cool air where she could think properly.

She shoved the phone into one of Luke's pockets and the pills back into the other. One of the bags missed and fell to the floor, but she just stepped over it and hurried down the stairs, pushing past another partygoer and yanking the mask from her tangled hair. The carpet squelched beneath her feet and the stench of spilled alcohol filled her nostrils.

Downstairs was chaos.

The rope that Scarlett had re-tied at the bottom of the stairs was gone and the hallway either side of the staircase was crammed with people. Shouts and screams rose up from the throbbing crowd as glass shattered somewhere at the back of the house.

It was then that Jess noticed the smoke.

It curled out from the dining room, white tendrils snaking past the doorframe and up to the ceiling where it had already formed a dense blanket. She turned back, reaching out to grab at the bannister and get back upstairs to warn Luke and Scarlett, but she was swept into the crowd which moved as one towards the front door.

'Wait!' She fought against the current of bodies, trying desperately to work her way back towards the staircase. 'There are people upstairs!'

An elbow slammed into the side of her head and she winced, stumbling again with the crowd as they lurched onwards towards the front door.

'LUKE!' she shouted, her voice lost in the shouts and screams of the masked partygoers surrounding her. 'SCARLETT!'

'We need to get out,' a voice next to her was screaming, rising in urgency with each syllable. 'Stop pushing, we need to get out.'

Jess turned again to see that the white clouds had been replaced with thick black smoke, billowing in waves from the dining room and obscuring the figures at the rear of the house.

Obscuring the staircase.

Cries were replaced with sounds of choking; hacking coughs that made Jess's stomach twist. She tried to pull away, but it was useless. The riptide of people carried her from the house as the smoke gathered behind them.

Spilling out the front door, the crowd surged on to the pavement, still shouting and screaming. The screams from inside the house were the worst; people were trapped, blocked by the bottleneck of those attempting to squeeze out through the front door.

One girl had fallen on the front step, her hands laced tightly across her head as masked partygoers poured from the house, trampling over her.

Dimly aware of the howling sirens in the distance, Jess ran across the street and turned to look up to Scarlett's bedroom window. For a moment there was nothing, no movement. Then, between the shadows of the curtains, Jess saw the shape of two figures.

Her hands flew up to cover her mouth as the wailing sirens grew louder.

Luke and Scarlett were trapped.

COOPER

A knock came from the partly open door behind where Cooper sat on a beanbag chair, video controller tightly gripped in his hands. It was a familiar knock, the old *shave-and-a-haircut* routine.

Without looking away from the screen, Cooper let go of the controller with one hand and completed the knock, *two-bits*, by rapping twice against the wooden bed frame beside him.

'Coop?'

Sam Cooper paused the video game, looking up from the frozen avatar that was preparing to bury an axe in a zombie's rotting head. 'What's up?'

Jag leaned into the empty room and looked around. 'Seriously? You're planning on staying in here all night?'

'Pretty much.' Cooper turned back to the video game. A shriek rang out as the zombie on the screen exploded beneath the axe, the screen spattering with green and red chunks while metalcore blared from the speakers.

Jag slipped into the room, closing the door behind him. 'Coop, have you seen the girls downstairs?' He sat on the unmade bed and stared at Cooper before pulling the controller from his hands.

'Hey,' Cooper cried. 'I was playing.'

'It's a party,' Jag said, pausing the game. Silence fell for a moment, only to be filled almost immediately with the wail of nearby sirens. 'A time for getting with hot girls you'll never see again.'

Wrinkling his nose, Cooper lay back on the crumpled duvet. 'No thanks.'

'It's time for you to get out there again. It's been, what? Two years? I miss my wingman.'

'One year, Jag. It's been exactly a year. And your wingman? Since when have you ever needed help with the ladies?' Cooper smirked, ducking as Jag hurled a pillow at him.

'I don't need help.' Jag smoothed his eyebrows. 'You know they can't resist me.'

Cooper took in the messy hair, the vintage shirt and the tight jeans that only Jag Nowak could pull off. It annoyed him no end to admit it, but Jag was right; the girls flocked to him. A Bangladeshi mother and a Polish father had blessed him with a perfect mixture of DNA that had produced a chiselled jaw and olive skin, though Cooper knew most of the looks came from Jag's mother's side.

But it was his father's genes, the slightly eccentric outlook on life that could make just about everyone around him laugh, which gave him the edge that meant he never had any problems finding a date.

'So what do you need?'

'What do I need?' Jag jumped to his feet. 'It's New Year's Eve and I want to see midnight in with my best mate. Is that too much to ask?'

Cooper stared, a single eyebrow raised in silent question.

'Fine,' Jag said with a roll of his eyes. 'We're almost out of beer.'

'Seriously? You want me to do a beer run at –' he glanced at Jag's bedside clock – 'eleven-twenty on New Year's Eve? Even if I got served, which I won't because I don't have a fake ID, everywhere will be closed by now.'

Jag grinned, pointing theatrically at Cooper with both hands. 'Crash and Dash.'

'No way.' Cooper was up and halfway to the door. He was done with the 'Crash and Dash', a move he and Jag had come up with when they were younger, braver and far, far stupider. 'You know what happened last time. And I'm not even talking about getting arrested, Jag, I'm talking about almost getting my head kicked in. Funnily enough, people don't take kindly to having their parties crashed and their drinks stolen.'

'You were just unlucky,' Jag soothed. 'Besides, it's not like she-who-shall-not-be-named will be around to call the police this time.'

Cooper sighed, annoyed at himself for giving in. 'Fine. Crash and Dash. But,' he said, jabbing a finger at Jag's chest, 'this is it. Time to grow up and move on from this stuff, OK?'

'Whatever you want,' Jag said with a smile. 'It can be our New Year's resolution.'

'It has to be, Jag. I can't be doing this stuff any more. I promised Amy.'

Jag's eyes misted over. 'Amy,' he said slowly, a smile spreading across his face. He focussed on Cooper again, grinning. 'What's she doing tonight, anyway? I take it she didn't get an invitation to Scarlett's big party?'

Cooper shook his head. 'Jess'll be there. It's ridiculous, but Amy sees it as betraying me. She's gone to Mulbrook instead.'

'Mulbrook?' Jag wrinkled his nose. 'She'd rather hang out with a bunch of greasy uni students than be here with me?' He glanced at the mirror and brushed some imaginary dirt from his shoulder. 'No worries,' he said, 'she'll come to her senses soon enough.'

'You've got to stop that,' Cooper said. 'That's my sister you're talking about.'

'You make it sound like you wouldn't want me as a brother-in-law.' Jag followed Cooper out on to the landing. A number of doors led off into various bedrooms and bathrooms, all of which were locked. This wasn't the first party Jag had thrown in his parents' house and Cooper knew from past experience that keeping the mess localised

23

to a small area would reduce the chance of Jag being discovered and grounded. Again.

They walked together down stairs that were covered in a luxurious cream carpet. The same carpet that would currently be getting trashed on the ground floor. Cooper wasn't looking forward to the next day, having promised Jag he would help clear up before his shift began at the Fill 'n' Save. He was actually looking forward to working New Year's Day; it would be quiet and Big Phil had promised double pay.

Downstairs was dark, noisy and filled with too many people. The perfect type of party for a Crash and Dash; crowds of people who didn't know each other, who would never pay any attention to a stranger walking in through the front door.

'Who are all these people, anyway?' Cooper asked as he sifted through the pile of jackets that had been dumped beside the mahogany hall table. Framed pictures of Jag's family had been knocked over and the mahogany table top was covered in empty cups and bottles. 'And where's my backpack? I left it here earlier and now it's—' He turned to see Jag holding out his bag and smiled gratefully as he took it.

Jag shrugged. 'They're friends of mine.'

Pulling his backpack on, Cooper nodded at the group of girls huddled together by the kitchen door. 'Oh really? So who are they?'

Jag's eyes narrowed as he peered through the darkness.

'I'm not sure,' he said, patting Cooper on the shoulder with a wide smile. 'But I should probably go and check.' Without another word he was gone, pushing his way through the crowd to where the girls stood.

Outside was cold, but fresh. The tang of smoke lingered in the air, perhaps from a nearby bonfire.

Pockets of mist hung in front of Cooper's face as he unchained his bike from Jag's front gate, and he was grateful to be away from the thick heat and incessant noise of the party.

He hadn't always felt like this about parties. In fact, this time last year he had probably been worse than Jag, the one who would volunteer to do the Crash and Dash at every opportunity because he liked the way it made him feel. He liked the adrenaline, the fear of crashing a stranger's party and grabbing as many bottles of alcohol as he could fit into his bag before running from the house and jumping on to his trusty bike.

Not any more.

Not since he'd lost *her*.

But now was different. Now he had a job and a course at college that would finally allow him to make something of himself. To erase all the dirt that was associated with his family's name.

He tossed the chain into Jag's front garden and tightened the shoulder straps of his backpack, then jumped on to his bike.

There was something symbolic about this last Crash and

25

Dash, so close to midnight on New Year's Eve. By the time Big Ben chimed, he should be back at Jag's party. His last petty crime would have been committed and he would wake up in the morning to a clean slate. One that he planned to maintain, no matter what.

At the end of the road, he stopped for a moment and looked around, listening. He could hear the conflicting beats of music from various houses along the road, but could see no crowds spilling out on to the pavement through an open front door. These types of parties were essential for a Crash and Dash; he needed a full house with an easy exit and preferably a crowd to disappear into.

Part of the problem was the neighbourhood. Jag's parents had a Victorian terrace in an affluent part of Bow, one of the nicer, tree-lined streets that was filled with professionals. Solicitors, graphic designers, doctors like Jag's parents. Teachers. The kind of people who would probably notice a seventeen year old stealing the beers from their kitchen.

Cooper knew where he needed to go. He turned the bike and began racing back the way he came. The parked cars lining the streets either side of him passed in a blur as he pedalled faster and faster. Without braking, he swung the bike to the right, hopping up on to the pavement and through the gap between two houses. The alleyway was dark and narrow, leaving only a few centimetres either side of Cooper's handlebars, but he had cycled this path countless times and, even without the light from the street lamps to guide his way, he was easily able to negotiate the passage without coming into contact with the brick walls rising up beside him.

Cooper burst out from between the two houses into a small park. The sudden lack of restriction spurred him on to pedal faster; there was only a short distance to cover before he got to the old churchyard, then it was only another couple of roads before he reached his destination.

Mulbrook Road.

A row of much shabbier terraced houses, most of which were occupied by university students. If there was one place guaranteed to offer a wild party with plenty of alcohol, it was Mulbrook Road. Better yet, it would give him the perfect chance to check on Amy. He knew which house to find her in; she'd given in and told him the address after he'd hounded her for it, but only on the understanding that he would leave her alone.

As if.

It wasn't like his twin sister had anyone else looking out for her and he knew that parties on Mulbrook were often drug-fuelled nightmares, so if he had a chance to make sure Amy was OK, he was damn well going to take it.

Cooper pulled up outside the churchyard and glanced at his watch. He had half an hour to check on Amy, crash a party, grab some beers and cycle back to Jag's. If he kept up his current speed, he'd be back in time for midnight.

There was a shorter route to Mullbrook, but that would mean cutting through Tavistock Square and he wanted to stay as far away from Scarlett's house as possible. The last thing he needed was to drive past the same house he'd partied in the previous year. And what he needed even less was to see *her*, with her new boyfriend. As happy as he had been when he was still with her.

The churchyard's iron railings had started to rust years earlier and the metal had twisted into a contorted skeleton that surrounded the collapsing church. Not that you could see much of the building any more. Weeds grew up almost as tall as some of the trees, twisting around the branches and choking the crumbling headstones beneath. Thick vines coiled in and around the building, like snakes attempting to squeeze the life out of a corpse with no life left to give.

Cooper jumped off his bike and lifted it over the railings. It was a pain to have to cut through the churchyard, but following the road would take at least another five minutes and time was not on his side.

He pulled himself up and jumped down into the overgrown mess. He yanked his bike from the grip of weeds that had managed to tangle themselves around the wheels. The remnants of a concrete pathway lay to his left and he moved towards it, lurching through the thick vines as though he were negotiating his way through a swamp.

The path was overgrown and fractured by the plants growing up through the concrete, but enough remained for him to be able to ride his bike to the other side of the grounds. Clouds had gathered overhead and a light drizzle had started to fall, closing the night a little tighter around him. He steadied his bike as he climbed on, then froze as something moved behind him.

Cooper turned. There was nothing but shadows, cast from the twisted tree branches and the crumbling remains of the church. To his right, something moved again. Cooper's heart drummed against his ribs in an unwelcome rhythm.

'Hello?' he called out, placing a foot on a pedal, ready to move.

There was no answer.

He started to cycle. It had probably just been a cat, or an urban fox. There were plenty of those around these days and, in all fairness, St Steven's churchyard was a pretty creepy place. It was no wonder he was a little freaked out.

A figure stepped out on to the path.

Cooper braked hard, his bike skidding out in an arc beneath him. He straddled the bike, his breath coming in quick bursts.

The figure stood motionless, slightly blurred behind the curtain of drizzle.

For a moment, Cooper stared. He swallowed, and it felt like he was trying to force a piece of cotton wool down his throat. The figure was dressed all in black, with a hood pulled up to cover a face that was looking right back at him.

Icy fingers of fear clutched at Cooper's belly. He wasn't

afraid of much, but he was afraid of this person. Something about the way they just seemed to be *waiting* for something.

Or someone.

Cooper glanced back over his shoulder.

There were two ways out. One was back the way he came, which would require jumping the fence again. The other, a gate whose rusty hinges had disintegrated, was blocked by the figure. Either way, he had to make a quick decision.

He never got the chance.

The first blow struck him just above his right ear. Pain exploded like white light as he blinked, shocked to find himself already on the ground, his legs tangled in the frame of his bike. His mouth filled with the taste of copper and he tried to spit, but the only thing to escape his lips was a weak groan.

When Cooper opened his eyes, he saw the world twisting around him as if he was looking through a kaleidoscope. A figure appeared above him, head tilting to the left like that of an inquisitive bird as it peered down to where he lay. The person said something, two words, but it was like they were talking in a foreign language and Cooper's brain just couldn't quite unravel the message.

The figure's hood slipped a little, revealing a face that Cooper was unable to focus on, the features blurred into a mess of nothingness. There, swinging casually by the stranger's side, what looked like a heavy glass bottle.

He reached up and swiped at the face, but everything

30

was moving and it was making him feel sick. Even his attacker's face was twisting, slipping towards him.

Cooper groaned again, squeezing his eyes closed as he tried to lift his head. But it was too heavy and it hurt too much and maybe if the ground would just stop spinning for a—

His jumbled thoughts were cut short as the second blow came down and everything went black.

JESS

Jess barely heard the fireworks.

Although they streaked the sky above her, lighting up in flashes of reds, blues and greens, she was unable to take her eyes away from the flames coming from Scarlett's house.

Fire spewed from the ground-floor windows, as plumes of thick smoke curled upwards, black against the whitewashed walls, while intermittent blue flashes from the fire engines pulsed in her field of vision.

In the back of her mind, she dimly acknowledged that it must be midnight.

The start of a new year.

'Jess?' A desperate voice came from behind and Jess turned to see Hannah pushing through the crowd towards her. 'Oh my god! You're OK!' She threw her arms around Jess, hugging her tightly.

Jess simply stared over her shoulder at the flames, her arms limp at her sides.

Why wasn't she freaking out? What was wrong with her?

'Where's Luke?' Hannah asked, moving back as she scanned the crowd. 'I can't find him.'

'He's still inside,' Jess replied, her voice sounding muffled, as though she were speaking underwater. 'With Scarlett.'

'What?'

'He's inside,' Jess repeated. She glanced at the crowd of people who, like her, had been in the burning house only minutes before. Many wore a wide-eyed expression similar to Hannah's, some with hands clasped over their mouths as they watched.

The firefighters moved quickly, silhouetted against the burning house as they dragged hosepipes, moved ladders and swarmed together in coordinated chaos.

All Jess could do was stare at the road beneath one of the fire engines. A puddle had appeared, growing rapidly as water dripped from the hoses.

She placed her hands into the pockets of Luke's jacket, her fingers brushing against the plastic bag of pills. When the sound of breaking glass shattered the night air, Jess turned back to the house, this time forcing herself to look up at the two sash windows on the first floor.

Jess couldn't see anyone inside, only the darkness and a steady stream of smoke that told her the fire had spread, despite the efforts of the firefighters she had watched run into the burning house.

To Jess's right, Hannah collapsed to her knees, hands over her mouth and the reflection of the sirens flashing in her tears as she watched everything unfold. Jess wanted to reach out, to take Hannah's hand, to tell her that it was going to be OK. But she couldn't move. Couldn't make the words form in her throat. She was just numb.

A voice rang out from the crowd. 'They've got someone!'

Jess looked up. Sure enough, a firefighter emerged from the front door, almost falling down the front steps as he held up a stumbling figure. Once they had reached the pavement, the figure collapsed to the ground and coughed violently.

Lurching to her feet, Hannah gasped as paramedics rushed towards the figure. 'Who is it?' she asked, turning to Jess and clutching at her arm. 'Did you see who it was?'

Jess shook her head. It was all she could do. She couldn't speak, couldn't move. Couldn't seem to *feel* anything.

There was more shouting as another firefighter appeared at the front door, carrying a smaller figure. An arm dangled loosely, lifelessly, bouncing in time as the fireman bounded down the steps.

'Scarlett,' Jess whispered.

The firefighter laid the girl on the pavement, beginning chest compressions as he shouted out to the paramedics for help.

'Is that Scarlett?' asked Hannah, her voice breaking.

'Oh god, is that Scarlett?' Her voice rose to a scream and she ran forwards, only to be met immediately by a police officer. 'Please,' she sobbed, 'that's my friend.' She turned her head to where the other figure lay and pushed forwards again, this time with more force. 'And that's my brother,' she shrieked, turning back to Jess. 'It's Luke,' she cried, 'they've got him. They've got Luke!'

The officer's hands tightened around Hannah's arms as he spoke to her in firm, reassuring tones.

Jess curled her toes, suddenly overwhelmed by the guilt of taking Scarlett's trainers. What if Scarlett had been looking for them? What if she and Luke *could* have got out, but had stopped to look for her shoes? The thought gnawed unpleasantly as she watched Hannah struggling with the officers, her emerald-green mask now lying in a puddle by Jess's feet.

Some of the crowd were still in their disguises; a boy with a clown mask, the blood-red smile betraying his shaking hands as he tried to comfort a female friend. A girl with a jewelled butterfly covering her face, her cream dress torn and blackened. And a single figure, standing away from the crowd in a black hooded top, wearing a featureless white mask; the kind you could buy at a craft shop to decorate yourself.

The same person who'd almost been knocked over by the naked Guy Fawkes.

'Jess?' A roar erupted from behind the crowd of police and paramedics. 'Jess? Where is she?' Luke's voice rose up again, verging on hysteria. Jess stepped towards him, her instinct carrying her forwards, before a flash, a memory of the night's events stopped her.

Then Luke appeared from within the crowd, pulling himself from the grip of a paramedic. He lurched into the road, stopping only when he made eye contact with Jess.

For a moment, everything slowed down.

Jess took in his torn shirt, blackened beyond recognition. The road between them glistened with water, the puddles reflecting the flashing blue lights, the fire, the fireworks popping and fizzing in the sky overhead.

'Jess?'

Jess said nothing, made no attempt to move towards him.

His eyes shifted to Jess's hand, still clutching the bag of pills. He stared for a moment and, when he finally looked at her again, his expression was one of horror.

This time, when the paramedic went to lead him away to a waiting ambulance, he didn't resist.

He didn't even look back.

And Jess felt nothing.

COOPER

Cooper was in trouble.

He drew a quick breath and reached up to touch his forehead. His fingers came away warm and sticky, but when he held his hand out in front of his face he was unable to see any blood.

In fact, he was unable to see anything.

He turned his head from side to side, sure that whatever was making his head feel like it was splitting in two must have also blinded him. He blinked again, this time catching sight of a dim red glow to his right.

Cooper took another breath, deeper and slower this time, as he tried to figure out what the hell had happened to him.

The last thing he could remember was being at Jag's party, playing that stupid zombie video game. He hadn't been drinking, so this wasn't the result of some alcohol-fuelled craziness, even though it felt like the worst hangover of his life. The world seemed to be spinning around him and it felt like he was moving, being carried at speed.

He was lying down. He tried to sit up, but only moved a short distance before his forehead collided with something above him. Cursing loudly, he fell back, reaching up again to clutch at his head. This time he felt a lump near his hairline, which he realized was the source of the steady trickle of blood oozing from his forehead.

He turned to his right once more, staring at the dim red glow for a few seconds before realizing it was the rear light of a car. Combined with the low throb of a running engine and the way the ground bumped and rolled beneath him, it could only mean one thing.

He was trapped inside the boot of a car.

And it was moving.

He squeezed his eyes closed, desperately searching for an explanation of how he had come to be here. Had Jag done something? Pulled some kind of prank? The throbbing pain in his head told him no. His friend had pulled some stuff in his time, but to go so far as to knock Cooper out and shove him in the back of a moving car? That wasn't Jag's style.

Which meant he was in *serious* trouble.

Cooper rolled on to his side and began to feel his way along the inside of the boot, hoping to come across some kind of catch that would open it from the inside. He didn't know who the car belonged to, or why the owner might have thrown him inside, but he was pretty sure he didn't want to hang around to find out.

The floor beneath him jolted again and Cooper was thrown to the opposite side of the boot before rolling back as the car swerved in a wide arc. Then everything went still and the engine fell silent.

A car door opened and slammed shut. A moment later came the sound of footsteps, though there was no urgency in the way the person walked. Whoever was outside was taking their time, like having a person trapped in their boot was the most natural thing in the world.

Then came a loud *blip-blip*, the sound of a car remote, and the boot flew open to reveal a clear, star-strewn sky.

Cooper didn't move. The heavy sound of crunching gravel told him there was someone close by, but at this point he wasn't going to make any sudden movements. His head throbbed and, if at all possible, he was going to try to avoid another crack to the skull.

Then, a silhouette appeared above him, framed by the moonlight. As Cooper's eyes grew accustomed to the darkness, he was able to make out some of the features of the person standing over him. When Cooper saw the shock of bleached hair that stood out from the figure's head, he groaned.

He knew exactly who this was, and he was in even deeper trouble than he'd originally thought.

His suspicions were confirmed when the figure smiled, revealing two gold front teeth that glittered in the moonlight.

Though he couldn't be any older than eighteen, Leon had obviously decided to continue the family tradition of gilded oral hardware. The last time Cooper had seen Leon, on another New Year's Eve four years ago, he'd been without any front teeth at all, so this was a marked improvement.

'Sam Cooper,' Leon said. His voice was husky yet gentle, a feature that in no way made Cooper feel any more relaxed. 'It's been a while. How's your dad?'

'You'd know as well as I would,' Cooper replied. He lay perfectly still, though he didn't take his eyes away from the person leaning over him. 'Considering he's been in jail for the last three years.'

'You don't speak to him any more?'

'I haven't spoken to Jimmy since he was arrested. Some of us don't really agree with what our fathers did.'

Leon laughed, though it almost sounded like the snarl of a dog preparing to fight. He moved closer to Cooper, his face falling into shadow. 'Who said I agreed with *anything* my father did?'

'So, have you seen Frank recently?' Cooper knew he was on thin ice, but he couldn't help himself. 'Has he even sent you a postcard from whatever tropical island he ditched you and my dad for? Because—'

'Keep talking,' Leon said, his voice low, dangerous. 'Because I don't really need much more of an excuse.' His hand shot forwards, grabbing a fistful of Cooper's shirt and yanking him up. He pushed his face close to Cooper's, so their noses were almost touching. 'Now, do you want to

40

tell me what you were doing on my patch?'

Leon's breath filled Cooper's lungs, a pungent mix of tobacco and chewing gum, but Cooper didn't pull away. Instead he shook his head. 'What? I don't . . .' He closed his eyes, disorientated by the sudden change in topic. 'I don't know what you're talking about.'

With his fist tightening around Cooper's shirt, Leon held up a bottle with his other hand. He swung it gently back and forth. 'How about now?'

Cooper winced, a flash of pain shooting to the cut on his forehead. He nodded. 'Yeah, that looks kind of familiar, now you mention it.' It wasn't the worst thing Leon had ever threatened him with, but this was different.

They weren't kids any more.

With a single tug, Leon yanked Cooper out of the car boot and on to the ground. The back of Cooper's head cracked against the concrete and stars burst before his eyes, reigniting the searing pain he had experienced when he had first regained consciousness in the boot of Leon's car. Leon straddled Cooper's chest before smashing the bottle hard against the ground next to his head.

Pieces of glass flew out in all directions and a quick, searing pain ripped through Cooper's cheek, followed by a gush of warmth that covered his face and neck. What had started as mild panic grew to abstract terror as he realized this was far more than just a little warning over setting foot on someone else's territory.

'Jesus Leon, you cut me! What the hell?'

41

Leon said nothing, only stared back at Cooper with the same empty eyes he'd always had. Just like his father.

'Look,' Cooper stuttered, unable to hide the waver in his voice. He'd been afraid of Leon in the past, sure. But that fear had stemmed from Leon's lack of control and common sense; he'd never really believed that Leon would harm him *intentionally*, despite the reputation he'd built for himself over the last couple of years. 'I don't know what this is about—'

Leon raised the broken bottle, the jagged edge sparkling in the moonlight. 'You know exactly what this is about,' he snarled, pushing the glass against Cooper's throat. 'And you're lucky I still consider you family, Sam, otherwise things would have ended very differently for you tonight.'

Barely even daring to breathe, Cooper squeezed his eyes closed, searching for the memory of how he had come to be here.

He had been at Jag's New Year's Eve party.

Jag had sent him out to go looking for beer.

But he never made it back. He never even made it into the unsuspecting stranger's kitchen, hence his empty backpack.

Come on, Cooper. Think.

'The churchyard,' he groaned. How could he have been so stupid? 'That's your dealing ground, right?'

Leon pushed the jagged glass a little harder against Cooper's larynx. 'The whole of London is my dealing ground,' he said, his husky voice dangerously low. 'Just like N is *my* drug.'

'N? I've never even heard . . .' Cooper's right ear had started to feel strangely blocked and, with a shudder, he realized it must be filled with his blood.

With the broken bottle still jammed tightly against Cooper's throat, Leon reached out to grab the backpack that had landed on the ground beside them. He dragged it up on to Cooper's chest before pulling out a small, clear plastic bag. Inside were a number of pills; small, round and red.

And Cooper knew exactly what they were, had seen them being dealt in the alleyway outside college. He'd also seen the zoned-out expressions of friends who had taken them at parties, the tell-tale smirk playing across their lips as they laughed at things no one else could see.

Nostalgex, the newest psychedelic drug on the market; a drug with a very high market value.

'What the . . .?' Cooper paused, desperately searching for how he had come to be here, trapped beneath the psycho son of a notorious drug dealer with a make-shift blade only a sneeze away from slicing through his jugular.

'*Mine*,' Leon spat, pushing the pills into Cooper's face.

'I swear, I have no idea how that got in my bag,' Cooper said. He turned his head carefully to one side. Given how angry Leon looked, he guessed now was a good time to start planning an escape route. To his left, a row of warehouses loomed up from the darkness and, with a sinking heart, Cooper realized where he was; the abandoned docklands, much further east than Cooper usually cared to travel.

'That's what they all say,' Leon retorted. '*Not my drugs, Leon*,' he said, his voice mocking. '*I swear, I've never seen them before.*' He pushed a little harder, the broken bottle digging a little further into Cooper's skin. 'You know how many times I've had to listen to that crap?'

Cooper closed his eyes. He'd never seen Leon like this. There was a good chance he was going to die here.

'OK,' Cooper said finally, his brain racing to find a way out. 'I'm sorry. I've obviously been very stupid.' He clawed at the ground either side of him, his fingers trailing over dirt and small stones, none of them large enough to do any damage.

Leon laughed, his eyes wild and his teeth glowing red as they reflected the rear lights of his car. He looked like a rabid animal, mid-attack.

There was a flash of memory as Cooper saw Leon, four years ago, in silhouette against a fire, his face illuminated in the same way, as he turned to look at Cooper. Leon's mouth had been red then too, but back then it had been from the blood that poured from where his two front teeth had been knocked out by his own father.

The pressure eased slightly from Cooper's neck. 'You're actually admitting it?'

Cooper dug his fingers into the ground, scooped up two handfuls of dirt and hurled them into Leon's face.

The broken bottle fell, clinking as it hit the concrete while Leon cried out, clawing at his eyes.

Cooper grabbed the lapel of Leon's jacket in his left

44

hand and swung hard with his right fist, his knuckles connecting with Leon's nose. It collapsed with a satisfying crunch as bone gave way beneath Cooper's knuckles and blood exploded from both nostrils. Leon howled and collapsed, clutching his hands to his face.

Cooper grabbed his backpack and staggered to his feet. The collar of his shirt felt hot and heavy, soaked with his own blood.

Then Leon was up, groping blindly as he lurched forwards, his face covered with dirt and blood as he swung his fists at the air in front of him. It would only be a matter of seconds before Leon was back in action, and Cooper suspected broken-nosed Leon would be even more dangerous than regular Leon.

Cooper spun left and right, unsure of which way to go. To his right, he was just able to make out the soft orange glow of a street lamp and he started to sprint in that direction, hoping it might lead him to a road or a way out of the docklands.

Within seconds there came the pounding of footsteps close behind, punctuated with the occasional expletive-filled death threat.

Cooper pumped his legs even harder, ignoring the pain that was beginning to take over every inch of his body. His backpack slammed rhythmically against his back and Cooper was thankful that he had been unsuccessful on his earlier alcohol run; a bag full of beers would have only slowed him down.

How *did* the drugs get in his bag? Perhaps someone had mistaken his backpack for their own at the party, or maybe he had put them there himself and, due to his obvious concussion, was yet to remember. He shook his head. He would never touch drugs, despite his otherwise generally lawless approach to life.

A guy had to have some standards, after all.

With loose gravel crunching beneath his feet, Cooper was unable to hear Leon chasing behind. He glanced over his shoulder and, sure enough, saw only the empty sprawl of concrete, save for Leon's car. In the distance the sky was illuminated with fireworks and, with a heavy heart, Cooper realized it was midnight.

He came to a stop at the corner of a deserted warehouse, his breath coming in quick bursts and misting in the freezing air. Placing his hands on his knees, he drew in deep breaths, waiting for his racing heart to slow as he tried to work out the best way to travel back into the city.

'Happy New Year, Cooper,' he muttered. As the fireworks continued to pop all around him, he felt sure there could be nobody else in London having a worse night than him.

When he stood up, ready to continue, a figure stepped out from the shadows.

There was just enough time to catch a glimpse of gold teeth before a fist filled Cooper's vision, returning him to the darkness he had only just woken from.

JESS

Time had become elastic.

Hours seemed to pass as she watched the paramedics work on Scarlett.

Time stood still when they grabbed the paddles she had only ever seen on TV.

Hours turned to years as they fired the paddles against Scarlett's chest and the screen beside her flashed in a set of confusing scribbles, which then returned to the terrifying straight green lines that had been there before.

She watched Hannah climb into the ambulance behind Luke, the doors slamming shut before it pulled away, sirens blaring.

Someone was shouting.

She turned back to where Scarlett lay on a stretcher, the monitors now turned away from Jess's view. They were running, pushing Scarlett towards another waiting

47

ambulance, while people followed either side, holding on to bags of liquid that were being fed into her veins.

It occurred to Jess, in some distant corner of her mind, that this might be the last time she ever saw her best friend. With that realization, time seemed to do another of its tricks and suddenly life was barrelling along at double time, the doors of the ambulance closing before Jess even had a chance to call out, to ask them to wait so she could say—

Say what, exactly?

Goodbye?

I love you?

I *forgive* you?

And within the blink of an eye, the ambulance was gone, the fire was out and the street was empty.

And Jess stood alone, staring at the charred, ruined remains of everything.

COOPER

A car horn blared as Cooper stepped out into the road, the driver swerving as he stumbled back, pulling his bike and its buckled wheel with him on to the pavement.

With a roar he lifted the bike and hurled it against the overflowing rubbish bin beside him. He blinked, wincing as he tried to open the swollen eye that had almost just got him run over. He hadn't realized quite how much the injury had impaired his vision and, after everything else that had gone wrong in the last few hours, it was the last straw.

It wasn't like it had even been worth going back for his bike. He had walked the five or so miles from the docklands back to the churchyard, limping from the bruised hip he had managed to acquire along with the rest of his injuries, only to find the twisted remains of his bike lying on the path beside the church.

It now lay in a mangled heap beside the bin, on top of a pile of relatively fresh vomit. He grimaced, then the grimace turned into a frown and he roared again, kicking at the bike. He missed and his foot collided with the bin, his toes crumpling heavily against the metal, making him howl again. A young couple walked past, crossing to the other side of the street without a word as they saw him hopping and cursing at the bin.

Cooper sank to the ground, clutching at his foot as he slouched back against the bin. He was probably sitting in something terrible, but who cared? It wasn't like things could get much worse. For a moment, tears stung his eyes, but he refused to give in to them. He exhaled a shaky breath, closed his one good eye and tried to work out just how he was going to get himself out of this mess. With a sigh, he removed his backpack and unzipped it. Though the sun was yet to rise, there was enough city light to let him see the contents. Ten plastic bags filled with small red pills; the same type of pills that Leon claimed Cooper had been carrying through the churchyard.

The deal was simple, Leon had explained. In exchange for the alleged crime of dealing Leon's drugs on Leon's patch, Cooper was to sell every single pill, all five hundred of the little red bastards that were now nestled in his backpack. Ten pounds per pill would rack up five grand for Leon, the price that would keep his face intact.

The *rest* of his face, Cooper thought, snorting with slightly manic laughter.

There had been more to the threat, of course, but Cooper couldn't think about the rest of it right now. If he thought about everything else Leon had threatened, Cooper would probably throw up himself, right next to the pile of vomit beneath his bike.

He zipped his backpack closed again, deciding that right now, he needed to sleep. Everything else could come after that. Besides, he had work in the morning and there was no way he was going to lose his job over one night's craziness. Energized by his decision, he rose to his feet and, deciding that the mangled bike was a lost cause, started walking. It would be another half an hour before he made it back to his flat, but it would take far longer if he tried to drag his wreck of a bike with him. His hands shook as he zipped his jacket up to his chin. The adrenaline that had got him this far was beginning to wear off and he was now cold and tired, desperate to get into his bed and sleep away the nightmare he had somehow been caught up in.

The sun began to rise over the city, flooding the grey skyline with a deep red hue and taking the vicious bite out of the cold wind.

By the time he returned to the block of flats he called home, streets which had been empty had begun to fill with cars and people passed by without even noticing Cooper and the blood that had dried on his face. He walked through the ever-full car park outside his block and started the long climb up the stairs to the fourth floor, breaking his cardinal rule of never touching the filthy handrail as he leaned heavily on it for support. The stairwell smelled as it always did; of stale cigarette smoke and urine, while the once whitewashed walls were covered in the same graffiti that had been there on the day Cooper and his sister had reluctantly moved in a few years earlier.

When Cooper finally reached the top, he paused to spit the coppery taste of blood from his mouth for what felt like the hundredth time, then reached into his jeans pocket for his key.

His pocket was empty.

Of course it was empty.

He pulled his backpack from his shoulders and rummaged through it, but he knew that the key was long lost.

'Perfect,' he muttered, his words somewhat slurred by the swelling to his face.

He pulled open the stairwell door, hoping that Amy had made it back from her New Year's Eve party and would be able to let him in, although his original plan had been to sneak in and get to bed before she noticed him or the injuries to his face. The time for explanations could come after he'd slept it off, when his head had cleared enough for him to come up with a story that wouldn't terrify her and send her into one of her manic spirals.

He stepped out on to the balcony that ran the length of the block of flats and groaned. Jag was sitting outside his front door, texting furiously. A thick scarf was wrapped almost entirely around his head and pockets of mist

52

clouded the air in front of him every time he exhaled.

There would be no sleep yet.

For a moment Cooper considered turning back to the stairwell, but he was cold, his head throbbed and his clothes were stiff with dried blood. He needed a hot shower and some paracetamol, and a very long sleep.

Jag didn't even look up from his phone. 'Coop, I'm not even telling you what you missed out on last night,' he said, grinning broadly. His phone pinged and he shook his head. 'Seriously, man. You've got to see some of these texts I've been getting. There was this one girl, Francesca . . .' He finally looked up at Cooper and his words hung in the air. 'What the—?' He jumped to his feet, colour draining from his face. 'What happened to you?' His thick south London accent seemed to soften as he looked Cooper slowly up and down. 'So I take it you didn't get the beers?'

'No, I didn't get the damn beers.'

'When you didn't answer any of my texts, I just assumed you'd hooked up with one of the chicks at the party,' Jag said, his eyes fixed on Cooper's bloodied face.

Cooper pulled the phone out of his pocket. 'Phone died,' he said, pressing at the blank screen. 'I need to charge it. Can we just get inside?'

'Yeah, sure.' Without taking his eyes from Cooper, Jag lifted the door knocker. A fake holly wreath hung from the handle and it swung in time with his knocks, the small bells jingling pathetically in time with his *shave-and-a-haircut* rhythm. The red paint on the door had started to peel away, revealing a dirty yellow beneath. 'I did knock earlier,' he confessed, 'but Amy wasn't too pleased to see me.'

Cooper managed a smile. 'Is she ever?'

'Jag, is that you again?' A voice called from somewhere deep inside the flat. 'I told you half an hour ago, Sam's not home yet.'

'Amy, it's me,' Cooper called through the door. 'I lost my key.' He rubbed his cold hands together. 'Happy New Year,' he added as an afterthought, as though it might soften her reaction to his battered face.

There was a moment of silence, followed by the rattle of a security chain being loosened and the clunk of locks being turned. 'I swear, Sam,' Amy's voice came from the other side of the door, 'one of these days you'll forget your own name.' The door swung open to reveal Cooper's twin sister standing in a pair of short pyjamas and a threadbare Chanel dressing gown, her hair twisted into a knot at the back of her head and her face clear of its usual makeup. Around her neck was the silver chain and heart pendant that Cooper had spent a month's wages on to buy her for Christmas.

Her only present.

'Oh my god.' She stepped forwards, reaching out to touch Cooper's face. 'Oh my god,' she repeated, this time with a little more panic in her voice.

'It's OK,' Cooper said, grabbing her wrist, 'just be careful, all right?' He stepped inside, letting Jag follow behind before closing the door.

'All right, Amy?' Jag asked, grinning at Cooper's sister. She wrinkled her nose in disgust and wrapped her dressing gown tightly around herself.

A piece of tinsel that had been draped across the coat hooks somehow became tangled around Jag's arm. 'That's a lot of blood, Coop,' Jag said, shaking the tinsel loose and nodding at Cooper's shirt. 'Where's it even coming from?'

Cooper reached up to touch his cheek, dismayed to find he was still bleeding. 'Here,' he said. 'And my head, too. I think.'

'Did someone cut you?' Amy asked, her voice trembling.

'It was an accident,' said Cooper, eyeing Jag and giving him a look that in no uncertain terms instructed him to stay quiet. 'I came off my bike.'

For a moment Amy stared, then her eyes narrowed. 'Kitchen,' she snapped. 'Now.'

Cooper followed her through the doorway into the cramped kitchen. The window looked out on to the balcony, with no blinds or curtains to stop passers-by from looking inside. The floor was linoleum made to look like wood, but it had started to curl away from the edges of the wall and had developed a strange bubbled appearance in front of the sink, where water from the leak that Cooper had so far been unable to fix had seeped into the floor beneath. Against the far wall stood a small table with two mismatched wooden chairs either side. Amy pulled one out and motioned for Cooper to sit down while she began opening and closing the various cupboard doors. They did their best to keep the place clean, but no matter how much they scrubbed, there was no way of bleaching away the years of neglect that had turned what had once been a smart ex-council property into a borderline health-hazard.

Placing his backpack on the kitchen floor beside him, Cooper watched on, feeling a familiar stab of guilt at the near-empty shelves. Maybe it was time to ask Big Phil for extra work at the Fill 'n' Save. Surely one more night shift wouldn't interfere *too* much with his college work?

'Ah-ha,' Amy declared, reaching into the small cupboard above the built-in oven. She pulled out a large Tupperware box and placed it on the table. 'Let's get you cleaned up and see what we're dealing with.'

Cooper nodded, too tired to argue.

Amy frowned, the lines on her forehead deepening as she worked. Finally she held up the blood-soaked piece of gauze and shook her head. 'Looks like stitches for you,' she said.

'No way,' Cooper replied, shooting Jag a look. 'No hospitals. And no police.'

'Police?' Amy's eyes widened. 'Why would the police get involved?' Her expression hardened. 'What the hell have you got yourself caught up in, Sam? I thought you said you came off your bike.'

Cooper sighed and closed his eyes. 'Nothing. It was a fight, that's all.'

'A fight?' She shot Jag an accusatory look. 'What kind of party was this?'

On the other side of the kitchen, Jag held up a hand to indicate they should stop talking. 'Prabir?' he said into his phone. 'It's Jag. Listen, I need you to find Dad's medical bag and bring it to Cooper's place.' Jag smiled at Cooper while he listened to his brother's response. 'No, no problems, just a little bit of a ding-dong with some of the lads on the estate.'

Cooper gave the thumbs up to Jag, and Amy scowled.

'Nice one. See you when you get here.' Jag slipped his phone back into his pocket and dusted off his hands. 'Job done. No hospitals, no police and we'll get you patched up before you know it.'

'He needs stitches,' Amy snapped. 'Not just a bit of patching up.'

'It's fine,' Jag soothed. 'Dad's got this special super glue, the same stuff they use in the hospitals. I promise, we'll get him back together in no time.'

Amy shook her head. 'You two are going to get yourselves killed one of these days. I swear, it's a miracle you've both survived this far.' She tossed the bloodied gauze into the almost overflowing bin and grimaced at the blood stains on her hand. 'I needed a shower anyway,' she said, looking at Cooper with concern. 'You sure you're all right, Sam?'

Cooper nodded. 'Honestly, I'm fine. And I'm sorry; I hate it when you're worried about me.'

'It's what sisters are for, right?' She turned and walked from the kitchen, scowling at Jag as she passed.

When they were alone, Jag hurried over to Cooper.

'She's warming to me, man. I'm telling you, one of these days you and I are going to be *real* brothers.' He held up a fist, waiting for Cooper to bump it. When he failed to reciprocate, Jag lowered his hand and shrugged. 'No worries. I know we're already family.'

Cooper forced a smile. 'Of course we are. Apart from Amy, you're the closest thing to a real family I've got.'

Jag leaned in, glancing over his shoulder to check that they were really alone, despite the rattling pipes telling them that Amy was already in the shower. 'So what happened? Did someone catch you trying to nick their beer?'

'I wish.' Cooper leaned back in his chair and grabbed his backpack. 'I'm in trouble, Jag. Big, big trouble.' He reached inside and pulled out a bag of pills.

'What the hell is that?' Jag stepped back. 'You know I don't mess with that kind of stuff.'

'I know,' Cooper said, dropping it back into his bag. 'But it's not like I've been given much choice in the matter.' He pointed at his face and Jag let out a long, low whistle.

'A smashed-up face will be the least of your worries if you get caught,' he said. 'And I'm not just talking about the police.' Jag glanced around them and leaned in close. 'You know Leon operates around these parts?'

Cooper raised an eyebrow.

For a moment Jag frowned in confusion, then his face dropped. 'You got yourself mixed up with Leon?'

He glanced at a non-existent watch. 'Is that the time?' He started to walk from the kitchen. 'Time for me to—'

'Jag!'

Jag stopped. Then he sighed. 'Yeah, OK.' He turned back to Cooper. 'But if you want me to stick around, you've got to tell me how the hell you got mixed up with that psycho. I thought we saw the last of him when Frank knocked his teeth out four years ago.'

'See this?' Cooper said, pointing at his sliced cheek.

Jag pretended to gag. 'Yes, Coop. I see the massive slash on your face. Exactly what I'm trying to avoid.'

'He thinks I was dealing on his patch. Says I owe him compensation for loss of earnings, or something.' Cooper swallowed. 'He said he'd come after Amy if I didn't sell his stuff.'

'What?'

Cooper glanced up. 'He said he'd kill my sister.'

'Amy? Why would he hurt her?'

'Because he knows that she's all I've got left. That if he wants me to do something for him, all he has to do is threaten her.' Cooper shook his head. 'He was always a psycho. Did I tell you that he pointed a gun at me when we were kids?'

'He what?'

'Yeah, it was crazy. His dad kept a gun in the spare-room wardrobe and he pulled it on me when we were eight.'

Jag whistled. 'Man. I knew he was nuts. Remember at school when he set fire to the bin under the teacher's desk?'

'I haven't seen him since that New Year's party,' Cooper said. 'Just before Frank did a runner and Mum and Dad were arrested. I swear he set them up. Not that I don't think they should be punished,' he added hastily.

'Frank was as nuts as Leon,' Jag said. 'Dad still goes on about how mental the whole thing was. He totally fell for the whole businessman act.'

'Everyone did. Even me. Seriously Jag, how could my father be a drug dealer without me knowing?'

'You were a kid. Don't be so hard on yourself.'

'And Mum was just as bad.' Cooper sat back in his chair. 'Money laundering. It's no wonder the police took everything: it was all bought with dirty money.'

'So Leon knows where you guys live now?'

'He knows our address, where I work.' He lowered his voice. 'He even knew about the necklace I bought her. He said what a nice neck she had, how it was a travesty for it to be covered in such cheap jewellery.' Cooper swallowed again. 'He said what a shame it would be to have to cut such a pretty throat.'

Jag grabbed the backpack and pulled out a bag of pills. He turned them over in his hands before looking up at Cooper. 'You need to go to the police.'

Cooper laughed. 'You're kidding, right? The son of Jimmy Cooper, East London drug lord, walks in to a police station with a backpack full of pills and a smashed-up face, and you think they're going to pat me on the back and tell me it's all going to be OK?'

Jag whistled. 'This is heavy.'

'You think I don't know that?' Cooper snatched the pills from Jag. 'Do you even have any idea what this is?'

Jag shook his head.

Cooper carefully pulled the ziplock at the top of the bag and took out a single pill. Laying it flat in the palm of his hand, he held it out to Jag.

'I'm not touching it,' Jag said, but he moved closer. 'What's that symbol?'

Cooper held it up and took a closer look. Sure enough, something had been stamped on to the top of the pill. 'That's an interrobang.'

'A what?'

'It's an exclamation point and a question mark placed together,' Cooper said. 'It must be the symbol for Nostalgex.'

Jag paused. 'Nostalgex?' He raised an eyebrow and took the pill from Cooper's hand. 'This is really Nostalgex? Damn.'

'Hey, I thought you weren't going to touch them?'

'These things have been all over the news,' Jag said, his eyes lighting up. 'Do you have any idea how much they're worth?'

'Yes,' Cooper snapped, plucking the pill from Jag's hand and placing it carefully back inside the plastic bag. 'And that is exactly why we need to sell them.' He paused. 'And he wants the first grand by tomorrow night.'

'How the hell are you supposed to manage that?'

Cooper shrugged. 'I wasn't thinking that far ahead.

I wanted to get away from him, so I just agreed to whatever he wanted.'

'You're crazy. Damn, *he's* crazy if he thinks you're going to be able to sell that many pills in twenty-four hours.'

'But we have to. Because if Leon doesn't get the money he thinks we owe him—'

'Whoa, whoa, whoa.' Jag stepped back and held up his hands. 'Who said anything about "we"?'

'What happened to us being family?'

Jag exhaled loudly. 'OK, fine. But you owe me, man.' There was a loud knock at the door and Jag looked at Cooper. 'That'll be Prabir,' he said. 'Here to save the day.' He disappeared into the hallway and Cooper heard the front door opening. There was a pause.

'Uh-oh.'

'Uh-oh?' Cooper stood up, a cold sweat prickling his skin as he shoved the bag of pills back into his backpack. Had Leon come for his money already? Or perhaps the police were here to do a raid. 'Uh-oh what? Jag?'

Jag appeared at the kitchen door, wearing a sheepish expression. 'Sorry, Coop.'

'Sorry for—' Cooper stopped when a short, wild-haired man appeared behind Jag. He peered at Cooper over a pair of wire-rimmed spectacles.

'Hello, Samuel,' the man said in a clipped Polish accent.

Cooper sank back into his chair as Jag's father pushed his way into the kitchen. 'Hello Dr Nowak.'

Dr Nowak tutted as he placed his medical bag on the

kitchen table. 'You've been a silly boy, I see.'

There was nothing like a visit from his friend's father to make Cooper feel like a kid again. He nodded, noticing that Jag looked just as uncomfortable.

'Your Uncle Barry isn't here, I take it?' Dr Nowak asked, peering out into the hallway.

'No, sir,' said Cooper. 'Not seen him in a little while. I think he's got business in Birmingham.'

'Business,' Dr Nowak repeated with a sigh as he glanced around the kitchen, at the plates piled high beside the sink and the single packet of cornflakes on the counter. 'You shouldn't be living like this, Samuel,' he said, prodding at Cooper's cheek. 'You do know there's help?' He stopped and placed his hands on Cooper's shoulders. 'You know that you and Amy can come and stay with us, anytime you like? You know how Mila loves to cook. She'd love a couple more mouths to feed.'

'I know,' Cooper said, wincing and sucking in a deep breath as Dr Nowak returned his attention to the cut on his face. 'We're OK. I've got it under control. And Barry'll be back soon.'

Actually, Cooper hadn't seen his uncle in six weeks, not that it was rare for him to disappear and leave Cooper and Amy to pay the rent and fend for themselves. He always looked a little surprised to see them when he returned, as though he'd forgotten they were even sharing his three-bed ex-council flat.

'Mmm,' said Dr Nowak, sounding unconvinced.

63

Jag leaned against the doorframe and ran a hand through his tousled hair. He mouthed the word 'sorry', but Cooper just smiled. Jag was like his father in so many ways: stubborn, slightly eccentric; and they both shared the same wild hairstyle.

Jag's father stepped back and frowned at Cooper. 'I can glue the cut,' he said, 'but I want you to get an X-ray to check for fractures.'

'So, hospital?' Cooper asked.

Dr Nowak nodded. 'Hospital,' he confirmed. 'I'm on call this morning anyway, so I'll drive you there just as soon as we've fixed you up.' He pulled a tube of glue from his bag and waved it triumphantly at Cooper. 'It's going to put you back together beautifully. You'll barely have a scar.' He paused, his eyes twinkling. 'Unless you want one for the ladies?'

Jag laughed and his father turned to face him. 'It's no laughing matter, Jagdeep,' he said, waving a finger at his son. Tutting, he turned back to Cooper. 'That boy of mine,' he muttered, leaning in towards Cooper with the tube of glue. 'Always dragging you down, getting you into trouble, hey?'

'No, Dr Nowak. It was nothing to do with—'

'Shh, sh, sh,' Dr Nowak chided, 'no talking now. Be still. It's going to sting, OK?'

'OK.' Cooper glanced over Dr Nowak's shoulder, to where Jag skulked sullenly by the kitchen door.

It was true, Cooper thought. Jag was the one who'd

always led them into trouble in the past, whether he meant to or not. But this time was different.

Glancing at the clock on the wall, then at his backpack, Cooper's heart sank.

The word 'trouble' had just taken on a whole new meaning.

JESS

Surely it was time to feel something?

Jess stared at her hands. Pink, filled with the blood that flowed through her veins; the very essence of life. How could it be that she was sitting here, alive and well, while her best friend lay somewhere close by, balancing precariously on the precipice between life and death?

Her best friend. Could she even call her that any more?

Of course she could. Whatever might have happened between Scarlett and Luke, it couldn't erase a lifetime of friendship. Could it?

She closed her eyes, trying to will away the thoughts of Scarlett, now hooked up to the machines that breathed for her, that were keeping the blood pumping around her body. How scared must she have been? How hard had she fought to get out? How many ragged breaths had she drawn before collapsing, unconscious and at the mercy of the flames that had torn through her home?

'Jess?'

She looked up to see Hannah standing in front of her, holding two steaming disposable cups. Hannah's eyes were red, her face flushed and blotchy from crying. Tears had run rivers through her makeup and the beautifully winged eyeliner was now smudged, giving her two black eyes.

'Thanks.' Jess took the cup, clutching at the container even though it was too hot. She could feel the heat, feel everything that touched her on the outside, so why didn't she feel anything on the inside?

She knew why. It was denial, one of the stages of grief.

She remembered a leaflet she'd found in the kitchen drawer, information her father had been given after her mum had died. This leaflet had been illustrated with a black dog, which was meant to represent grief. The dog was drawn with different facial expressions for each stage, starting with denial, until it reached acceptance.

At this point, the black dog was drawn to look like a puppy. Jess thought it was a stupid leaflet, like the acceptance of death was something cute and fluffy.

She supposed she was in denial.

'You should call your dad. Get home and get some rest.' Hannah pulled her black and purple hair up into a ponytail and secured it with one of the bands she always wore around her wrist. Always practical. 'Scarlett's dad said they'd call me if there was any news.'

Jess knew what that meant. It meant they'd call if Scarlett

67

died. At this point, while the machines were keeping her alive and her body was being pumped full of drugs, there really couldn't be any other news.

'I will,' Jess said. 'Soon.' Then, after a moment, 'Do you need a lift? You've been here all night.'

Hannah shook her head. 'I'm going to wait for Luke.'

'Oh. Yeah. Of course.' Jess sipped at her tea. It was too sweet, but she swallowed it anyway. The waiting room was packed, had been full from the moment they arrived. New Year's Eve was obviously a busy time for A&E, although the crowd had thinned somewhat by the time the sun came up. Now, at ten in the morning, it was once again at full capacity. Sad looking Christmas decorations hung from the ceiling and tatty paper snowflakes were stuck to the windows, though most of them were either ripped or half peeled off. In one corner a security guard leaned against the wall, swinging a key lazily around his finger while he laughed with two police officers.

'So are you going to tell me what happened?'

Jess turned to see Hannah staring at her from behind her own cup, her eyes unblinking. She seemed to be looking for something in Jess's eyes, searching for an answer to a question she couldn't quite come up with. It wasn't usually like Hannah to hold back her thoughts, so seeing her hesitate put Jess instantly on edge.

'What do you mean?'

'I mean,' Hannah said carefully, 'what happened with you and Luke? I know it's kind of awkward, because

I'm his sister. But I'm also your friend, so . . .'

Jess looked away. 'What makes you think something happened?'

'I've known you all your life, Jess. We grew up next door to each other. I have this kind of interior alarm that goes off when something's up with you. And if it also concerns my little brother, that alarm goes off the chart. So what's going on?'

'I . . .' Jess swallowed. 'He did something.'

Hannah coughed out a small laugh. 'He did something? Seriously Jess, what could he have possibly done to make you act this way?'

'What way?'

'Are you kidding me? You didn't even ask to ride in the ambulance with us. I figured you were waiting behind for Scarlett and that when you got here you'd be kicking the door down to be with him.' Hannah nodded at the set of double doors leading through to the treatment area. They burst open and a nurse came rushing through. She glanced at the clock on the wall before disappearing through another set of doors. 'Whatever he's done,' Hannah said, her eyes fierce, 'he needs you.'

Jess turned away. What could she say? How would any of it make any sense? Hannah had no idea what her brother was capable of. What he was really like when things got tough.

'I need some air,' Hannah said, standing up. 'I can't just sit here doing nothing.' She looked down at Jess with a mixture of confusion and accusation, as though it were Jess's fault they were even here in the first place.

Unable to think of anything to say, Jess just nodded. She raised her cup to her lips and took a sip in an attempt to hide her face from Hannah. Where were her own tears? Perhaps she was in shock and the emotion would strike later, hard and fast like a car slamming into a brick wall.

Like that stupid black dog. Lurking somewhere behind, ready to rip her throat out.

Jess watched Hannah leave through the automatic doors, a gust of freezing air blasting in as they opened. The doors began to slide shut, then swished open again as two boys walked in. One of the boys wore a black sweater and jeans, his hood pulled up over his head, partly obscuring his face. Blood seeped through a bandage on his forehead and his cheek was covered with similarly stained gauze.

Inwardly, Jess groaned. She looked away, hoping he would continue to walk by without saying a word.

Of all the people she had to bump into on one of the worst days of her life, it just had to be Sam Cooper. And surprise, surprise, there was his shadow, Jag. Cooper looked as though he'd been in a fight, though it wouldn't be the first time he'd been on the wrong end of someone's fist.

He turned to look at Jess as he passed, his piercing blue eyes cutting through her for a second before they widened in recognition. He paused for a second, as though he were about to say something, then he drew the strings to gather his hood and continued walking.

Jess scowled. He was as cocky as ever. Obviously just the same self-involved, immature kid he had been back when—

'Are you Jessica?'

Jolted from her thoughts, Jess looked up to see a nurse in front of her. When Jess remained silent, the nurse glanced at the paper she was holding.

'Or Hannah?'

'No. No, I'm Jessica.'

The nurse smiled. 'Luke's asking to see you.'

Jess glanced at the empty seat beside her. 'Sure.' She nodded and stood up, stealing a final glance at Cooper and Jag, now settling into a pair of the red plastic seats in the waiting room. Once again, Cooper's eyes met hers, though he quickly looked away. Jag, on the other hand, had fixed her with a cold stare, one that she could feel burning into the back of her neck as she walked.

The nurse led her through the double doors into the bustling A&E department. The room stretched onwards and outwards, a maze of cubicles, most of which had curtains pulled either partly or fully around the beds. Nurses gathered around a row of desks, a mini Christmas tree twinkling beside a computer, the screen lit with an X-ray of an obviously broken leg.

The department was filled with sounds; talking, groaning, bleeping machines and ringing phones. From some curtained-off corner came the sound of quiet sobbing.

71

Jess thought she would rather hear screaming. At least screaming indicated life, a desire to fight. The quiet sobbing just sounded so hopeless.

'Here we go.' The nurse pulled a curtain back with a loud swish and turned to Jess with a kind smile. 'Can I get you another cup of tea?'

'No thank you.'

And with that, the nurse was gone, disappearing into one of the other cubicles.

'Hey.' Luke lay on the bed, his right forearm wrapped in clean, white bandages. His hand was left uncovered, his scarred knuckles purple and angry looking. Jess thought back to the day he had earned those scars, by punching out a car window.

A saline drip fed into his left hand and sticky tabs were arranged on his bare chest, the skin there mapped with a constellation of freckles that Jess knew so well. The rest of him was covered in a patterned hospital gown and a sheet that was as white as his dressings. He looked so clean, much cleaner than when he had been pulled from the fire.

'Hey,' Jess said weakly. Then, looking at the bandage, 'Are you OK?'

Luke shrugged a shoulder. 'As OK as I can be, I guess.'

Jess nodded.

'Are you going to come in?' Luke held out a hand, offering the plastic chair beside his bed. He seemed so stiff, so formal.

Jess looked back at the double doors she had come through and shook her head. 'No, I don't think so.'

'We have to talk.' Luke leaned forwards, his voice lowering. 'I have to explain something to you.'

'I'm not sure—'

'Jess, please.'

Jess couldn't stand the desperation in his voice, the same kind of emotion she had heard in that quiet sobbing. She pulled the curtain closed behind her and stepped into the cubicle beside Luke's bed. He reached out and took her hand in his, the same one that was connected to the IV. In that moment, feeling his skin against hers, Jess felt it, just like she had imagined.

A car against a brick wall.

Her knees buckled beneath her but Luke was there, sitting up and pulling her towards him as the tears finally started, her body shaking with each sob as she pressed her face into his shoulder. Hannah was right; she needed Luke as much as he needed her.

Whatever had happened, whatever Luke had done, it wasn't worth losing him over. She realized that now and she hated herself for every second she had been in that waiting room when she should have been in here, with the one person she loved more than anything, more than *anything*.

'I'm sorry,' she cried, 'I'm so, so sorry.'

'No,' Luke said, his hand stroking her hair as he shook his head against hers. 'You didn't do anything wrong.' He pulled away, kissing her cheeks, her forehead.

'She's got to be OK. She'll be OK, right?'

'I don't know,' he whispered. He took her hand. 'I don't know.'

'What happened? Why didn't you get out?'

'We couldn't open the door. I don't know if there was something trapped against it, but it wouldn't open.'

'The door was locked,' she said. 'You locked it.'

Luke shook his head. 'No, we didn't. And we tried the key, but it wouldn't turn. They had to break the door down to get us.' His voice dropped. 'We thought we were going to die, Jess.' He sniffed, then his eyes shifted. 'The pills,' he said suddenly, glancing over her shoulder to where the curtain remained pulled tightly across the cubicle.

'Not now,' Jess said, shaking her head. 'We can talk about that another time.' She sat on the bed beside him, taking his hands, running her fingers across his scars.

'No,' Luke said, his eyes darting to the pocket of the jacket Jess was still wearing. 'I mean, do you still have them?'

Jess paused, her hand frozen around his. 'Yes,' she said, unable to stop the icy tone creeping into her voice. 'But it's OK, I'll get rid of them. We'll talk about it later.'

Luke's hand tightened around hers, the scars on his knuckles whitening. 'No,' he said, his voice urgent. His throat clicked as he swallowed, then he spoke again, softer this time and with a reassuring smile. 'Just leave them in the jacket.' He nodded at the chair beside them. 'Leave it all just there.'

Jess stared. Luke's eyes were wide, filled with a panic that contrasted terribly against the calmness in his voice. She pulled her hand from his.

'Jess,' Luke hissed, leaning towards her and grabbing at her arm. 'Take off the jacket.'

'No,' she shot back, pulling her arm from his grip. She stepped away. The colour had drained from his face, a thin film of sweat beading over his top lip.

He slammed a fist against the bedside table. 'I said take it off!'

Jess stumbled back again and the curtain swished open. A nurse, different to the one who had led Jess in, stood outside. 'Everything OK?' she asked, looking from Luke to Jess.

'It's fine,' Luke said, waving a hand as he fell back against his pillow, eyes closed in resignation.

Jess nodded, but didn't take her eyes from Luke. For a moment the nurse didn't move, then she slowly pulled the curtain closed around them.

'I can't explain it all now,' Luke said, reaching for her hand again, 'but I'm asking you to trust me, Jess. Please. You owe me that much.'

For a moment the familiarity had been enough to make everything OK; the closeness of his skin, his smell. It had been enough, until the claws of hatred tightened around her heart once more and she pushed his hand away, the memories of the previous night returning like a slap to the face.

'I have to go,' she said, reaching for the curtain. 'I can't do this any more.'

'Jess,' he said, 'please, don't do this to me. Not now. Not again.'

'No,' she cried. 'Don't put it on me, don't make it sound like I'm choosing this.' She swallowed the rising lump in her throat. 'You chose this, with *your* actions.'

'I'm sorry. I don't know what else to say. Please, Jess. I can't stand the thought of being without you, I can't cope without you in my life, you know that.'

It was all so horribly familiar, but this time there was no car window to punch out.

'And I can't stand the thought of what you've done,' she spat. 'You've been *lying* to me, Luke.'

'Please, just let me explain.'

'Explain what, exactly? Why I found a stash of pills in your jacket pocket?'

'You don't understand, please, just let me—'

'Let you what? Go on then, explain it to me. Tell me why you had them.' She reached into the jacket pocket and pulled out Luke's phone. 'Tell me why I find these messages from Scarlett on your phone.' There had only been one, but by the uncertain look on Luke's face she knew there had been more, long since deleted, no doubt. 'Tell me why you and Scarlett were locked inside her bedroom when I couldn't find you.'

Luke opened his mouth, but no words came out.

'Yeah, that's what I thought. I heard it all, everything you said to her.'

'Jess . . .' He lunged towards her in an attempt to grab her again, but Jess raised her hands and stepped back.

'No, don't. Don't touch me. Don't try to deny it.'

'I'm not going to deny anything,' he spat. 'And you know what? I'm not going to try to explain it either, because you've obviously made up your own mind about what happened.'

'I heard everything, Luke. I know you've been cheating.' She threw the phone at him and it struck his shoulder before falling on to the bed beside him with a soft clump. 'I don't even know who you are any more.'

'I'm still me,' he said, clutching a hand to his chest. 'I'm the same boy who's always loved you. Everything I've done has been for you, you know that.'

Jess's hand tightened around the bag of pills as her stomach twisted with rage. 'No,' she said. 'Don't you dare say that. None of this has got anything to do with me.'

'If you don't give me those pills,' Luke said, 'then everything is over for me. For us. Everything. There's this guy . . .' His voice trailed off.

'You mean Leon?' Seeing the look on his face, she continued. 'I saw the message. And who the hell is Whiteface? What kind of a name is that anyway?'

'You have no idea how serious this is,' Luke said. 'I need those pills, Jess.'

Her fingers twitched around the plastic and there was something about the terrified look on Luke's face that made her doubt herself, made her take a step towards him, but the way in which his eyes lit up when she did made her stop.

'No,' she said. She lifted her chin, forcing an end to the tears she was wasting on him. 'Consider this the last thing I do for you.' She shoved the bag back into her pocket and turned before Luke had the chance to say anything to her, pushing the curtain aside as she strode from the cubicle.

He shouted her name more than once as she walked out, but Jess didn't break her stride. She didn't even look back. She pulled the bag of pills from her pocket and clutched them tightly – they would go into the first bin she could find.

Marching through the waiting room, with her head down and her vision blurred from crying, she didn't see the running boy until it was too late.

He turned the corner and collided with Jess, knocking the bag from her hand. The plastic burst against the floor, sending the small red pills scattering across the blue linoleum.

'What the . . .?' The boy grabbed at her to stop them both from tumbling to the ground, his eyes locking on the pills strewn over the floor.

It was Cooper.

Now, with their faces inches apart, Jess was able to see

the full extent of his injuries. His left eye was almost swollen shut and surrounded by an ugly bruise. She didn't want to think about what might lie beneath his bandages.

His grip loosened and his expression shifted from one of shock to puzzlement. 'Are those—?'

'Just leave me alone,' Jess snapped, sinking to her knees as she quickly began scooping up the pills, forcing a smile for the people in the waiting room who had turned to stare. The security guard on the opposite side of the room was no longer leaning against the wall, but was now standing poker straight, his eyes locked on them both and his hand resting lightly against the radio attached to his belt. The police he had been talking with earlier were nowhere to be seen.

Cooper sunk down beside her and picked up one of the pills. His expression turned to one of horror as he lifted it closer to his one good eye. 'Do you know what these are?' he whispered, glancing back over his shoulder and along the empty corridor.

Jess paused. 'Of course I do,' she snapped, stuffing the pills into Luke's jacket pocket. The split bag was useless, but she stuffed that in as well.

'I doubt that somehow.' He scooped up a handful of pills and she tried to snatch them back, but he quickly lifted his hand out of the way, grabbing her shoulder to hold her back.

'Give them back,' Jess snapped, barely able to contain tears of anger, frustration and the embarrassment that out of the millions of people who lived in this city, it had to be Sam Cooper who was witnessing her at her very worst.

'Listen to me,' he said, his grip tightening on her shoulder, 'and listen closely. You see this?' He pulled his hood down to reveal his mangled face. 'The person who did this to me is a very dangerous man.' He opened his hand to reveal Jess's pills. 'And he did it to me because of these.'

'What?' Jess reached for the pills, but Cooper snatched them away. 'I don't know what you're talking about. It's just medication. Now leave me alone, please.' She glanced up again to see the security guard speaking into his radio, his eyes still fixed on Cooper.

Cooper pulled a backpack from his shoulder and unzipped it. Inside was a familiar looking plastic bag filled with the same red pills. Not just one; a whole pile of them. Jess leaned closer and gasped. 'Where did you get those?' she whispered.

From somewhere behind Cooper came the sound of heavy footsteps. He turned, just as the two police officers who had been talking with the security guard appeared at the opposite end of the long corridor.

'I have to go,' Cooper whispered. 'Those guys seem to want to talk to me. Are you coming?'

Jess looked at his face again, into the piercing blue eyes that were filled with, what? Fear? She shook her head, unsure of what else to do. Then she glanced up to see the security guard, edging closer to where she and Cooper were kneeling on the floor together, surrounded by the last few pills.

Cooper quickly scooped up the remaining drugs, shoved them into his pocket and zipped his bag closed. 'Do what you want,' he said, pulling his hood up and lowering his head as the officers approached. 'But I'm pretty sure those guys don't want to talk to me about the weather, so I'm out of here.' He took two steps towards the exit before a voice rang out.

'Hey, you! Just wait there!'

In that moment, everything seemed to happen at once. The security guard rushed forwards, pushing past an empty wheelchair and almost colliding with an elderly couple. The police officers began to jog towards them, one shouting into the radio attached to her vest. And Cooper took two long strides towards the exit.

Then he stopped and turned back to look at Jess. 'Last chance,' he said, reaching out a hand that Jess swore a year earlier she would never hold again.

Without even looking back, Jess reached out and let Cooper close his fingers around hers.

They ran.

JESS

Jess's feet burned as she ran, the back of her borrowed trainers rubbing blisters into her soles and heels. But Cooper was much faster than her and she was more concerned that she might fall flat on her face as he pulled her through the crowds. The streets were filled with shoppers, all looking for their New Year's bargains.

Jess looked over her shoulder for what felt like the hundredth time, certain that the police must be closing in on them. Sure enough, the flash of a yellow vest appeared as the officers emerged from within the crowds, pausing for a moment as they searched the street.

'Where are we going?' Jess cried as Cooper dragged her around yet another corner. Cars rushed past and she had to shout to make herself heard over the roar of traffic.

Without answering, he slowed just long enough for a black cab to pass by them, then he dragged Jess out into the traffic, weaving through moving cars as he pulled her towards the other side of the road.

'Cooper, wait!' Jess screamed. Her hand tightened around Cooper's and she pulled him back as a motorbike sped past, narrowly missing him.

'Thanks,' he shouted back, then he was off again, back up on to the pavement, the distance between them and the hospital growing with every step. Shops and restaurants passed by almost in a blur as they weaved through the crowds, then Cooper suddenly turned into a narrow alleyway beside a cafe, pulling Jess past overflowing dumpsters while vents spewed steam all around them.

Jess stumbled again, her ankle wrenching painfully beneath her. Her lungs were burning and her feet were on fire, pain shooting through them every time they slapped against the concrete. She pulled her hand from Cooper's, jerking away and bending double as she dragged in breath after breath. 'That's enough,' she panted, leaning against the grimy brick wall as she willed her racing heart to slow.

'We haven't gone far enough,' he said, reaching for her arm again. 'Come on.'

'No,' she snapped. 'No. That's enough.' She looked towards the end of the alleyway, to where the crowds passed by without so much as a glance in their direction. 'If they find us, they find us. But no more running.' She lowered herself to the floor, clutching her knees to her chest, her ankle throbbing in time with her heart. The ground was freezing, but her body was still on fire, her muscles threatening to cramp up at any second.

Cooper raised his hands in defeat, nodding as he too fought for breath. His bag fell to the floor as he sank down beside her and tilted his head towards the sky.

Neither of them spoke. The air was thick with the stench of rotting garbage and Jess was sure she saw something moving underneath one of the two large wheelie bins beside them. Despite the alleyway being totally empty of any passers-by, Jess couldn't help but peer around the side of the bin, sure that the two police officers who had chased them out of the hospital were about to round the corner at any given second. But they didn't appear. Instead, a steady stream of people passed by, not one of them even glancing into the dim alleyway.

When her heart no longer felt like it was about to burst through her ribcage, Jess turned to look at Cooper.

'So are you going to tell me what's going on?' she asked, taken aback once more by the severity of the injuries to his face. This wasn't the Cooper she knew, but somehow she was unsurprised that he had got himself into whatever kind of mess this was. It was a feeling of vindication, a validation of every negative thought she'd ever had about him, and of every reason she'd used to convince herself to end their relationship last year.

He turned to her and she realized she had forgotten just how blue his eyes were.

And just how withering his voice could be. 'I told you.

84

I got on the wrong side of someone you really don't want to get on the wrong side of.'

'That tells me nothing.'

'As pedantic as ever, I see.' When Jess said nothing, he sighed. 'You wouldn't believe me, even if I told you the truth.'

Jess's eyes narrowed. 'Why wouldn't I believe you? It's not like you've never lied to me before.'

'You mean the one time I told you I was sick because I didn't want to come to your little revision session?'

'A lie is a lie.'

The tiniest of smiles played over Cooper's lips. 'Still holding a grudge, then?'

'No,' Jess shot back. 'Holding a grudge would mean I still cared.'

Cooper placed a hand over his chest, as though he had just been shot. 'Ouch.'

In spite of herself, Jess smiled. Then, as quickly as it had appeared, it was gone, replaced with a frown. 'I mean it, Cooper. You need to tell me what's going on with you. Especially if you think I'm caught up in it too.'

'So, what? Mr Perfect not around to protect you these days? He was there pretty quickly after we broke up. You know, it's kind of crazy how you quite literally fell for the boy next door.'

'That's not fair.' Jess looked away and shivered, the adrenaline receding and suddenly leaving her cold, despite the jacket she was already wearing. 'And our break up has got nothing to do with any of this.'

'Fine.' Cooper removed his own jacket. 'Put this on first.'

'No thanks.'

'You're cold. Put it on, then I'll tell you everything.'

He held out his coat and Jess paused before taking it from him with a mumbled thanks. She threw it around her shoulders and pulled it across her body, the material covering Luke's jacket and the pockets containing his pills. As she closed it around herself, she caught a familiar scent; one that instantly recalled a memory of her and Cooper together on a park bench one bright autumn day, his arm around her and her head on his shoulder, his jacket smelling exactly the same as it did now.

She pushed the image away, surprised by the sudden arrival of something that was so unwelcome. For a moment she considered passing his coat back, but realized the action would say more than she wanted it to. 'So?' she asked instead. 'Are you going to tell me what we're doing in a stinking alleyway on New Year's Day?'

'All I can tell you is what happened to me,' Cooper said, wincing as he reached to touch his battered face. 'And even I can barely believe it.'

Jess nodded, hoping it would be enough encouragement for him to continue. It was.

'I was at a party. At Jag's,' he said, with a wry smile. He looked at her as though he knew what was coming and Jess rolled her eyes, unable to help herself. Of course he'd been with Jag. The permanent third wheel in their relationship. 'Yeah. I'm sure you guessed that already. Anyway,' he continued, 'next thing I know, it's almost midnight, I'm out on my bike to get –' he paused, his eyes shifting in the way they always used to when he was about to cover something up '– to crash someone's party to get some more alcohol,' he continued, looking her straight in the eye. He waited, as though he were expecting some cutting remark from Jess; one that was on the tip of her tongue, but she bit it back, refusing to prove him right. With a tiny raise of his eyebrow, Cooper continued his story. 'I was on my way through St Steven's churchyard and I swear Jess, this guy just came out of nowhere.'

'What guy?'

Cooper shrugged. 'I can't remember.' He reached to touch the dressing on his forehead and frowned. 'He smashed me on the head with something, but I was on the ground when he did it. It was dark and I know he looked at me, but . . .' He stopped for a moment, his brow furrowing deeper. 'I can remember the black hoodie he was wearing. I remember almost everything but, and I know this is going to sound crazy, it's like there's just this white space where his face should have been. Just, I don't know. Nothing.' He waved his hand, but something about this image gnawed at Jess, an unpleasant feeling that came from somewhere deep inside her gut. 'Anyway, the next thing I know, I wake up in the boot of a car with a bleeding head and—'

'In the boot of a car?'

'Oh, it gets worse.' Cooper smiled that wry smile again. 'Turns out this is the boot of a drug dealer's car. And it also turns out that my bag –' he reached out to grab his backpack – 'is filled with the same drug he's dealing. Oh, and as if that wasn't enough, St Steven's churchyard is his dealing ground.'

Jess paused for a moment, allowing Cooper's story to take shape in her mind. 'Let me get this straight,' she said slowly, unable to stop the sceptical tone from creeping into her voice. 'You, out of nowhere, find yourself in a drug dealer's car, with a bag full of drugs? And you're completely innocent in all of it?'

With a roll of his eyes, Cooper gave a snort of laughter. 'I said you wouldn't believe me and I was obviously right.' He got to his feet and grabbed his bag. 'But there are two sides to every story, Jess. You don't always have to believe the one that makes me look bad. And you can keep the coat.'

'Cooper, wait.' Jess got up and followed after him, though her ankle screamed in pain with each step. 'Cooper!' She grabbed at one of the straps of his bag. He turned to face her.

'I know what you think of me, Jess. You made that very clear last year. I couldn't convince you otherwise back then and I'm sure as hell not going to try again now.' He went to turn away again, but she pulled on his bag once more.

'What happened between us has nothing to do with

88

what's going on now,' she snapped. 'You know that as well as I do. I just want you to tell me what you know, so I can get rid of these pills and worry about more important things.'

Cooper snorted. 'Like what? Let me guess, you need to go back to studying, right?'

Rage boiled in Jess's stomach. 'You think that's all that matters to me? You have no idea, Cooper, you . . .' She choked on her words, as surprised by her sudden tears as Cooper seemed to be, his eyes widening like those of an animal caught in a trap.

'Jess? What is it? What's happened?'

'Did you even think there might have been a reason why I was at the hospital too? Did you even think to ask?'

Cooper's throat bobbed as he swallowed, his deer-in-the-headlights look making a sudden reappearance. 'I guess I thought . . .' He swallowed again. 'So why? Why were you there?'

'Because there was a fire.' Jess felt a new pang of anger as Cooper's face fell. He really didn't have a clue, did he? 'Scarlett and Luke were trapped, they were upstairs and they couldn't get out.' Her hand flew to her mouth as fresh tears sprung from her eyes and Cooper stepped forwards, pulling her against him and wrapping his arms around her in the way he always used to, all that time ago. For a second it was enough, then she pushed him away as a new wave of anger washed over her. 'So that's why I want to know,' she shouted, her hands balling into fists at her sides. 'That's why I want to know if you have any idea why our costume party ended with me at the hospital, unsure if my best friend is going to live or die while my boyfriend . . .' She paused, her stomach turning as she forced out the next words, 'while my *ex-boyfriend*,' she corrected, 'demands that I hand back his secret drug stash while he lies in a hospital bed.'

'Luke?' Cooper laughed. 'Luke's taking N?'

'Dealing it,' Jess said, her voice small. 'And there was this message on his phone, from some guy called Leon—'

Cooper held up a hand. 'Whoa. Luke's working with Leon?'

'You know him?'

'That's the guy who did this to me,' Cooper said, gesturing towards his face. 'He's the one I'm now supposed to be working for. What the hell is going on?'

'I don't know,' Jess said. 'All I know is that I found this bag of pills, and another in Luke's coat . . .' She paused and looked up at Cooper, a wave of panic washing over her as she clambered to her feet. 'There was another bag. I dropped it outside Scarlett's room when the fire started. It'll have my fingerprints all over it.'

'Jess, nobody's going to believe that—'

'That what? I could be handling drugs? Would you have believed that Luke was dealing them?' She started to stride towards the road.

'Well, no.'

'Then I need to find them. You don't think the fire's

90

going to be investigated? You don't think the police will be interested in a bag of drugs found at a party?'

'They've probably been destroyed in the fire.'

'I need to check. I can't just leave them there.'

'Jess—'

'No,' she cried, turning to face him. 'I've got enough to worry about already, Sam. Can't you see that?'

He seemed to flinch at hearing her call him Sam. It felt equally strange to feel the word forming in her own mouth. He was Cooper now; she hadn't called him Sam since the break up.

'You can't control everything,' he said. 'No matter how much you want to.'

'Exactly.' She wiped the unwelcome tears away with the palm of her hand. 'I can't control whether Scarlett lives or dies. I can't control what happens with Luke. But this is something I can control. I can go back to the house and find those pills and then I can walk away from the whole mess if I want to.' She paused. 'I can walk away from Luke.'

For a moment, Cooper said nothing. Then he nodded. 'If that's what you want.'

'It is.'

Cooper fell in step with Jess. 'Then let's go.'

LEON

A bloody whirlpool span over the ancient plughole, twisting in the crimson water before it was sucked down into the pipes.

The cracked mirror misted under Leon's breath as he examined his face, his swollen nose whistling with his failed attempts to exhale through it. A blood-bubble appeared at one nostril, before it burst and spattered against the mirror. He cursed and grabbed an already-stained flannel to wipe the droplets away, then roared with frustration as the cloth drew a much larger, much bloodier smear across the surface. He hurled the flannel into the sink and reached for the bottle of whisky that stood on the window sill, among the half-empty shampoo bottles and deodorant cans. Taking a slug straight from the bottle, he eyed himself in the bloody mirror. It wasn't his first broken nose and it probably wouldn't be his last.

He couldn't even remember how many times his own father had broken his nose. Not to mention the fractured ribs, black eyes, cracked cheekbone and the fractured arm he'd received on his ninth birthday. His two front teeth.

Not any more.

Frank was gone now; not on some tropical island as Cooper had suggested, but really gone.

He swallowed the fiery liquid and licked his lips, grimacing at his reflection. The gold teeth glinted, a permanent reminder of what had happened, paid for with his father's money before the police seized everything.

Leon glanced at the cracked, mildewed tiles above the bath. It was a far cry from the sprawling Georgian mansion his father had raised him in, before Jimmy Cooper had got himself arrested and the shit had *really* hit the fan. Anything bought with the 'drug money' had been seized, so when Leon was sent to his first foster parents, all he had with him were the clothes on his back and the gold teeth in his mouth.

He spat into the stained sink and a huge glob of bloody mucus clung to the fibreglass like a dollop of jelly. With a grimace, he took another mouthful from the bottle of whisky and walked through to the lounge.

Things were getting out of hand, he knew that, but he didn't have a choice. Whoever was pulling his strings had done a fine job of tangling him in whatever the hell this mess was.

Falling back on to the sofa, Leon cradled the whisky

bottle against his chest. All he wanted to do now was sleep. He could deal with everything else later, figure out exactly how he was going to get himself out of this for good. Reaching into his jeans pocket, he pulled out a small plastic baggie containing five red pills. His phone slipped out with the baggie, the screen lit up.

NEW MESSAGE FROM: Whiteface

With an agitated sigh, he tipped three of the pills into his open hand, tossed them into his mouth and chased them down with a slug of the whisky. Then he picked up the phone and opened the message.

Luke Vaughan is alive.

Leon's thumb hovered over the keypad. He wanted to type *What do you want me to do about it?* but he knew what the answer would be.

Killing was never part of the deal. Can't we just give him a few more days? He doesn't owe that much, he's just a stupid kid.

A moment later another text came through.

If you really want out of this, you kill Luke. He's had enough time to pay and we need to send a message.

Leon took another sip from the bottle. The pills would begin to take effect soon and he'd be able to sleep, even if it was an artificial sleep filled with memories instead of dreams.

It'd be easier if I had the gun.

You think I'm going to give you the gun? The one with your fingerprints all over it?

He'd never expected to get the gun back, but it had

been worth a try. And now he was stuck in a situation he'd never intended on getting himself into, destined to kill Luke Vaughan.

Just like he'd killed his own father.

COOPER

The street looked like a war zone.

Streams of police tape crossed the road, tied between trees and wrought iron fences. The blue and white plastic flapped in the breeze like party streamers. In the middle of all the tape stood the charred shell of a house, the ground-floor windows gone and the outside walls blackened.

Cooper let out a low whistle.

'Yeah,' Jess said. 'That's pretty much how I feel.' She took two more steps towards the house, drawing Cooper's coat tighter around herself. It swamped her, making her look tiny and fragile, but Cooper already knew that Jess's delicate appearance was a deep betrayal of what went on beneath the surface.

At least, it used to be. There was something different about the way she held herself now, her shoulders a little more curved, her head a little lower.

On the pavement in front of the house, two policemen stood, arms folded, with their backs to Cooper and Jess.

'You think they've been in yet?' Jess asked.

'Don't know. But I guess we'll find out soon enough.'

One of the officers threw his head back and laughed at whatever the other had just said and, by instinct, Cooper reached out to touch Jess's arm. It was intended as a comforting gesture, one to counterbalance the insensitivity of the officers, but when he felt her flinch beneath his touch, he moved his hand away.

'Are you sure this is a good idea?' he asked.

Jess paused, chewing her lip. Then she nodded, stoic. 'And given that those two idiots seem to be the only ones here, I'd say now is as good a time as any.' She began striding towards the end of the street and Cooper immediately realized she was heading for the back of the house. He trailed after her, deciding not to mention the way she was still limping. He knew what she was like; when she had her mind set on something there was no convincing her otherwise, twisted ankle or not. Once she'd decided on what she thought was the right course of action, she was going to follow it.

The alleyway at the back of the houses ran between a brick wall on one side and a neat row of wooden fences on the other. Cooper had made this journey a number of times before, back when he and Jess first started dating and when he would follow her almost anywhere, though that usually meant either to study in the school library or here, to Scarlett's house.

'Won't the police have the back taped off, too?' he asked as they neared Scarlett's fence.

'Why?' Jess asked. 'It's not like she has a gate or anything. Remember how we used to get in through the back?'

Cooper did remember. The memory was instant, as quick and as sharp as a bee sting; running down the alleyway with Jess, stealing kisses by the fence before sneaking through to see their friend. They used to sneak in this way if Scarlett was grounded, or sometimes just because the bus stop was closer to the back of the house.

Jess was right, as always. There was no tape, no police officers, nothing to suggest anything untoward had happened on the opposite side of the creosoted fence they were now standing by. Jess paused, shivering as she trailed her fingers along the fence. At the second panel, she stopped and reached over the top of the fence. Her shoulder moved while she worked on loosening the panel from the other side and within a few seconds, whatever she had undone caused the fence panel to come away from the support post that had been holding it in place. Without looking back, she slipped through the gap and disappeared. Cooper stared for a moment, caught off guard by the strange feeling that had come over him. It was like he had gone back in time and was watching another memory unfold in front of his eyes, a memory he hadn't even realized existed. Then Jess's face appeared in the gap and he was launched back to the present.

'Are you coming?' There was something in her voice that was so different to what he remembered, but he couldn't quite figure out what it was.

'Sure,' he said, turning sideways as he attempted to push himself through the impossibly small space.

'You've put on weight.'

He turned to Jess just in time to catch a glimpse of a smile.

'I think the gap's got smaller,' he shot back. 'And you've definitely got sassier.'

This time she laughed and when she looked at him, her eyes bright and her cheeks dimpling, he felt another surge of discomfort. But it was more than that. It was a hollow feeling, a sense of something missing. Something lost that he knew he could never get back.

On the other side of the fence lay the true extent of the devastation.

There was a sharp intake of breath beside him and when he turned, he saw Jess's shoulders hitch before she exhaled a steady breath.

'You OK?' he asked.

She nodded.

'Jeez,' Cooper breathed, looking back at the building. 'It doesn't even look like the same house.'

Where the front of the house was charred but mostly intact, the back looked as though a bomb had hit it. Windows and their frames were completely missing from the ground floor and water dripped steadily within.

'It's not the same house,' Jess replied, hugging herself as she began climbing the stone steps that led up to the rear door. It was hanging from a single hinge, the red paint bubbled and blistered from the heat.

Cooper followed her up the steps and was immediately greeted by the bitter tang of old smoke mixed with a sickly-sweet chemical smell. He wrinkled his nose. 'It stinks in here. Aren't loads of toxins released in a house fire?'

'It's more of a problem when the house is actually burning,' Jess said.

The carpet squelched beneath her feet as she stepped inside. 'Ugh, it's soaked through.'

'You think the floorboards are OK?' Cooper poked at the carpet with his foot, noting the slight give.

Without a word, Jess continued through to the main hallway and stamped her foot on the floor. 'Happy?' she asked.

Cooper looked around at the blackened walls. 'I can think of happier places to be on New Year's Day,' he muttered, carefully stepping after her.

The ceiling bulged above them and water dripped steadily through the plaster. To their right, an empty doorframe led into what was left of the dining room.

'It started in there,' Jess said quietly.

Cooper peered over her shoulder at what remained of the room. If there had once been any furniture inside, it had since been reduced to ashes. Cooper was acutely aware of the change in the way Jess was holding herself, her arms folded tightly across her chest as though she were hugging herself to keep warm. 'You OK?'

'I'm fine.' Jess placed her hands on the doorframe and leaned in, keeping her feet in the hallway. She stepped back and Cooper followed her from the dining room to the other side of the doorless partition wall that separated the hallway from the staircase. She stopped, so suddenly that Cooper almost ran into the back of her.

'What is it?'

Without a word, Jess turned and pushed past him back to the dining room. 'Look at this,' she said, stepping back and pointing at the walls around her.

'I'm not sure what I'm looking at.'

'The damage,' Jess said. 'Look at how bad it is in the dining room, then compare it to the hallway.'

'Oh-kay,' Cooper said slowly. He joined her beside the dining room and glanced in, once more taking in the extent of the damage and the gaping hole that opened the side of the house out into the garden. Then he stepped back into the hallway and looked around, making a mental note of the walls, blackened but in no way as severely damaged as the dining room.

'Now look,' Jess said, taking Cooper by the arm and guiding him around the partition wall to the foot of the stairs. The stairwell was split by a small landing, where the staircase then doubled back on itself up to the next floor.

Most of the lower bannisters were still intact. White paint grinned through the soot in places. The spindles on the upper portion of the staircase had been reduced to blackened stumps and the walls around and above the small landing were cracked and crumbling.

'Can't you see it?' Jess asked, almost excitedly.

It took Cooper a moment, but then he nodded. 'Yeah. Looks like the fire started in the dining room, but there's no way it could have done this much damage to the stairs without the hall being in the same kind of state.' He reached out to touch one of the more intact lower spindles. 'And how come these are still OK, while the higher ones have been destroyed?'

'Exactly.'

He turned to look at Jess. Her eyes were wide and she nodded in encouragement, as though she wanted Cooper to confirm whatever it was she was thinking.

'You think another fire started on the stairs?' he asked. 'Two separate fires?'

'That's exactly what I'm thinking,' Jess said. 'Which can only mean one thing.'

Cooper nodded. 'It means it was arson.'

LEON

Three pills and a decent helping of whisky.

It wasn't enough to pull him into the hallucinatory depths he'd experienced after taking five, but enough for the drugs to wrap him in a warm chemical blanket. Enough for his brain to close off to the noise of the traffic outside his open window and keep him balancing the precipice between sleeping and waking.

In recent months he'd learned to control the dreams, though he supposed memories were a more accurate way of describing them. As he felt the first surges of the chemical tide washing over him, he would begin to think about the memory he wanted to relive, though he really didn't have too many options. There were the interactions he'd had with countless, faceless girls, though even those had begun to lose their appeal. More often than not, he'd find himself thinking back to the first Christmas morning he'd had at his foster parents' house, though he'd never been able to feel the same warmth he'd felt that day. While there hadn't been the usual huge pile of store-wrapped gifts from his parents, or the lavish meal prepared by a hired chef, there had been something Leon realized he'd been missing his whole life.

But no matter how much Nostalgex Leon took, he'd never been able to recreate the feeling of that day. That wasn't what the drug did, it didn't make you *feel* the same, it just replayed the memories as if they'd been recorded and replayed on a TV screen.

Now, as the drugs began to take hold, he found himself unable to think of anything but the day his father had died.

The memory appeared as if it were smoke, gently invading the periphery of his vision at first, almost undetectable. But as the chemicals continued to pass from blood to brain, the smoke became a shimmering haze, the images fading in and out of focus as his grip on reality began to falter.

He was fourteen.

Walking through the garden in the dark, almost tripping over the empty firework box.

In the distance tyres crunched on gravel, the sounds of the last guests leaving. Fire cracked and popped nearby, while a lone firework screamed in the distance.

His mouth was filled with the metallic tang of his own blood, his tongue absently probing the newly acquired space where his two front teeth had once been. Soft, like raw meat.

He could smell the cold in the air, but it wasn't as cold as the metal in his hand. A faint breeze lifted a few strands of hair and the crackle of the fire briefly intensified as the gust continued its journey.

Behind the pagoda that had been installed that summer he could see his father standing beside the barbecue pit. The flames had been turned up to dispose of the remains of the hog roast and the stench of burning meat clung to the air.

Frank turned, his eyes immediately locking with Leon's.

Ice clinked against glass as Frank raised a tumbler to his lips and took a sip, his lips curling against the gold teeth as he sucked in his breath. The firelight shone through the cut crystal in his hand.

'That's good whisky,' he said, his eyes flicking to the gun in his son's hand. He laughed. Husky. Mocking. 'What are you going to do? Shoot me?' Frank sniffed and turned to look at the fire. 'It's not even loaded.'

Leon raised the gun, his finger twitching at the trigger. 'What's the golden rule, Dad?'

Frank turned again, snarling as he prepared to say something in return. What that had been, Leon would never know.

Under the effects of the Nostalgex, every sense was heightened.

Even down to the contracting sinews of the tendons in

his fingers, Leon felt everything.

The click of the safety under his thumb.

The indent of the trigger against the fleshy pad of his right index finger.

The pressure, building in his wrist and forearm as he squeezed, his other hand tightening around the grip.

The sparks from the barbecue pit, dancing like fireflies behind Frank.

The drum of his heart, the blood thundering through his body, almost deafening and yet barely noticeable beneath the explosion of the gun.

The recoil, lifting his hands into the air.

And then his father's face, his curling, sneering lips briefly dropping as his mouth fell open in surprise. The explosion of flesh and bone a centimetre below and to the right of his left eyebrow, the bullet carving out layers of skin, muscle and cartilage as it disappeared into Frank's head. The larger, messier explosion from behind as the bullet made its exit.

For a heartbeat, Frank didn't move. Nothing happened. Then black blood began to pour from the hole where his left eye had been and Frank fell backwards, the flames embracing his body as he disappeared into the barbecue pit.

What happened next was something Leon had been unable to remember until he'd taken his first hit of Nostalgex. The gun slipped from his hand, the rough grip almost like sandpaper against his skin under the effects of the drug. It clumped gently against the grass as he turned back to the house and ran.

The first few times he'd taken the Nostalgex, he hadn't noticed the person standing beside the pagoda. But once he'd noticed, he'd found himself returning to the memory time and time again, pausing as his head whipped around and his eyes focussed somewhere just to the right of the figure. Yet no matter how many times he returned, no matter how hard he tried, he'd been unable to make out the person's face.

But there was no doubt in Leon's mind.

This was the person who had picked up the gun.

The same person who had contacted him, two years later, telling him they had the evidence needed to put Leon behind bars for life unless he did what they said.

The person he called Whiteface.

The person who was trying to make him kill again.

JESS

'You sure you don't want me to go first?' Cooper asked.

Jess's hand tightened on the charred bannister and she turned to face him with a forced smile. 'I'm sure I'm just as capable of this as you are, thanks.' The words came out with more venom than she'd anticipated and she steeled herself for Cooper's response. She'd never speak to Luke in that way, but something about being with Cooper brought out her feisty side.

'Yeah, sorry,' he muttered.

She looked at him for a moment longer, sure that he was preparing to add something else. When he only stared back, she turned and continued up to the next landing.

The damage on the first floor was even worse than it had been in the dining room. Wind blew in through the remains of the back of the house, and the stairwell that led up to the second floor was completely destroyed from the mezzanine upwards. The spindles must have acted as kindling, spreading the fire rapidly upwards.

Jess continued, picking her way across the landing to the doorway of Scarlett's bedroom. She placed a hand against the doorframe and peered in, her eyes flicking from the exposed springs of Scarlett's charred mattress to the tattered piece of pink fabric that hung from the curtain pole above a glassless window, flapping in the breeze like a piece of bunting. On the ruined carpet below, one of Scarlett's teddy bears lay looking up at the ceiling with glassy eyes.

'Here,' Cooper called out from behind. 'Is this it?'

Jess turned to see Cooper holding a plastic bag, the outside grimy with soot.

'Yes!' Jess snatched the pills from Cooper's hand. She ran her fingers across the blackened surface to reveal the clear plastic beneath and the red pills within. Without a word, she threw her arms around Cooper's neck, hugging him tightly.

'Hey,' he said, patting her awkwardly on the back. 'It's OK.'

'Thank you,' she whispered.

His hand came to rest on the small of her back, the other on the back of her head. For a moment she felt safe, like she had found her way home after a terrible storm, then, before she could think any more, she pushed him away and turned back to Scarlett's ruined bedroom. This was her reality now, this was the mess she was supposed to be dealing with.

'Looks like the firemen had a bit of trouble getting in here,' Cooper said, kicking at something on the floor.

'What is that?' Jess asked, frowning at the pieces of wood beneath Cooper's foot.

'The door,' Cooper said. He reached down and picked up a shard of wood, splintered and broken. 'They must have broken it down.'

Jess took the piece of wood from Cooper and turned it over in her hands. She looked to her left and, sure enough, part of the door remained attached to the hinges. It had most definitely been smashed down. 'When the fire first started, Luke and Scarlett were in there with the door locked.'

'Any particular reason?' Cooper asked, stepping inside the room and looking around. When Jess failed to reply, he turned to her with a sympathetic look. 'Ah,' he said.

'What's that supposed to mean?'

'There aren't many reasons why a guy and a girl lock themselves in a bedroom, are there? Especially at a party.' He paused. 'Is that why you called Luke your ex earlier?'

Jess turned away. 'I don't want to talk about it.'

'Fair enough.' Cooper's eyes remained on her for a second longer, then he moved back to the doorframe.

'I don't understand why Luke or Scarlett couldn't unlock it from inside?'

'Maybe they couldn't get to the door,' Cooper suggested.

'No, Luke said they tried the key but it wouldn't turn.'

Cooper shrugged in response, unhelpfully.

'But don't you see? That doesn't make any sense.'

Jess kicked at the charred remains of the broken door. Then she gasped, grabbing at Cooper's arm. 'The key was missing from the bathroom.'

'So?' Cooper looked at her like she was mad.

'They have universal keys! I know because we used to mess around with them as kids. Someone must have used the key from the bathroom to lock Scarlett's door from the outside!'

Cooper sighed. 'Seriously, Jess? You've got to stop obsessing. This was just an accident. A horrible, tragic, accident.'

'No! Luke said something was stopping the door from opening. What was it?'

Cooper said nothing for a long time. 'I guess I don't have an answer for that,' he said finally.

'Because the answer is that someone locked them in from the outside.'

'Do you realize what you're suggesting? That someone was trying to kill them? You're talking about attempted murder. Who could possibly want to kill Scarlett? She's one of the sweetest people I've ever met.'

'Who said anything about Scarlett?' Jess lifted the sooty bag of pills, holding them up in front of Cooper's face. 'These things almost got you killed last night, right?'

'I'm not sure about killed,' Cooper said, reaching up to touch his swollen eye. 'But yeah, I get what you're saying.'

He closed his eyes and gently massaged his temple, as though he were trying to rub away a headache.

'The message on Luke's phone, the one from Leon? It said he owed money.' She glanced at the pieces of shattered door at her feet. 'Do you think he was the one who did this?'

Cooper said nothing.

'I don't know how this is related,' Jess said. 'But it is. I can feel it and I need you to say that you believe me. Don't you think it's weird that this happened on the same night that these drugs get planted on you? It's not like the churchyard is too far from here, either.'

Cooper opened his eyes again and looked at Jess. This time she ignored the sting of tears because it was more important that Cooper agreed with her. Hell, he didn't even need to agree with her, she just wanted to hear him say that she wasn't imagining it all. That she wasn't going crazy.

'Jess,' he said. 'You're the smartest person I know. If you think this is all connected, who am I to argue?'

Without even thinking, Jess lunged forwards and wrapped her arms around Cooper's neck. 'Thank you.'

He patted her and the awkwardness was enough to make her smile.

'We should probably start thinking about . . .' Cooper paused, then took a step through the doorway. He turned back to Jess, a finger over his lips and a hand up to indicate she should stay where she was.

'What is it?' she mouthed, but her question was answered

112

when she heard the sound of voices below. An instant rush of adrenaline kicked her heart into double time and she looked at Cooper, eyes wide. He crept over to the empty window frame and, keeping himself pressed against the wall beside it, carefully leaned around to look out. Without a word, he covered the distance between the window and the doorway where Jess stood in only a few strides. 'We have to go,' he whispered.

Jess nodded and for the second time that day she placed her hand in his. She followed him as he stepped carefully towards the stairs. A floorboard creaked beneath her and they froze, Cooper's hand tightening around her fingers. Only when she was sure that there had been no break in the conversation going on below them did Jess nod for Cooper to continue. The stairs seemed even more difficult to negotiate on the way down than they had on the way up, but they managed to reach the mezzanine before Cooper paused, holding his hand up again for Jess to wait.

Now able to make out two separate male voices, Jess strained to locate where they were coming from.

'Dining room,' Cooper whispered, as though he'd read her mind. With his eyes fixed on the bottom of the staircase and the opening in the dividing wall that led out into the hallway, Cooper continued his descent.

Not like he's inexperienced at creeping around, a voice said in Jess's head. She quickly pushed away the unwelcome thought, frowning at the viciousness of it. It made her want to pull her hand away from Cooper's, as though by touching him, he might be able to sense what she was thinking.

She was over it, she told herself. Everything that had happened with Cooper was done with and forgotten about.

So why did she still feel a flare of anger towards him?

At the bottom of the staircase, Cooper released her hand and peered around the dividing wall. With a quick nod, he beckoned Jess and she followed him into the hallway. The voices were still coming from within the dining room, but their owners were out of sight, somewhere near the back of the house.

No longer caring about the floorboards, Jess chased after Cooper as he ran through the hallway and out of the back door. More than once, he glanced over his shoulder, to check that Jess was still behind him.

'Hey,' a voice suddenly called from within the house. 'Hey, you kids get back here right now!'

Without even daring to glance behind her, Jess raced to where Cooper was already by the fence, his face fixed on a point somewhere behind her.

'Quick,' he shouted, pulling open the gap in the fence panel. 'Get out, quick!'

As she pushed her body through the small space, Jess turned to see a man in a dark blue uniform leap down the steps by the back door. 'Hey!' he shouted again, sprinting across the grass towards them. 'You two need to stop!'

'Cooper, come on!' Jess reached over to hold the fence panel as he slipped through after her. She grabbed his arm

114

and pulled with all of her strength, and he came tumbling through to the sound of splintering wood.

'Run,' he said, without even turning to look.

Jess took off, her feet pounding the concrete. She concentrated on the rhythm of her steps and the way they matched Cooper's, listening intently for a third set of running feet. But they never came. Once they'd reached the road, Jess glanced back down the alleyway. It was empty.

With his hands on his hips, Cooper drew a deep breath. 'We seem to be getting into a nasty habit of being chased,' he said through a half-smile.

'Yeah,' Jess replied. 'Funny how you've been back in my life for less than a day and you're already getting me into trouble.'

Cooper raised an eyebrow. 'I'd say you were in trouble way before I arrived. If anything, you're the one who seems to be leading *me* astray.' He paused. 'Which would be a first, in all fairness.'

Unable to stop herself, Jess smiled. There seemed to be a new side to Cooper these days, a self-awareness that he'd lacked when they were together. 'You didn't ever lead me astray,' she said. 'I tolerated your antics from afar.'

'That's probably the nicest thing you've ever said to me.'

Jess laughed. 'Probably.' She glanced over her shoulder once more. 'Any idea who those guys were?'

'Fire Investigation Unit,' Cooper said. 'I saw their van outside.'

'Surely they only get those guys out if they're suspicious about a fire?'

Cooper shrugged. 'Who knows? But we should probably get out of here. What do you want to do next?'

'I want to sleep,' Jess said. 'Then I want to wake up and have everything back to normal. You think you can arrange that for me?'

He smiled at her sadly. 'I would if I could.'

'Yeah. I know.'

A silence hung in the air between them, almost palpable.

'I have to go,' Cooper blurted out. 'I have to work.'

'Really? You're going to work like that? You've not even slept.'

'It was good to see you again,' Cooper said, ignoring her question. 'Even if it's because of all this craziness.' He paused. 'Do you still have my number?'

'Yes. Do you still have mine?'

'I do. I mean, my phone's at home on charge so I can't check, but I'm pretty sure it's still there. I don't remember deleting it.'

'OK then. So, I guess we'll talk later?'

'I think that's a good idea.' With a nod, Cooper turned and began walking away. For a moment Jess wanted to call him back, to beg him not to go to work and to stay with her, because she couldn't stand the idea of being left alone with her thoughts and the memories of the previous night.

But she said nothing.

Once she had turned the corner, Jess pulled her phone out of her pocket to check, even though she knew full well that Cooper's number was still saved in her contacts. The screen lit up with a number of missed calls and texts, most of which were from Hannah and her dad. She opened the first and most recent message.

Scarlett's awake. Call me.

JESS

Jess's shoes squeaked on the linoleum floor as she crossed the ITU ward to where Hannah sat beside Scarlett's bed, wearing the same plastic apron the nurses had asked Jess to put on when she'd arrived. A curtain was pulled halfway across the length of Scarlett's bed, so Jess was able to make out the shape of her friend's legs under a blanket, but her upper body was hidden.

The scent of the alcohol rub she'd used to clean her hands mixed in with the other hospital smells. The overhead lights were too bright and machines bleeped and pinged all around her. Jess's stomach rolled in protest at the sudden assault to her senses and she drew in a deep breath to quell the nausea as she approached the bed.

If it weren't for the small whiteboard above the bed with *Scarlett Ahlstrom* scrawled on it in black pen, Jess would never have believed it was her friend lying there.

The puffy face didn't look like it belonged to Scarlett. The blonde hair fanned out on the pillow behind her was the only part of her that still looked like it always did. Her mouth was obscured by a tube that led to a ventilator, the machine hissing and sucking as it pushed and pulled the air from Scarlett's lungs. Tubes fed clear and corn-yellow liquids into her arms, while wires connected her to a myriad machines that Jess thought wouldn't look out of place in a NASA launch control room.

Trying to focus on her friend's eyes, Jess forced a smile. 'Hey,' she said.

Scarlett blinked, but the rest of her face remained motionless.

'She can't speak,' Hannah said. 'But I guess you probably figured that out for yourself.' She stood up and crossed to the other side of the bed where Jess stood, pulling her into a hug. 'I was worried about you,' she whispered. 'Where did you go? Why didn't you answer your phone?'

'I'm sorry,' Jess whispered back. She felt Hannah nod against her before she pulled back, wearing a smile that looked as fake as Jess's felt.

'You should call your dad by the way. I told him you were OK but didn't know where you went.'

Jess nodded weakly.

'So,' Hannah's voice was heavy with fake enthusiasm as she turned to look at Scarlett. 'The doctors have said that this breathing tube should be out in a day or two. Isn't that great?'

Scarlett lifted one of her bandaged arms a few centimetres and gave a shaky thumbs up.

'That's really great,' Jess said, her voice as ridiculously cheery as Hannah's as she returned Scarlett's thumbs up. Seriously, it was like the world's worst audition for a pair of kids' TV presenters.

She lowered herself into one of the plastic moulded chairs beside Scarlett's bed and gently touched her friend's hand. 'I'm so glad you're doing OK,' she said to Scarlett's eyes. It was the only part she felt comfortable looking at; every other inch of her was bloated and bandaged and covered in the equipment that was keeping her alive.

Scarlett blinked again, though her eyelids appeared heavy, her pupils dilating and giving her the appearance of someone who wasn't quite managing to focus either physically or mentally.

'Your mum and dad around?' Jess asked. Of course she knew that Mr and Mrs Ahlstrom would be close by, but she needed something to talk about. Something that would push away the memories of the previous night.

Scarlett managed a single, slow nod and her eyes moved to the left, where the doors led out of the ITU.

'They've gone to get coffee,' Hannah said, reaching to brush a strand of hair from Scarlett's forehead. 'The police have just left and they've been here all night so I said I'd wait with Scarlett while they took a break.'

Jess took in the bags under Hannah's eyes and her clothes; the same outfit she'd been wearing since the party.

'You look like you could do with a break yourself. Have you been home yet?'

'No.' Hannah shook her head. 'And you don't look like you have either.'

Jess looked down at her dress; crumpled, torn and completely filthy. She knew her make-up was probably everywhere on her face except where it should be and that her hair had turned into a frizzy nightmare, but she didn't care. 'No,' she said. 'I guess I haven't.' She glanced back at Scarlett, whose eyes were now closed.

'She does that a lot,' said Hannah. 'They're giving her a lot of drugs, so she's in and out of sleep.' She looked at Jess. 'So where did you go? Luke said you had a fight.'

It was always like that with Hannah. No messing around, always straight to the point. Not that Jess ever got used to it, and perhaps that was why Hannah continued to be so forthright. There was something about her blatant honesty that caught people off guard and gave her the best chance of having them be honest in return.

'What else did he say?'

One of the machines by Scarlett's head began to beep obnoxiously, a two-tone siren that made Jess jump to her feet. 'What's happening? Is she OK?'

One of the nurses hurried over and pressed a few buttons. 'Nothing to worry about,' she said with a smile. 'They do that sometimes, like to keep us on our toes.'

With the machine quiet, Jess returned to her seat, though her heart was now beating double-time.

'He said that you thought he was cheating,' Hannah said.

The words hit Jess like a slap to the face.

Hannah didn't even wait for a response. 'He said it's not true. But I'm not going to side with him automatically, just because he's my brother. You should know that.'

'Thanks.'

'I love you both, but you know what? He's completely in love with you, Jess. I just can't see him doing something like that.'

Scarlett's eyes fluttered.

'Is now really the time to be talking about this?' Jess asked.

'Given that my brother is lying in a hospital bed and that I can't do anything to stop his physical pain, I would say that now is the perfect time to discuss this.' She spoke in measured tones, not taking her eyes from Jess. 'And you're in pain, too. I can see that.'

'I heard him,' she said, her voice low. 'I heard him and Scarlett talking about cheating.'

'You think he cheated on you with Scarlett? Are you crazy?'

'How am I the crazy one?' Tears stung Jess's eyes. 'I overhear my best friend and my boyfriend talking about cheating and I'm the crazy one?'

'Shit.' Hannah bit her lip, but she wasn't looking at Jess any more.

Scarlett was looking at Jess with wide, bloodshot eyes.

Jess could only stare back. 'Scarlett. I'm sorry, I didn't want to talk about this now. It's not the right time.'

Scarlett shook her head.

'Well, you kind of *have* to talk about it now,' Hannah said. 'You can't just leave it like that.'

'She's on a ventilator,' Jess snapped. 'It's not like she can say anything.'

Hannah turned to Scarlett. 'Is it true?' she asked, ignoring Jess. 'Were you and Luke seeing each other?'

Once again, Scarlett shook her head, this time with more vigour. She looked at Jess with wide, pleading eyes, the beeps of the machines around her increasing in tempo.

'I'm not doing this now. I can't.' Jess stood up. 'It's not fair on anyone.'

'What's not fair?'

Jess turned to see Scarlett's mother, holding a styrofoam cup. Wisps of steam rose up in front of her pale and drawn face, which was now crumpled in confusion. Her usually immaculate hair, as blonde as her daughter's, hung around her face in matted tendrils and the remains of the previous night's mascara streaked her cheeks. Scarlett's father lurked behind, his face a waxy grey and looking a good ten years older than the last time Jess had seen him.

'What's going on?' Mrs Ahlstrom asked, placing the cup on the table at the end of Scarlett's bed. 'Why is she crying?' She stepped forwards and stroked her daughter's face. 'Jess? Why is Scarlett crying? Is she in pain?'

'Can we get a nurse over here please?' Jess's dad glanced

about the ward for a member of staff before moving to his wife's side.

Jess looked from where Hannah sat with her arms folded, to Scarlett. Neither of them were looking at her.

A hand landed on Jess's arm. 'Honey, are *you* OK?' Scarlett's mum was looking at her with such concern, it made Jess want to curl up into a ball of shame. She should never have come, not until Scarlett was better and at least able to talk. 'Does your dad know you're all right? The police said that everyone had been accounted for after the fire, but nobody knew where you'd gone.'

'I have to go,' Jess said. 'I'm sorry, I shouldn't have come.'

Before anyone could stop her, she turned and walked away. She felt sick. Not only had she just come from breaking into the burned-out house of these poor people, the same people who'd welcomed Jess into their own home like she was a part of the family, she'd just accused their daughter, her *best friend*, of having an affair with her boyfriend. When she couldn't even defend herself.

When she was on a *ventilator*.

In the corridor outside, Jess leaned against the wall and exhaled in an attempt to stop the gathering tears.

'Jess?'

Jess looked up to see Luke standing a couple of metres from where she stood.

He was still in his hospital gown, but his arm was now strapped to his body with a sling. In his other hand, he clutched a pole on wheels which held his drip.

124

'What are you doing here?' she asked, eyeing the doors around her in an attempt to determine which would make the best exit.

'I came to see Scarlett.'

'Of course.' The words dripped sarcasm, but Jess couldn't help it. She'd had enough.

'Where did you go?' he asked, levelling his eyes with hers. 'After you left me here?'

'After I left you here? What was I supposed to do, Luke? Take you with me?'

'You could've stayed. I've been on my own.'

'What about Hannah? She's been to see you, right?'

His eyes moved slowly down her body and Jess felt the need to pull Cooper's jacket tighter around her. 'Whose coat is that?'

'It doesn't matter.'

'Did I say it did matter? Or did I ask you a question?' His voice was low, his lips thin, both warning signs that things were about to get very bad for Jess.

She started to walk away, but Luke reached out to grab her arm. She looked down at his hand, at the tube that was feeding liquid into one of his veins.

At the purple scars he'd gained on the night he grabbed her in just this way.

'Get your hands off me, Luke.' She looked into his eyes, something she realized she'd lost the courage to do in recent months when they argued. Not now, though. In the last twelve hours, she'd begun to recover a strength she'd forgotten she'd ever had.

His grip tightened as a hospital worker in a green tunic walked past, eyes flicking in their direction. 'Stop making a scene,' he whispered. 'Just calm down.'

'I said get your hands off me.'

'Why are you acting like this, Jess? Do you know how dramatic you sound? Stop making out like I'm the bad guy here.'

'Get. Your hands. Off me.'

For a moment his grip tightened, but she held his gaze and his hand fell away. He cupped her face, looking into her eyes with an all-too-familiar intensity. 'Let's go to the canteen,' he said. 'I'll buy you a coffee and we can talk, OK?' He smiled and took her hand in his and for a moment she allowed herself to be led away as she always had done, until she pulled her hand away.

He turned to look at her, his lips thinning again.

'We're over,' she said, before he could speak. 'And this time, I mean it.'

She allowed herself one last look at the scars on his knuckles, from a time when he'd convinced her that a break up could only be a mutual decision.

As she walked away she realized just how wrong she'd been.

COOPER

Cooper tilted his head back, letting the hot water run down his face and into his mouth.

Though he'd been told to leave the dressings on for a few days, he'd decided that it was worth losing them for the sake of a decent shower. His wounds stung under the heat, but it was a good kind of pain, a feeling of washing away the previous night's events. With the warmth seeping back into his aching bones, he was finally beginning to feel human again.

There was a sharp knock at the bathroom door. 'Sam? You want a cup of tea?'

Spitting out the mouthful of water he'd collected, Cooper reached to turn off the shower. 'Yeah, cheers.' He grabbed the towel that was hanging over the radiator and glanced at himself in the partly misted bathroom mirror. There was a huge scrape across his left shoulder, though he

127

had no recollection of how that particular injury had happened. Turning slowly, he examined his naked body, marvelling at the numerous scratches and bruises that adorned his skin.

'Serves me right,' he muttered, drying off his torso before wrapping the towel around his waist. He took a step closer to the mirror to examine the wounds on his face. It appeared that Dr Nowak had been right; despite the amount of blood that had poured from the gash on his cheek, it looked like it shouldn't leave too much of a scar, if anything at all. His face was still swollen though, and a nice purple bruise was beginning to form beneath his eye.

From the opposite side of the thin wall came the sounds of cupboards banging and the fridge door opening as Amy prepared the tea. Cooper slipped out of the bathroom, tracking wet footprints across the laminate flooring as he crossed the hall to his bedroom. The curtains were still drawn, but they usually were in Cooper's bedroom. He shut the door behind him before pulling the wardrobe door open to check that his backpack was still lying at the bottom. It was. As if anything could have happened to it in the fifteen minutes he'd spent showering. Still, he reached down and unzipped the top section, pulling it open to reveal the stash of pills.

'Sam?' There was a knock at the door.

'Hang on!' Heart hammering against his ribs, Cooper quickly pulled the zip closed and shut the wardrobe. 'I'll be out in a sec, OK?' With the sound of Amy's footsteps retreating, Cooper reached for the nearest pair of boxers in his clean washing pile. As he pulled them on, he glanced down at his phone, which was flashing incessantly. He pulled the charger cable out and opened the messages, most of which were from Jag.

Dude, where the hell did you go? You still at the hospital?

Cooper, seriously – you need to call me.

Right, I'm leaving. Call me NOW or I'm going without you.

Cooper continued to scroll until he reached the final message, sent about half an hour earlier.

That's it. I'm coming to yours. If you don't already have a good excuse for bailing on me, I'd come up with one now!

'Jeez,' Cooper muttered. He hit the button to call Jag back, but it went straight to voicemail. Which probably meant that Jag was on the tube. He replaced the phone on the bedside table, beside the framed photo of him and Amy on one of the many Caribbean beaches they used to holiday on. It was the only picture he kept of their past life, while Amy's bedroom wall was covered in photos of them and their parents.

'OK,' he called, opening his door. 'I'm ready.'

'Tea's in the kitchen.'

Cooper joined Amy at the kitchen table and winced as he lowered himself into one of the mismatched wooden chairs. On the table was his mother's teapot and two sets of cups and saucers. It was ridiculous, drinking from delicate bone china in a damp kitchen beneath a bare lightbulb, but the tea set was one of the few things Amy had salvaged from the house after almost everything else had either been seized or sold to pay for the legal bills.

'You look like hell.'

'Thanks.' Cooper took a sip from the cup and exhaled. 'That's great, Amy. Thanks so much.'

'No problem.' Amy pointed at a letter on the table next to Cooper. 'We got post yesterday, by the way.'

Cooper picked up the envelope and his stomach dropped. 'That's not a letter.'

'I know,' said Amy, watching as Cooper ripped it open. 'Which is why I waited for you. I couldn't face opening it alone.'

Scanning the bill, the heaviness in Cooper's stomach mutated to a feeling of his guts being turned inside out. 'Shit.'

'It can't be that bad,' Amy said, reaching for the letter. Her eyebrows shot up and she dropped the bill on the table like it had just burned her fingers.

'What are we going to do?' she asked, her eyes wide. 'We barely made rent last month. How are we going to pay for this?'

'We don't really need electricity, do we?' Cooper asked, only half joking.

Amy buried her face in her hands. 'When's it going to end, Sam? It's like we're constantly swimming upstream. I feel like we're drowning.'

'I know,' Cooper said, reaching out to take his sister's hand. 'But we're going to be OK.'

'How? How are we going to be OK? We have no money, we have barely enough food for three meals a day and god only knows where Uncle Barry is.'

Cooper scratched the back of his head. 'You know Jag's dad said we could stay with them. Maybe we should—'

'No,' Amy snapped. 'We're not a charity, Sam. And we'd lose the flat if we stopped paying rent. Then what? We can't stay at Jag's forever and we'll never find anywhere cheaper than this.'

Looking around at the stained walls, at the mildew gathering in the corners of the room, Cooper had to concede that Amy was right. Staying at Jag's could only ever be a temporary measure and through whatever dodgy deal their uncle had made with the landlord, there was no doubt that this was possibly the cheapest flat in London.

'I just want to go home,' Amy said in a small voice.

'We are home.'

'That's not what I meant.'

'I know what you meant. But you can't say stuff like that,' he snapped. He knew he was being harsh, but the truth was that he too wanted nothing more than to return to the last place they had called home. The sprawling mansion they had lived in with their mother and father, up until they were arrested and Cooper and Amy were sent to live with their errant uncle, who wasn't even really their uncle. Barry was their mother's step-brother, but the closest thing they had to a living relative who'd been willing to take in two teens. Though as it turned out, he'd been more interested in the child support and tax credits than in reconnecting with his long-lost step-niece and nephew.

'It was ours,' Amy said, shaking her head. 'They had no right to take it from us.'

'It was never ours. Everything we owned was paid for with drug money, Amy. You know that.'

Dissolving into a fresh round of tears, Amy nodded. 'But we were just kids, Sam. We didn't know any better, so why did we have to suffer?'

Cooper limped to where his sister sat and wrapped an arm around her shoulder. 'You're right,' he said. 'We were just kids. But it's all going to be OK, I promise. We'll figure something out, all right?'

'All right.' Amy wiped her eyes with the palm of her hand. 'I'm sorry,' she said, half laughing. 'I shouldn't be dumping all this on you. It's not like it's your fault.' She touched the heart pendant that hung from her neck, a far cry from the jewels that used to drip from their mother. 'And you worked so hard to buy me this. Really, I should be grateful for everything you do.'

'It's OK.' Cooper kissed the top of her head. 'And we're going to be OK.'

Amy nodded. 'And you know, I can always quit college if it means—'

'No, we stay to the end; that was our deal. It's not long, only a few more months. It would be such a waste to quit now.'

'OK.' Amy smiled. 'You really are the best.'

A figure passed by the kitchen window before a loud knock came from the front door.

Shave-and-a-haircut.

'Oh man, it's Jag,' Cooper muttered. 'And I think he's pissed off with me.'

'What? Why?' Amy walked into the hallway and Cooper followed.

She opened the front door and Jag stepped past without even a hint of flirting. In fact, his eyes were locked on Cooper.

'What the hell, man?' Jag pushed past Amy to where Cooper stood, placed his hands firmly against his chest and shoved, hard.

Cooper stumbled back, his bruised shoulder colliding with the doorframe. 'Hey,' he said, straightening himself up. 'Take it easy!'

'Take it easy?' Jag's eyes darkened, his lips thinning as his voice began to rise in pitch. 'You bail on last night's party, turn up this morning with a smashed-up face and a bag full of drugs, then disappear again two hours later?' Jag stepped forwards, jabbing a finger at Cooper's bare chest. 'And you're telling me to take it easy?'

Cooper slapped Jag's hand away. 'Don't touch me,' he snapped. 'You have no idea what happened, so don't come round here getting all up in my face when you don't even know the facts.'

'That's enough.' Amy appeared behind Jag, grabbing at his jacket as she attempted to pull him back towards the front door. 'Time for you to leave.' She looked Cooper square in the eye. 'Sounds like my brother and I need to have a talk.' She pulled Jag towards the front door, but he twisted his body, releasing himself from her grip.

'I'm here to see Cooper,' he said, more softly this time, though he avoided making any kind of eye contact with Amy. 'Not you. He's the one who gets to say if I should leave.'

'This is my flat too—' Amy snapped, before Cooper cut her off.

'It's OK. Just give him a minute. Please.'

Amy levelled her eyes with Cooper's. 'Fine. But you need to tell me what's going on. For real, this time, OK?'

Cooper sighed, closing his eyes and rubbing at his temple. 'It's not how it sounds, Amy.'

'So you don't have a bag full of drugs? Jag was lying about that?'

'He . . .' Cooper paused, turning to glare at Jag, who was looking innocently at the ceiling. 'No, he's not lying, but—'

'Jesus, Sam!' Amy threw her hands up in the air. 'I thought we were over all this?'

'Over what?' Cooper snapped. 'Nothing like this has ever happened before – what are you talking about?'

'I'm talking about all the trouble you were getting in the last couple of years. Getting arrested for all the stupid crap you two were pulling.'

'I've been arrested twice, Amy.' Even as he said it,

Cooper realized how stupid it sounded. As though getting arrested once or twice was no big deal. But he couldn't help himself. 'And you know one of those times wasn't even really my fault.'

Amy glared. 'If you're talking about last New Year's Eve, how was that not your fault? Just because Jess was the one who called the police, it doesn't make it *her* fault.'

'She had no reason to—'

'She had every reason, Sam. Things got out of control. Just because I took your side, it doesn't mean I think you were right. I lost some of my best friends because of your stupidity.'

'Nobody's stopping you from seeing Hannah and Jess.'

'Whatever.' Amy shook her head. 'You know what, Sam? If you want to end up like Dad, be my guest. I'm not going to stop you.'

'I'm not going to end up like Dad. This whole thing has just been a huge misunderstanding, OK?'

'A bag full of drugs is a misunderstanding?'

'As if he'd get involved with Leon on purpose,' Jag scoffed.

'*Leon?*' Amy looked from Jag to Cooper. 'You're involved with Leon? He's as crazy as his dad! What were you thinking?'

'His dad can't be that crazy,' Cooper snapped. 'Seeing as how ours is in prison while Leon's is out there somewhere, living the life of Reilly.'

'Frank knocked Leon's teeth out, Sam. His own son's

135

front teeth. If that's not crazy enough for you, I don't know what is. And what? You think you're untouchable? That you're not going to end up like Dad?'

Without a word, Cooper turned and walked into his bedroom. Flinging open the wardrobe door, he yanked the backpack from the bottom, unzipping the top compartment as he returned to where Jag and Amy stood in the hallway. 'Here,' he said, tipping the bag upside down. The bags of pills slid out, landing at Amy's feet. Tossing the backpack aside, Cooper pointed at the packages. 'You really think I'd deliberately get involved with this stuff? With *Leon*? You think I'd deliberately put myself in a position where I have to somehow conjure up a grand by tomorrow night, so he doesn't—' Cooper stopped himself, shocked at the way his voice had risen, at the heat raging in his belly. His shoulders were lifting and falling in time with his breathing and it suddenly felt like everything was closing in on him, like the weight of the last twenty-four hours had taken on a physical, palpable form that was crushing him from above, that was—

'Sam?'

Cooper opened his eyes to see Amy kneeling on the floor in front of him, her eyes full of concern. Somehow he had gone from standing to sitting, his knees tucked up to his chest and his hands covering his face. Jag was crouching next to him, his eyes fixed on one of the bags of pills.

'I'm sorry,' Cooper said, his head throbbing steadily in time with his heart. 'I'm really sorry.' He didn't even know what he was apologising for, or who he was even apologising to, but it felt like the right thing to say.

'What are we going to do?' Jag asked, picking up one of the bags and weighing it in his hand.

'We?'

'Of course, man,' Jag replied with a wry smile. 'You know I've got your back. Look, I know I came in here shouting and everything, but it was only because I was worried about you. You just disappeared from the hospital and I had no idea why.'

'I was with Jess,' Cooper said.

'You were with Jess? Your ex-girlfriend, Jess? The one who broke your heart and—'

'Yes,' Cooper snapped. 'That Jess. Looks like she's somehow got caught up in this mess too . . . Not that it makes any sense.'

'What makes you think she's involved?' Amy asked.

'She had some of those,' Cooper said, pointing to the pills in Jag's hand. 'Looks like Luke had been dealing and somehow she ended up with them.' He closed his eyes again, leaning his pounding head back against the wall. 'One thousand pounds,' he said slowly. 'How am I going to get my hands on that much money by tomorrow night? It's not like I can do anything about it today. I have to work.'

'I don't know,' Jag said slowly, in measured tones. 'Maybe you could borrow the cash.'

Opening his one good eye, Cooper turned to Jag.

'Oh yeah? And who's going to lend me that kind of money? You?'

Jag shrugged. 'If it's just a loan, then why not the Fill 'n' Save?'

Cooper laughed. 'Yeah, right. Can you imagine me asking Big Phil? Hey man, any chance you could front me a grand to stop this drug dealer from cutting me up any more?'

'I never said anything about asking him.'

'Jag!' Amy cried, though her voice carried little conviction.

'You're talking about stealing?' Cooper asked. 'From Phil?' He paused for a moment, then shook his head, hating himself for even entertaining the idea.

'It's not stealing if you pay it back,' Jag said, tossing the bag of pills back on to the pile. 'And there's enough merchandise here to pay him back tenfold if you want to.' Jag raised his hands. 'Look, I'm not telling you what to do, Coop. I'm just giving you options.'

Cooper stared at the pile of drugs on the laminate floor, then turned to look at Amy. Her face was drawn, pale, and her eyes were wide with fear. As much as he hated to admit it, Jag was right. Taking the money from the Fill 'n' Save was certainly an option.

And right now, it was the only one he had.

JESS

The warm aroma of chicken soup filled the lounge.

Without opening her eyes, Jess groaned and pulled the blanket up over her head before turning to face the back of the sofa.

'You've got to eat sometime.'

'It's too early.'

'It's afternoon, actually.' The end of the sofa dipped beneath the weight of Jess's father. 'And since when has it ever been too early for my chicken soup?'

'Since today.'

There was a sigh, followed by the clink of a bowl being placed on the coffee table. 'You haven't even been to bed. If you're not going to sleep, at least eat something. It's your favourite.' Jess's father spoke softly, the remnants of his Jamaican accent giving his voice a richness that never failed to comfort her.

She peered out from under the blanket. 'I'm not hungry.'

There was a pause. 'If you need me to come back to the hospital with you later . . .'

'I don't know when I'm going back.'

'Then sleep. I know you don't think you'll be able to, but I promise you, sleep will come. Problems don't go away by you staying awake and worrying about them, but they're far, far easier to deal with once you've rested.'

'OK,' she said, standing up from the sofa and dragging the quilt behind her. 'I'll try to sleep.'

'Thank you,' Michael said, and he did look truly grateful. 'I'll be right here if you need me.' He took her hand and planted a kiss on her palm, and Jess smiled at him.

'I know you, Jessica. And I know when something you can't talk to me about is making you sad. I know I'll never replace your mum, but I'll always be here if you need me.'

'I'm OK.' Jess leaned in to kiss her father on the cheek. 'And you should know that having you as a dad means I still have more than some other kids whose parents are both still alive.'

She passed by the mantelpiece on her way out of the living room and, though she tried not to look into the mirror, she couldn't help but steal a glance. Her reflection stared back at her, pale and wild eyed. Her hair was even wilder, the curls tightened from the previous night's rain and sticking out from her head at crazy angles. In the reflection beside her was their Christmas tree, its branches drooping and the bare wooden floor around it covered with dropped pine needles. It was a sorry-looking picture, set in the mirror's ornate silver frame.

'Sleep,' Michael repeated, firmer this time.

Jess met his eye in the mirror and she nodded, dragging her quilt out of the room and up the uncarpeted staircase. They were decorating the hall, or at least that's what her father kept telling her every time she bugged him about the bare wooden steps. 'All in good time,' he'd tell her with a smile. 'Everything in good time.'

On the way up the stairs, she trailed her fingers along the chipped plaster. Sometimes she could hear Luke's or Hannah's music through the wall, but today all was quiet.

She pushed open the door to her bedroom.

On one of her painted white bedposts hung two masks; the two choices she had rejected the previous night. One was white, a phantom-of-the-opera style that covered half her face. The other was masquerade style, like the one she had ultimately chosen, but this one was a fiery red, and was adorned with silver sequins.

As she stared at the masks something in her brain seemed to spark, like the flash of a firework in her peripheral vision. But as quickly as it had appeared, it was gone, buried deeply within the recesses of her memory.

Luke's and Cooper's jackets lay on her bed where she had dumped them on first arriving home, before dragging her quilt downstairs to the sofa.

Jess lay back on her bed, closing her eyes as she massaged her temples. How had everything gone so wrong in such a short space of time? She turned her head to come face to face with Luke's jacket. Unable to help herself, she pulled it close to her face and inhaled. It still smelled just like him. She closed her eyes and breathed deeply, letting the scent fill her head, clouding her mind with memories of happier times. Aimless walks, hand in hand through the cobbled back streets of the East End. The park in the summertime, when they'd climbed fully clothed into the fountain and kicked water at each other. Lying on Jess's bed studying, Luke with his eyes closed and stroking her hair while she read to him from her chemistry revision guide. In fact, now that she thought about it, there were few times she could remember being without him in the last few months.

They'd spent almost every waking hour together, something she'd thought had been so romantic. So why did the thought now make her feel so claustrophobic? Maybe because he was *always* there, and even when he wasn't, he was always—

On her bedside table, beside a half drunk glass of water, her phone buzzed.

'Go away,' she whispered, but still she reached out to pick it up.

Call me. Please.

It was Luke. Of course it was. It was *always* Luke.

Leave me alone.

The reply came almost immediately. **Where are you?**

Jess paused. **I'm out**, she typed.

With Cooper?

Her stomach twisted. How did he know she'd been with Cooper?

Her phone buzzed again. I know you were with him. What are you playing at, Jess? The moment we have a fight you go running back to him?

Jess knew she shouldn't reply, but she couldn't help herself. I didn't go running to anyone. And it's none of your business, I told you we're over.

Of course it's my business. Is he there now?

What could she say? If she didn't reply, she knew what would happen next. Luke would be out of that hospital and at her door within the hour.

No. He's gone to work.

For a moment her phone was silent, then it buzzed again.

Does he still work at that petrol station?

Jess tossed her phone back on to her bedside table. It was time to stop replying. She looked at Luke's jacket, then pushed it away. A few of the loose pills spilled from the pocket. She scooped them up and shoved them back inside. She had to get rid of them, for now at least. She could stash them away somewhere, hide them, just so long as she didn't have to think about them for a while. Not until she was able to get her head around everything else that had happened.

Until she was able to figure out how she was involved in the same mess as Cooper.

She grabbed her phone, her fingers dancing over the keys as she typed out a text message. She knew he'd be at work, but that never used to stop him from replying when they were dating.

Though things were different now. *He* was different now, too.

How do these pills work, anyway?

She found Cooper's number and hit the send button before she had a chance to change her mind. Then she pulled out some of the loose pills that she had shoved so unceremoniously into Luke's pockets.

They were bright red; so bright they almost looked like a child's sweets. Or vitamins. They certainly looked harmless enough, though she knew that looks meant nothing when it came to drugs. She turned one over in her hand and looked at the symbol, a question mark overlaying an exclamation mark. She ran her finger over it and felt the way it was stamped into the pill, an indelible mark that would only be destroyed by the digestive juices of whoever decided to swallow it.

Her phone buzzed and she reached for it.

People use them to hallucinate memories. Why?

Jess frowned as she typed her reply. **What does that mean?**

A couple of minutes passed before the next message came through, containing nothing but a website link. Jess clicked on it and a Wikipedia page opened on her phone.

NOSTALGEX, alternatively known by its colloquial term of

'N', or 'Reds', is a synthetic psychedelic drug known for its ability to create realistic hallucinations of the user's past, providing what is described as a mind altering, spiritual experience. In smaller doses (one to three pills), Nostalgex can be used to recollect vast amounts of information, and conspiracy theorists believe it has been used for military purposes, allowing humans to be used as biological computers for the purpose of smuggling data without the need for hardware and its associated hacking risks. There has also been speculation that Nostalgex is used by law enforcement agencies for extracting information from witnesses, either with or without the witness's cooperation.

It has been reported that Nostalgex abuse is a growing problem among students during exam periods, used to help them recall information when sitting tests.

Nostalgex is more commonly known for its recreational use, for the enhanced experience it gives users who want to relive past experiences. For some this may be a particular event that has given the user pleasure, or for those wishing to simply experience the heightened, often euphoric experience reported by users.

Jess read the information, then read it again. She looked at the tiny pills lying in the palm of her hand.

How could something so small do so much? She returned to the text-message conversation.

So it's a memory pill?

Moments later, her phone buzzed.

It's more than that. They say it's like real life, but in HD. I dunno, never taken it.

Jess looked at the pills again. Could they really allow her to relive her memories? Like she was watching them on a TV screen? Maybe she could figure out where everything had gone so wrong.

Maybe she could figure out how to fix it all.

Well, she typed, **I guess there's only one way to find out.** She tossed the pills into her mouth and took a big gulp from the glass of water on her bedside table. She had made a New Year's resolution to be more reckless, to be more like Luke, so why not stick with it?

The moment the water hit her stomach, her gut twisted with regret. A wave of nausea hit her, the contents of her stomach threatening to make a very sudden reappearance.

Which actually seemed like a very good idea.

Her phone buzzed beside her and she looked down to see Cooper's number calling, but she was already up and making her way out of her bedroom to the bathroom.

She burst through the door, hunched over the toilet and shoved two fingers down her throat. She gagged, but nothing came up. Suddenly terrified, she tried again but achieved nothing more than a painful retching. Why did she take so many? She must have swallowed five of them, maybe even six. How many should she have taken? The article said three was a small dose. Had she overdosed?

She'd never taken anything stronger than paracetamol before. What had she been thinking?

Her vision began to pulse. It was too late; the drug was in her system and she was going to have to ride it out.

She staggered from the bathroom onto the landing. Maybe she should call for her father?

Everything was getting hazy, the outline of the stripped wooden bannisters fuzzy and warped. Lights flashed behind her eyes and she squeezed them closed. She could see the bannisters clearly, but they were now covered in their original glossy white paint. The walls beyond were covered in light blue and yellow wallpaper, the colours popping against the bright white of the staircase.

She opened her eyes again and looked at the now-bare walls, the ancient plaster cracked and uneven. She hadn't seen the old blue and yellow wallpaper in over a year, had barely even paid attention to it when it was there, but if she closed her eyes she could see the pattern perfectly. She could even count how many yellow flowers covered one width of paper: exactly seventeen.

With the room spinning around her, Jess lurched towards her bedroom. Every time she closed her eyes, images from her past flashed into her mind, like a movie was being projected on to the insides of her eyelids.

There was her father at the top of the stairs, telling a much-shorter Jess to pick up the toy he was about to trip over.

And there was her bedroom, decorated with a Noah's Ark wallpaper that Jess had long forgotten about, complete with wooden cot and matching furniture.

Flash after flash of memories, each one different, but as clear as it had been the first time round.

In the next flash, her room was as it was now, but Scarlett was sitting on her bed, laughing at something on the laptop beside her. So vivid that, for a second, Jess thought it was real and she reached forwards, stumbling a little as she tried to touch Scarlett, but she melted away only to be replaced by Luke, laying against her pillow. He smiled and beckoned her over, and Jess's heart leaped and fell into her stomach all at the same time, because right now she wanted nothing more than to go back in time to that day, when she had been so happy.

But his hand was bandaged, the white material stained from the red that was seeping through. Now, when she looked at him, at the way he was smiling at her, she felt sick and scared.

Jess blinked and the image swam away. Her room seemed to be collapsing in on itself and she couldn't focus properly, could barely tell what was real and what was not. She opened her mouth to call for her father, but even in her disorientated state she knew that it was a terrible idea.

Instead, Jess reached for her phone. It swam in and out of her vision, but she found that if she concentrated enough, she could just about focus. There were four missed calls, all from Cooper. With a shaking hand, she pressed the button that would call him back, but her vision was fading and pictures of her past were demanding to be seen.

'Hello?' The voice seemed to be coming from far away,

but it didn't seem to matter any more because suddenly Jess was in Luke's arms and the sky above was dark, but filled with stars.

'Hello?' Her voice was slurred, but she was caring less now; all the fear had gone and the distant voice was nothing more than a minor irritation. And Luke was there, taking her hands and telling her how much he loved her, how he'd do anything for her. *Anything*.

'Jess? Can you hear me? Oh shit, you really took it, didn't you?'

'I—' Jess looked down to where Luke's fingers intertwined with hers. Where was that other voice coming from? It wasn't Luke. 'Who is this?' she asked, though her mouth didn't seem to be moving. Instead, she was looking at Luke's hands, at the rivulets of blood that were running from his knuckles.

'Jess, this is Cooper. It's Sam. Remember?'

Cooper.

Luke's hands slipped through her fingers like sand and suddenly Jess was in the corridor at college. She turned. Where was Luke? A classroom door swung open and a boy walked out into the corridor like he owned the place. His hair was closely cropped to his head and when he looked at her, she saw familiar piercing blue eyes.

So, so blue.

'Cooper?'

'If you can still hear me, just lay down and close your eyes.' He had turned away, was walking towards the double doors at the end of the corridor, but still she could hear his voice. 'Think of something good, OK? Something happy.'

Something happy.

The whitewashed walls of the college corridor melted away and Jess looked down. Her toes curled beneath her in wet grass, her painted toenails glistening beneath the dew drops while the hem of her favourite yellow sundress shifted in the summer breeze. Morning sun kissed the back of her neck, warm.

Yellow's not her colour.

Someone was shouting at her, but from very far away.

'—be fine, I promise. Everything's going to be—'

Then the boy she loved was behind her, his arms circling her waist and his lips kissing the same spot on her neck that had been warmed by the sun. Jess closed her eyes for a moment, then she turned to look at him.

And she was happy.

COOPER

Cooper slipped his mobile back into his pocket.

She should be fine, he told himself. If she just took one or two, she'll be fine.

But what if she's not?

It was the last thing he would ever have imagined Jess to do. She hated drugs, could barely even stand to talk about them, so what had changed?

On the opposite side of the Fill 'n' Save, Big Phil grunted as he set a large box of Coke cans in front of the fridge. He pulled a tissue from his pocket and mopped the sweat from his brow before hitching his jeans up over his monstrous belly.

'You need a hand?' Cooper called from behind the till. He looked at his watch. It would be hours before his shift ended, before he could check on Jess.

'Nope,' Phil replied, his breathing laboured and

wheezing as he reached to pull open the fridge door with his meaty fingers. 'You shouldn't have come to work in the first place,' he said sternly. 'And I'm telling you, if I find who it was that did that to you . . .' He paused mid-sentence to cough, a breathless hack that seemed to linger all year round.

Jag looked up from the magazine he was reading. 'Really, Phil? What're you going to do, sit on him?'

'You going to buy that or not?' Phil snapped, turning to pluck the magazine from Jag's hands. 'And why are you still here? If you're not going to buy anything, you can leave.'

'Fine.' Jag rolled his eyes and made his way to where Phil had left the box of Coke cans and started to stack them in the fridge.

Phil watched on for a moment, as though making a decision about what to do with Jag. 'Fine,' he said, his voice icy. 'But I'm not paying you.'

Jag grinned at Cooper, but Cooper was watching as a red Nissan pulled into the otherwise empty forecourt, stopping at the petrol pump that was furthest from the shop. The driver got out, pulling a cap low over his eyes before picking up the dispenser. Cooper pressed the button to authorize the pump and glanced outside again. The driver was staring right back at him.

'OK,' Phil wheezed, making his way to the back. 'If you need me I'll be in the office.' He pointed at Jag. 'And you keep an eye on him, OK? Make sure he stacks those cans properly. Facing *out.*'

Phil punched in the code to unlock the door, then let it slam shut behind him, the automatic lock clicking into place.

Jag saluted the closed door, then opened one of the Coke cans he'd been stacking and took a long swig. 'So,' he said, before expelling one of the loudest burps Cooper had ever heard. 'How did Leon look?'

'The same as ever,' Cooper said. The Nissan driver had looked away and was now concentrating on filling his car. 'Bit older. And he's got two gold teeth now.'

'Man, how crazy was that party?' Jag laughed and shook his head. 'Remember that punch?'

'Of course I remember the punch. Or, actually, I remember how much my head hurt the morning after drinking that punch. Whichever idiot thought it'd be a good idea to spike it should be shot.'

'Those guys used to throw the best parties,' Jag said wistfully. 'Remember the hog roasts? I don't miss Leon, but I do miss hanging out at his place.'

'I never even think about it,' Cooper said. 'It feels like a different life now.' He turned his attention back to the Nissan driver, who was now shaking off the petrol pump. He leaned in to the open car door and it was then that Cooper noticed the person sitting in the passenger seat, dimly lit by the car's interior light. The passenger was also wearing a cap that obscured most of his face.

Something turned in Cooper's stomach as the driver

looked up again, nodding at whatever the passenger was saying to him.

'You're paying for that, by the way,' Cooper said to Jag, not taking his eyes from the man who was now walking across the forecourt.

The door rattled as it opened, the small bell above the frame jangling as it announced a new customer. The man stepped in and glanced briefly at Cooper before he turned to browse the magazine shelf. He flicked through the same magazine Jag had been reading, his eyes occasionally moving up to glance at Cooper. Then he replaced the magazine before striding towards the glass partition that separated Cooper from the front of the shop.

'Are you Cooper?' he asked. His voice was low and his eyes shifted from the door to Cooper, then to the car parked outside. The windows of the Nissan were dark, the interior light out, but a red security light flashed behind the windscreen. The passenger must have locked the doors from the inside.

Placing his finger over the panic button under the checkout, Cooper nodded slowly.

The man, who couldn't be any older than nineteen, maybe twenty, repositioned his cap and licked his lips. He was sweating.

'Pump number one,' he said, then, much more quietly, 'and ten.' He shoved a handful of notes at Cooper, far too much for the few litres of petrol he'd pumped into his Nissan.

Cooper stared at the money. 'Ten what?'

'Come on,' the cap man said, laughing nervously. Then he leaned in closer to the partition. 'Ten reds, man.' His eyes shifted again and he glanced out of the window at the Nissan. A bead of sweat rolled from somewhere beneath his cap.

'Who sent you here?' Cooper asked, shoving the money back at the cap-man. 'I have no idea what you're talking about.' His eyes shifted to the backpack by his feet, as though somehow it may have opened without him realizing and spilled its contents out for everyone to see. He didn't like having it with him at work, but couldn't let it out of his sight; somehow the idea of having to explain the loss of the pills to Leon was worse than the thought of being caught with them. Cooper could feel himself starting to sweat just as much as the guy in front of him. He rang up the cap-man's petrol purchase on the till and looked him squarely in the eye. 'That's eleven eighty-two,' he said.

'But—'

'Eleven eighty-two,' Cooper repeated. His head and face throbbed and all he could seem to think about was Leon and the threats he'd made against him. Against his sister. Could he really turn down an opportunity to make the money he so desperately needed?

The cap-man nodded and pushed a twenty-pound note through the small gap in the partition.

Cooper collected the man's change and passed it back. 'I finish at midnight,' he said, keeping his voice low.

The cap-man's eyes lit up. 'Yeah?'

Cooper paused. 'Meet me at one, by the fountain next to the skatepark.' He eyed the passenger in the Nissan, whose face was still obscured by the cap he was wearing. 'And come alone.'

The cap-man nodded. 'Sure thing.' He pocketed his change and walked quickly from the shop, the door rattling as it closed behind him.

Jag approached the counter, leaning in close until his breath misted against the glass panel. 'What was that about?' he asked, watching as the Nissan pulled away.

'Looks like I've just made my first deal,' Cooper replied quietly.

'What?' Jag looked out at the empty forecourt. 'With that guy? He bought some pills?'

Cooper shook his head. 'No, but I told him I'd meet him after my shift. By the fountain.'

'Seriously? A proper drug deal?'

There was something about those words, 'drug deal', that turned Cooper's stomach. He opened his mouth, ready to protest that this was part of the plan, but as he did so the door to the back office swung open.

'I'm going for a smoke,' Phil said, pulling a coat around his huge frame. 'I'll be five minutes, OK?'

'Yeah,' Cooper said, nodding. 'Sure, no problem.' He watched as Phil made his way to the front door, his palms slick with sweat. He had known this moment was coming, but had tried to push away the thoughts of what he was preparing to do. Now that the time had arrived, the surge of adrenaline struck like a tidal wave. Could he really do this? The bell above the door jingle-jangled as it opened, then closed, but Cooper found himself unable to move. Instead, he watched as Jag covered the distance from the counter to the office door in three strides.

'Are we doing this?' Jag asked. Phil was out of sight, but Cooper knew that he was only metres away, around the back of the building by the stack of wooden pallets by the rear office door. He glanced at the clock on the wall behind him, a clock that could be set by Phil's smoke breaks. There was less than four minutes before Phil would reappear, four minutes of opportunity that Cooper knew he had no other option but to take.

'Let's do it.' Cooper unbolted the partition that separated him from the shop front and stepped out to meet Jag. With hands that didn't feel like his, he quickly typed the code into the lock and pushed open the office door. 'Hold it,' he said to Jag, stepping into the office.

Inside the office was a desk, an office chair that had foam spilling from both the back rest and seat, and piles upon piles of folders, all filled with papers and receipts. They were everywhere; on the desk, on shelves, in higgledy-piggledy piles on the floor . . . and on top of the large green floor safe that was pushed up against the far wall.

Despite Cooper's urging, Phil still refused to record his finances on a computer. There was a laptop somewhere beneath one of the many piles, but Cooper had never seen

Phil using it as anything but an expensive paperweight. Instead, he would often walk into the office to see Phil sat at the desk, working meticulously through each receipt and carefully copying down numbers with a Biro, in his thin, spidery handwriting.

Cooper scanned the corkboard hanging on the wall above the desk. As cluttered as the rest of the office, it was covered with small pieces of paper, Post-it notes and letters, all held in place with brightly coloured push pins. And at the very bottom, in a neat row, were a number of keys hung upon the pins with small loops of string.

Cooper considered the keys. He'd opened the safe once or twice before to get change, so had a vague idea of what the key looked like. He settled on three likely looking suspects, carefully removed them from their pins and carried them to the safe where he sank down in front of the lock. He looked at the keys for a moment, pulled one out and pushed it into the lock. Having already decided it wouldn't open, his eyebrows shot up when the key actually turned, clunking heavily. The door swung open to reveal a number of bags. Most were small, clear plastic baggies containing various types of change, all piled up on top of three or four larger, fabric bags. Without stopping to think about what he was doing, because if he did it would end with him slamming the safe door closed and getting the hell out of that office, Cooper reached in and grabbed one of the fabric bags. The baggies of change clattered on to the floor in front of him and he quickly scooped them up and shoved them back inside, then closed the safe and locked it. The fabric bag was heavy and he laid it on the desk while he replaced the keys on the corkboard. He hadn't even realized he was sweating until a bead of it ran into his eye, making him blink. He stared at the keys, suddenly filled with panic. He hadn't taken the time to study which key was on which pin before taking them. What if Big Phil had a system? What if he always hung the safe key on the blue pin? Looking now, he couldn't even remember which was the key that unlocked the safe.

'Cooper?' Jag's voice came from behind the half-closed door. It swung open and Jag leaned into the office, his eyes immediately fixing on the fabric bag. 'Damn,' he said, making eye contact with Cooper. '*Damn.*'

'Damn is right,' Cooper muttered, grabbing the bag. He stepped towards the open office door before a familiar *jingle-jangle* stopped him. A customer? Jag turned his head and when Cooper saw his eyes widen with surprise and fear he knew it wasn't a customer at all.

'What are you doing there?' Phil's voice called from the front of the shop. 'Where's Sam?'

'Uh . . .' Jag turned to look at Cooper, grimacing in a *what do I do now?* kind of way.

Without thinking, Cooper grabbed the bag and shoved it into the waistband at the back of his jeans, before pulling the hem of his shirt down to cover it. Then, taking a deep breath, he grabbed the cordless phone that was lying on the desk and strode out of the office.

'Yeah,' he said into the phone, fixing his eyes on Phil's. 'We're open twenty-four hours. That's all day and all night.' He rolled his eyes theatrically, ignoring Phil's quizzical look. 'No, I mean, we don't ever close.' He covered the mouthpiece and pointed at the phone. '*You want this?*' he mouthed at Phil, rolling his eyes again for extra effect.

Phil raised his hands. 'No way,' he said, 'I've had my fair share of crazies this week.' He headed towards the counter, shaking his head and muttering about people wasting his time. Turning sideways to fit through the partition, he inhaled as he slid through, then reached for the button to authorize a pump.

'Come on, Sam,' he called, 'just hang up. We've got customers.'

Sure enough, there was another *jingle-jangle* as the door opened at the front of the shop.

'OK madam,' Cooper continued, backing into the office. 'I will certainly let you know if anything changes.' He looked at Jag, shaking his head as he lay the phone back on the desk. The bag in his waistband was too bulky not to be noticed, but there was nowhere he could hide it without being found out. Before he had the chance to come up with a plan, a loud crash came from within the shop, followed by cursing.

'Sam?' Phil's voice carried through to the office. 'How many times have I told you not to leave your bag lying around for me to trip—'

Cooper was out of the office before Phil had a chance

to finish his sentence, but it was too late. As the office door swung closed behind him, Cooper froze when he saw Phil standing beside the partition, holding his backpack in one hand.

And a bag of pills in the other.

JESS

It was happening again.

But this time, Jess knew that Luke and Scarlett wouldn't get out. The fire was growing, the smoke was getting thicker, but she was being pulled towards the front door and there was nothing she could do to stop it.

Spilling out on to the street, she saw the masks littering the floor, the other partygoers standing around watching, doing nothing. The person in the white mask and black hooded top on the opposite side of the road, just *staring*.

She tried to scream out, to tell the crowd around her to stop, to turn back because someone was going to get hurt, someone might be dying and they had to help. Jess tried to scream at the person in the white mask, but her mouth didn't move, didn't make a sound. Instead, she was running from the house, just as she had done when it had first happened, just like the first time she saw the masked figure—

Wait.

She stopped.

Everything around her froze, as if she were inside a movie screen that had been paused by an unseen hand.

That masked figure, in the corner of her eye. It wasn't the first time she had seen that person, she knew that. With her heart thundering, she searched the depths of her memory, sure that somewhere—

She was back in the house, before the fire had even started. In front of her, Scarlett was laughing as she spoke to Luke.

'I've got a slinky sequinned number that would look just *divine* on you.'

Jess wanted to grab her, to pull her out of the house, to shout at her to get out, anything that could stop the tragedy that was about to unfold.

'Well,' Luke was saying, 'I've been told that sequins do make my eyes pop.'

And just like she had done before, Scarlett grabbed Jess's hand and led her and Luke through the crowded hallway that would soon be filled with smoke. Jess could feel the warmth of Scarlett's hand, as real as it could possibly be. Then the skinny guy in the Guy Fawkes mask streaked through the corridor with his strategically placed beer can, shoulder checking Jess on his way past.

Luke's hand shot out almost instantly and grabbed his

arm. Jess watched on as everything seemed to slow down. She saw Luke's mouth twist into a snarl, the spittle flying from his mouth. 'Hey,' he snapped. There was an edge to his voice that Jess hadn't picked up on before. She watched as Luke's fingers continued to sink into Guy Fawkes' arm; she could almost see the blood vessels burst beneath his skin as Luke continued to apply pressure. 'Take it easy, *mate*.' He spat the last word, making it perfectly clear that this was in no way a matey situation. Then he released Guy, the bruises already forming where his fingers had been.

A pattern of bruises that Jess herself had sported in the past.

The room began to fold in on itself and Jess blinked in the sudden darkness. But it wasn't dark at all, the sky was spattered with stars and she could feel fingers digging in to her own arm and she was begging, asking Luke to please let go, because he was hurting her.

'Oh, I'm hurting *you*?' he sneered, his voice carrying the exact same edge she'd just heard when he'd been talking to Guy Fawkes. 'You don't answer the phone for two hours and you say I'm the one hurting *you*?'

'I'm sorry,' Jess could hear herself saying, though she was just as bewildered now as she had been back then. What was she apologising for? 'It was on silent, I didn't hear it.'

'So why was it on silent? You didn't want to talk to me?'

'Of course I did, but—'

'And who were you with again?'

'I told you, I was with Sarah. From college. We were in the library revising, so I had to have the phone on silent.'

'Revising again. Being a good girl for Daddy?'

'That's not fair.'

'Why? You always want to please him, but you don't give a toss about what I think or what I need. You know I need to revise too, I could have come with you. You act like you don't want me to do well in my exams.'

'That's ridiculous! Of course I—'

'The least you can do,' he interrupted, 'is have your phone on you when you knew I'd be calling.'

'I'm here now, aren't I? And I did have my phone – it was on silent, I told you already.'

'You could have had it on vibrate. And why haven't I heard about this Sarah before?'

'You're acting like I'm lying to you.'

Luke smiled. 'Are you?'

'No! Why do you always think I'm lying to you Luke?' Jess's voice had risen an octave and she could feel the way her hands were curling into balls, her nails digging into her palms. It was something she'd always done when she felt stressed, ever since she was a kid.

'Hey,' he said, his voice now soft. 'Why are you shouting? Stop getting so worked up. Did I say you were lying?'

'No, but—'

'I'm not the bad guy here, Jess.'

'So you're saying I am? I've done nothing wrong!'

'Stop shouting,' Luke said again, this time looking around the car park as if someone might be around at this time of night to hear. 'You're embarrassing yourself.'

Jess turned and started to walk away.

'Where are you going?' he snapped. 'Come back and talk about this! You're acting like a kid.'

'I can't. I don't have anything to say to you right now.'

His footsteps crunched on the gravel behind her. 'Don't walk away from me, Jess.'

'Leave me alone.'

'You want me to leave you alone? Fine. That's it. If you can't even act like an adult then we're through. I can't keep doing this, over and over again.'

'Fine,' she shouted back. 'If that's what you want.'

For a moment there was a silence so big, it seemed to fill the night. But Jess kept on walking. Then came the sound of glass shattering, instantly followed by the shrill whooping of a car alarm.

Jess spun to see Luke, hunched over beside a Volvo and cradling his hand. She ran back to him, the blood already dripping from his knuckles and spattering on the gravel in thick black spots.

'What did you do?' she cried, reaching for him.

'I'm sorry,' he whispered, reaching for her and pulling her against him. 'I'm so sorry.'

And her arms were wrapping around him, just like she remembered. Though now, watching it all unfold for a second time, Jess wanted nothing more than to turn and

166

run as far away as she could. How could she have fallen for it? How could she have been so manipulated?

'I'm sorry. I'm so sorry. I love you so much,' he was saying, stepping back and taking her hands in his own, the rivulets of blood trickling from his knuckles on to her skin, snaking around their entwined hands like vines. Bonding them. 'I'd do *anything* for you, Jess.'

She stared at him, at the tears in his eyes and at the way his lips thinned against his teeth, at the way he spoke with just so much damn passion.

And for the first time, she saw him for what he really was.

'I love you,' he said.

She stared at him for a long time. When she spoke, her voice was firm. 'If you ever put your hands on me again, we are over. Do you hear me?'

Luke nodded. 'I'm so sorry,' he whispered. His lower lip trembled and he looked so sad, so lost. 'I just love you so, so much.'

'I love you too,' she replied. And she had meant it, she really had. Because she had fallen for all his tricks, for all the manipulative, cowardly ways in which he'd tried to make her his.

He never did put his hands on her again, but he'd found other ways to get the reactions he wanted from her. Ways that didn't leave bruises.

Not on the outside, anyway.

The stars began to fade and she found herself back at

the party, watching again as Luke released the arm of the kid in the Guy Fawkes mask. Guy stared back for a second before running off towards the front door and down the steps into the street, almost knocking over the figure in the white mask.

Once again, everything froze. The figure in the white mask was staring right at her, the eyes hollow, black indents in a face that gave nothing away.

The face contorted slightly, as though a heat haze were rising up in front of it. The image faded briefly and she saw Luke, under the starlit sky, black blood dripping from his knuckles. Then Cooper, walking away from her in the college corridor. The images twisted, each one disappearing like smoke as it was replaced by a different memory.

Were the drugs wearing off? They couldn't be, not yet, she still hadn't—

Then she was back inside Scarlett's house, in the crowd being pulled towards the front door while the fire grew behind her. She was losing control, even though it felt like she had only just learned what the drugs really allowed her to do. It wasn't time yet. She hadn't figured it all out yet.

She tried to scream, but there was no way to control her body. She was a passenger along for the ride, trapped inside her own head and looking out through eyes that could see only what they had seen before.

The crowd surged again and this time she could actually feel the rise in temperature as the smoke rolled across the ceiling. The pulsing lights from the lounge lit the twisting smoke and the music filled her head, and this time when she screamed, she heard it, heard herself making the noise.

She screamed again, louder this time, and someone called back, though they sounded very far away.

'Jess? Jess, it's me.'

'Please,' she cried, 'please help them, they're upstairs, they're trapped.'

Invisible hands clutched at her, but the crowd still pulled her towards the front door. 'No,' she shouted from somewhere inside her own head, 'let me go, we have to get them out.'

'Jess, open your eyes, everything's OK.'

The walls of Scarlett's hallway bulged, a terrifying undulation that convinced Jess the whole house was about to collapse.

'Jess, I said open your eyes.'

She did. Blinking, she looked up to see her father sitting on the bed beside her. He pushed her hair, matted with sweat, from her face.

'It's OK,' he soothed. 'You were having a bad dream.'

Jess glanced around. It was dark outside but the light from her bedside lamp was soft and warm. 'It was so real,' she whispered. 'I couldn't get back to them – I tried, but I couldn't.'

Her father pulled her towards him, stroking her hair and kissing her forehead. 'It's OK,' he said. 'It's all going to be OK.'

She burrowed against him, soaking in his warmth, but

every time she closed her eyes the images returned, swimming quickly into focus. It was like jumping from one world into another, instantly immersed in all the sounds, smells and feelings that went with them.

It was exactly like Cooper had said it would be.

She had been dreaming, but the dreams were all memories, so vivid it was like she was reliving them. Like she was watching them on a TV screen, able to pause, rewind, focus in on things she hadn't noticed the first time around.

Like the black eyes in that white mask, looking directly at her.

BIG PHIL

Big Phil had one rule after eleven p.m.: he didn't unlock the front door for anyone or anything.

No exceptions.

Every night would play out the same way. At eleven o'clock sharp he would lock up the front and back doors, then he would settle himself behind the counter with a family sized bag of crisps, a two-litre bottle of cola, and switch on the radio. Any customers who came in after eleven would fill their cars with fuel, then approach the small service window that separated Phil from the forecourt. He would either take money through the small gap in the window, or the customer could pay with a credit card on the pinpad mounted on the outside. Sometimes the customer would ask for a snack, or some tobacco, and Phil would haul himself out of his chair and wheeze his way from behind the counter to fetch the item before shoving it back through the gap. On the rare occasion that someone asked Phil for something that was larger than the gap, he would shake his head regretfully but ask with all sincerity if he could get them anything else that might fit through the slot. Sometimes the customer would argue and sometimes they would ask him to unlock the front door. But Phil would just shake his head again and tell them to have a good night and to please come back soon.

Big Phil did not unlock the front door for anyone after eleven, not even the police.

No exceptions.

So far, Big Phil's night had not been different to any other. He had locked up, grabbed his snacks and tuned in to his favourite radio show. The flow of customers had been steady but now, at one a.m., things had slowed down. Phil knew he was getting too old to pull off a night shift after having already worked all day, but money was tight and he did love his job. He liked the banter with his regulars and he had great staff.

Or rather, he *had* had great staff.

Big Phil sighed as he reached into his crisp bag and rummaged around.

Perhaps firing Cooper on the spot had been too harsh? Though it wasn't like Sam had argued to keep his job; if anything, it was like he couldn't wait to get out. Having snatched the backpack from Phil's hand, he had all but ran out of there, with that Jag trailing right behind him. Maybe he'd thought that Phil was going to call the police?

It had certainly entered his mind. But Phil liked Cooper, knew that kids like him made stupid mistakes. Besides, Phil had made enough mistakes of his own and where would he be now if he'd been turned in to the cops at the first sign of trouble?

But drugs? He knew that Sam had had his fair share of trouble, but he would never have pegged him as a drug dealer.

He would have to call Cooper in the morning and talk it out. Perhaps they could work something out, reach an understanding that if Cooper agreed to stop dealing, he could have his job back?

Phil leaned back in his chair, then noticed the person outside, standing beside one of the petrol pumps.

For a moment he watched, waiting for them to move. But the person, dressed in a black sweater with a hood pulled up over their head, simply stood, their body slightly turned away from Phil.

Phil leaned closer towards the window, looking for the customer's car.

The forecourt was empty.

Probably someone on their way home from a club or party. Stopping to get cigarettes or a snack to soak up whatever kind of alcohol the kids were drinking these days.

There was a knock at the window.

Phil jumped, clutching at his chest. He looked up, but the customer was not at the service window. Scanning the length of the shop, he finally caught sight of them standing beside the door.

'Door's locked,' he called out. He banged the service window. 'You need to come here.'

The figure remained frozen.

'It's locked,' Phil called again.

No reply.

'Damn junky,' Phil muttered. He heaved his frame up from the chair and made his way around to the front of the counter. He stopped. The window was now empty, the figure completely vanished.

'What the—?'

Another sharp knock made Phil spin around to the service window.

This time, what he saw made him take a step backwards. The figure had reappeared, still wearing the same hooded top, but now he could see their face.

Or rather, what was covering their face.

A white mask, expressionless apart from two black eye-holes above the smooth nose and lips. The figure tilted their head slightly, regarding Phil through the window like a child watching a fish inside an aquarium.

Phil forced a laugh, though it was more of an uncomfortable snort. He shook his head in a *kids these days* way and walked back round to the business side of the counter.

'Can I help you?' he asked, keeping his voice deliberately even and trying to ignore the uncomfortable pounding in his chest. It was just one of the local teens messing around, no need to be so jumpy.

The figure stared back through the black eye-holes, unmoving.

Then Phil noticed the smell.

Working in a fuel station, one quickly becomes accustomed to the bitter tang of diesel and petrol fumes. After fifteen years, Phil's brain had somehow wired itself to completely ignore it, but this was different. The shop was filled with the rich stench of fuel, enough for Phil to know that there had been a spill somewhere close by. A big spill at that.

He reached for the emergency shut off, but froze when another, heavier round of knocking shook the service window. He looked up to see the masked figure holding up a small box of matches.

A thin film of sweat had broken out on Phil's forehead, but that was nothing compared to the growing patches of moisture beneath his armpits. He stepped towards the phone. 'I'm calling the police,' he shouted. 'Unless you leave right now.'

The figure turned away from the road and back towards the main door.

'It's locked,' Phil said, but mostly to himself, a reminder that whoever this was and for whatever reason they might be messing with him, they would not be able to get inside. With his hand resting on the phone, he watched as the figure stopped beside the door and picked up a small green canister, with a black nozzle attached to one end. The nozzle appeared through the small letter box and liquid glugged from the container, splashing against the floor as Phil watched on in horror, his hand frozen to the phone. Within seconds, the canister had been emptied and the masked figure tossed it aside, stepped back and pulled the matchbox from a pocket in the black sweatshirt. Phil simultaneously lifted the phone from its cradle and retreated towards the back office, his hand shaking as he punched in the code. Sweat poured from his head, dripping down his back and soaking into the waistband of his trousers. The pounding in his chest had progressed to a disconcerting tightness, one that seemed to travel into and down his left arm.

He tried to open the door, but in his panic had entered the wrong code. With sweat dripping into his eyes, he blinked, moaning in terror as he tried the code again.

The tightness in his chest grew stronger and his breath came in short, sharp bursts.

This time the door opened and Phil stumbled into the office, grabbing at the keys hanging from his corkboard.

He slid the back door key into the keyhole and turned it, the ancient internal lock clunking as it opened. Phil pushed the handle, leaning heavily against the door in anticipation of his imminent freedom, but it did not move.

He fumbled with the key again, almost blinded from the sweat and panic, and turned to look again at the front door, visible from his position in the office. The pool of petrol had spread, trickling across the floor in rivulets that reached towards Phil like liquid fingers. Outside, the figure still stood, head cocked in that curious way, watching as Phil attempted to secure his escape.

Turning back to the lock, a terrible sense of dread began to creep up his spine.

He pushed the door again, but this time he knew it would not open. Something was blocking it on the other side. That was why the figure was watching, not moving. They knew that Phil was trapped like a rat.

With a shaking hand, Phil reached for the phone and lifted it to his ear. It was silent, the line dead.

It was only then that the figure struck the match. Phil watched, almost in a trance, as the flame blossomed. He watched as the figure tossed it towards the locked door. He watched as the fire grew outside, trailing along the edge of the store, the flames licking at the windows. And he watched as the puddle on his freshly cleaned lino floor erupted in the most beautiful way.

But the last thing he saw, as the fire danced towards him and the now-crushing pain in his chest drove him to his knees, was the expressionless white face somewhere behind the flames.

The face of the person who had come to watch him die.

COOPER

The park's fountain was still.

It had been switched off some months earlier, after some of the local kids decided to fill it with washing-up liquid as a summertime prank.

'I still don't get why they haven't switched it back on yet,' Jag said, tossing a stone into the stagnant water pooled at the bottom of the fountain. He smiled and turned to Cooper. 'Such a good night, though. Remember all the girls running through the bubbles? It was like one of those Ibiza foam parties.'

Cooper shot Jag a withering look. 'Jag, I'd hardly compare a load of drunken Hackney girls jumping around in Fairy Liquid to a night out in San Antonio.'

'All right,' Jag muttered. 'I just thought it was cool, that's all.'

'Sorry. It's been a very long twenty-four hours.'

'You know it's all going to be OK, right? Like, your job at the Fill 'n' Save and everything? It'll all work out. Big Phil won't leave you out in the cold – he sees you like you're his own son. Just like you're basically my brother, right?' He spoke quietly, almost mumbling, but Cooper knew it was just Jag's way of showing he cared. Jag had never been one for big speeches or emotions, so it made it all the more special when he made the effort.

'Thanks Jag.'

Resting against the concrete base of the fountain, Cooper closed his eyes. The stone was cold, even through his layered clothing, but at least it was keeping him awake. His mind kept wandering back to thoughts of Jess. His phone had remained silent, but it was late and the Nostalgex would still be coursing through Jess's system. He knew she was safe at home, so there was nothing he could do but wait.

Other than the sound of Jag tossing the occasional pebble into the water, the night was as silent as it ever got in London. The distant whisper of traffic provided a calming undertone to the rhythmic barking of a dog that hadn't shut up for the last half hour. Though only a handful of people had walked past, Cooper had started to wonder if he should have chosen somewhere a little more discreet for his first deal. That was until Jag had pointed out that more discreet meant fewer witnesses if anything went wrong. And so they had settled, close enough to one of the park's lit pathways to see the faces of anyone walking by, but far enough away that nobody really paid them any attention.

When Cooper became aware of the distant beat of heavy bass music, he opened his eyes. 'You hear that?'

Beside him, gravel crunched underfoot as Jag turned to look. 'Yeah. Headlights.'

Sitting up straight, Cooper scanned the blue-black horizon, split by the skeletal, wintery remains of the park's trees. Sure enough, a pair of headlights arced across the uneven ground as a car moved slowly towards the otherwise empty car park. A police car sped past on the main road, sirens blaring, though it neither stopped nor slowed as it passed by the park's entrance. Cooper watched as its lights disappeared, half expecting it to turn back and head right for them. His heart felt like it was trying to escape from his ribcage and it didn't slow even when the police car was out of sight.

He turned his attention back to the car that had just pulled into the car park.

It rolled to a stop and, for at least a minute, nobody moved. The car's headlights remained on, pointing almost directly to where Cooper and Jag sat together by the fountain. The bass music continued to pound away. Inside the car was a tiny red light, barely noticeable from where Cooper was sitting, but it was most definitely there. He squinted and stood up. What was it?

'Should we go over there?' Jag asked, standing up and taking a step.

Cooper reached out a hand. 'No. We stay here, in the open. They come to us.'

The bass continued for another few seconds, then the car seemed to just shut down. Music, lights, engine, all switched off, leaving a very still silence. The red light continued to glow.

'Now what?' Jag asked. His voice was strong, but Cooper wasn't fooled. He'd known Jag for long enough to detect the slight tremor, the only clue that gave away just how scared he was. Which happened to be just as scared as Cooper was.

'We wait,' Cooper said. He knew his voice sounded as confident as Jag's, but his heart was hammering with enough force to send the blood thundering through his ears. It was almost deafening. 'They come to us,' he repeated.

The driver's door opened.

A figure emerged from the car, leaned in to speak to the passenger, then slammed the door closed behind him. The park lights were just bright enough to fill in some of the shadows on the right side of his face and Cooper watched as the driver licked his lips before reaching a hand deep into his jacket pocket.

Instinctively, Cooper took a step backwards.

The figure looked over to where Cooper and Jag stood, then glanced towards a small copse of bare trees. He stared for a moment, then turned back to Cooper and Jag, and began striding towards them.

'Here we go,' Cooper muttered. 'Just keep cool, OK?'

'As if I could be anything else,' Jag replied.

Cooper smiled at this answer, grateful that his friend had agreed to come along.

As the figure approached them, hand still thrust deeply into his pocket, he glanced again at the cluster of trees. Within seconds, he was within spitting distance of Cooper. 'You got someone else out here? Who was that?'

Cooper paused. This wasn't the same, nervous, cap-wearing guy he'd met in the Fill 'n' Save earlier that night. This guy was a few stone heavier, a few inches taller and his voice was a good few octaves deeper. His shaved head sported a number of tattoos that spilled down on to his face.

'Wh—' Cooper cleared his throat and glanced towards the copse. 'What do you mean?'

The new guy stared at Cooper for a moment, then shrugged a shoulder. 'Thirty red, yeah?' He pulled his hand from his pocket and Cooper flinched. The guy smirked at this, his eyes glinting in the half light as he counted from the wad of money he had just produced. 'You're a straight-up gangster, huh?' he said, with a hearty chuckle that in no way calmed Cooper. He plucked a stack of notes from his huge pile and held them out.

'What happened to the guy in the cap?' Cooper asked.

The new guy stared. 'Not here.'

'In the garage he asked for ten reds.'

The new guy shrugged. 'Now we want thirty. Anyone who's got ten stacked up ready must have thirty stacked up ready.' He fixed Cooper with a stare. 'Tell me I'm wrong?'

Jag reached out, pulling the notes from the man's hand. 'You're not wrong.' He licked a finger and started to count. 'Thirty reds, Coop.' He shot Cooper a look that in no uncertain terms said 'get this guy out of here.'

With a nod, Cooper reached for his backpack. As he unzipped it, he realized how stupid he'd been to come with the entire bag. He was going to have to count out thirty pills in front of this guy and there was no way he'd be able to do that without revealing his entire inventory. Turning away, he placed his bag on the edge of the fountain and reached inside, hoping his body would go someway towards shielding the contents. As quickly as he could do so in near-darkness, he counted thirty pills into his hand.

He froze as somewhere in the distance came the wail of another siren.

Cooper turned to see another police car race by, immediately followed by a fire engine.

'Cooper—' Jag started.

'Wait.' Cooper clutched the pills tightly, zipped his backpack closed, then turned back to the new guy. 'Here,' he said, holding out his clenched fist.

The new guy was staring at something over Cooper's shoulder.

'Cooper,' Jag repeated, pointing at something in the distance. 'Check it out.'

Cooper glanced back again, this time noticing the plumes of smoke curling up into the sky from somewhere behind the tree line.

'Are we doing this or not?' The guy held out his hand to Cooper. 'Too many cops around to be playing games, son.'

'Uh, sure.' Cooper tipped the pills into his outstretched hand.

'What the hell is this?' The guy looked at Cooper, almost smiling, though there was a look in his eyes that made Cooper confident it wasn't a laughing matter. 'You don't have any baggies?'

'Sorry.' Cooper's eyes flicked back towards the rising smoke. 'I'll make sure I get some for next time.'

For a moment the guy said nothing. Then he turned and started walking quickly towards the parked car, muttering under his breath about kids and amateurs.

'That looks close,' Cooper said, over the sound of more sirens.

'Yeah,' Jag said, his now-empty hand falling to his side. 'Looks like—'

A huge explosion swallowed up the rest of Jag's words, the sound hitting Cooper with enough force to make him stumble backwards.

'Oh shit!' Jag shouted, unable to take his eyes from the blossoming flames rising up from whatever had just been blown apart.

The skyline had taken on a dull orange hue. The air was thick with the sound of sirens, pouring in from all directions, while a number of car alarms were blaring, discordant alongside the frenzied barking of dogs.

'The Fill 'n' Save.'

It was all Cooper was able to say before his legs were moving and he was running, his arms pumping as he charged towards the rising plumes of black smoke. He could hear Jag calling from behind, telling him to wait, that he'd left his bag, but Cooper didn't care. He'd covered the distance between the fountain and the iron railings of the fence within seconds and he launched himself forwards, grabbing at the railing as he pulled himself up and over on to the pavement. The road, normally filled with traffic during daylight hours, was empty as Cooper propelled himself forwards. He skipped up on to the pavement opposite and ran through the network of alleyways that he knew would lead him to the next main road, the one directly opposite the Fill 'n' Save. Jumping across overflowing bin bags and weaving around the bins and dumpsters, he almost fell on more than one occasion, but soon enough he was there, the smell of the fire reaching his nostrils before he even laid eyes on the Fill 'n' Save.

Or rather, what was left of the Fill 'n' Save.

Though much of the view was obscured by the many fire engines, ambulances and police cars, Cooper could see that the shop was gone, as were the pumps in the forecourt, which were now spewing fire from the ground. Heat haze distorted the night sky and Cooper winced against the blazing heat that seemed to be scorching his skin even though he was thirty or forty metres from the fire.

Cooper stumbled and sucked in breath after breath as he attempted to slow his racing heart and quell the pain of the stitch he had only just noticed. He scanned the growing crowd for a familiar figure, but Big Phil was nowhere to be seen.

'Cooper!'

Cooper spun to see Jag behind him, hunched over and also fighting for breath. Leaning against the brickwork of the shop wall beside him, Jag pointed to the straps across his shoulders. 'I got your bag,' he said, between puffs of breath.

Without a word, Cooper took his backpack and turned back to the remains of the Fill 'n' Save. 'Do you think he got out? He got out, right?' He looked back at Jag, but the expression on his friend's face was one he didn't want to see. He stepped out into the cordoned-off road and approached one of the many police officers.

'Hey, did the guy get out?'

The officer turned to Cooper, his young, clean-shaven face pulsing blue beneath the flashing lights.

'You knew someone who was working there?'

Cooper opened his mouth ready to speak, but something told him to close it again. He stepped back, scanning the crowd once more. His phone buzzed in his pocket and he pulled it out to see a text from Leon.

Don't talk to the police. We have a video of your deal – I'm sure they'd be very interested to see it.

The red light inside the car.

Someone had been filming him.

'Son? I asked if you knew who might have been inside?'

Suddenly very aware of the weight of his backpack, filled with drugs and the money he had stolen from the shop that had been razed to the ground in front of him, Cooper could only shake his head.

The officer continued to stare at him, his eyebrow twitching as he watched Cooper move back to where Jag stood.

'We should get out of here,' Cooper muttered to Jag, slipping his phone back into his pocket. 'Before anyone figures out that I work here. Or, rather, that I used to work here.'

Jag shifted his gaze. 'Looks like someone might already be wanting to ask you some questions.'

Cooper glanced over his shoulder to see the officer speaking to one of his colleagues. Both were looking in their direction.

'I'd say that's our cue to leave,' said Cooper. 'Last thing we need is for them to find stolen money from a burned down building in my bag.'

'Don't forget about the shitload of drugs,' Jag said with a smirk.

'It's not funny, Jag.'

'I never said it was.' Jag leaned in closer, so his lips were almost against Cooper's ear. 'But what you need to remember is that with the Fill 'n' Save burned down, there's nothing to tie you to that cash. Nothing to even suggest that any money was stolen.'

Then Jag stepped back, his smirk now a full-blown grin and his usually dark eyes ablaze.

JESS

She was caught on the stairwell between the hallway below and Scarlett's bedroom above, with fire coming towards her from both directions. But she couldn't run. The carpet had turned into thick treacle, her feet sinking a little further with each step as the flames drew nearer, her breathing quickening, then stopping altogether as the heat finally engulfed her.

She tried to scream, but the fire was in her lungs, her skin bubbling and blistering in the heat.

And then it was gone.

Now she was in a forest, the treacle floor replaced with earth, littered with sticks and stones that cut into her bare feet as she ran.

Luke was close behind, chasing her through the trees as branches whipped at her naked body. She glanced back to see the blood dripping from his hands as he screamed at her to stop, that he loved her and that he was sorry and that he would never,

188

ever do anything to hurt her because he loved her, he loved her.

But when she finally stopped and turned to him, his eyes were covered with a white mask and he was smeared with blood from head to toe; crimson rivulets ran down his face and dripped into his grinning mouth, blackening his teeth as he stepped towards her with outstretched arms.

Jess stumbled back, her calves hitting a fallen branch which sent her sprawling to the ground as Luke lunged for her.

But it wasn't Luke any more. It was Scarlett, the bandages falling from her charred skin as she reached out for Jess, clawing at her face and screaming, 'Why did you leave me behind? What did I ever do to you? Why? Why would you do this to me?'

Jess opened her eyes.

She blinked, her chest rising and falling, as she scurried back against the wall, certain that Scarlett was still in the room with her.

But there was nothing but the tiny dust motes, dancing and spinning in the sunlight that streamed in through the gap in her curtains.

Cursing the brightness, she closed her eyes and turned her back on the light, burying her face into her pillow. Her head was banging, her mouth dry and her limbs felt heavy, almost detached. Though she'd never had a hangover in her life, she felt like this must be on a par with what her dad always referred to as 'post-party trauma'.

She reached for the glass of water on her bedside table and groaned when she discovered it was empty. As she withdrew her hand, she knocked her phone from the table to the carpeted floor, but made no attempt to pick it up.

If anything important had happened, her father would have found out by now and woken her.

Her night had been broken; periods of wakefulness interspersed with terrible nightmares, twisted versions of reality, ones she was able to manipulate or ones that told a different story to what had actually happened. Nothing like the stark visions of truth she saw after taking Nostalgex.

She exhaled slowly and her stomach rolled beneath a wave of nausea. Could have done with that last night, she thought, remembering the way she had forced her fingers down her throat in an attempt to vomit up the Nostalgex. No wonder her throat felt so sore.

If this was what it was like to be hungover, she could quite happily go her whole life without touching a drop of alcohol.

Cupboards banged in the kitchen downstairs. Her father must be making breakfast.

She should go down to see him. Maybe a nice hot cup of coffee would stop the pounding inside her head.

Luke's jacket still lay at the foot of her bed. Jess stared at it for a moment, then leaned forward to grab it. She slid her hand into the pocket and pulled out a couple of the loose pills.

The red hue seemed even brighter than the night before. Maybe the drugs were still in her system; the colours had certainly been brighter in her dreams. Or were they memories? Hallucinations?

Whatever they were, they were unlike anything Jess had ever experienced. Not just the colours either; the sounds, the smells, the feelings . . . Every sense was heightened under the effect of the Nostalgex.

Jess rolled the pills in the palm of her hand. She licked her lips, her mouth dry. She needed water.

Maybe she felt so bad because she'd taken so many pills last night.

Maybe the drugs needed to leave her system slowly, not all in one go. Perhaps if she just took one pill now—

Her thoughts were interrupted by a sharp knocking at the front door.

Jess jumped up from her bed, grabbed her red and white heart-motif dressing gown, and ran down the stairs, past where Michael stood at the bottom step about to open the door. Despite the frosted glass panels in the front door, there was no mistaking who was outside.

'It's Hannah,' Jess said, her voice rising with panic. 'Oh god, it's Hannah.'

Michael placed a hand on her shoulder. 'It's OK,' he said. 'I'm here.' He gave her a gentle push, steering her towards the door. Jess realized she was shivering and in the back of her mind she wondered when it had got so cold. With a shaking hand, she reached for the handle and pulled the door open.

'It's not about Scarlett,' Hannah blurted out, before

dissolving into uncontrollable sobs. Michael took a step forwards, scooping Hannah up into his arms and bringing her into the house. She buried herself in his chest, her shoulders heaving as she cried.

Jess's eyes widened as she looked from Hannah to her father, her heart and mind racing, her mouth suddenly so dry that she was unable to swallow.

'What is it?' she asked, her voice a near whisper. 'What's happened? Hannah?'

Pulling herself back from Michael, Hannah took the tissue he seemed to have pulled from nowhere and dabbed at her eyes. 'I'm sorry,' she said. 'I didn't mean to scare you guys. It's just been such an awful time.' She sniffed and exhaled a shaky breath before turning to Jess. 'It's Luke,' she said.

'Luke?' Heat rushed to Jess's face. 'What's happened to Luke?'

'That's just it,' Hannah said. 'Nobody knows. He disappeared from the hospital in the night.'

'How can someone just disappear from a hospital?' Michael asked.

Hannah shrugged. 'Have you heard from him, Jess? Did he call you?'

Without a word, Jess turned and ran up to her bedroom. Her phone was where she had left it, lying on the floor beside her bedside table. She picked it up and, sure enough, the screen was filled with messages. Most were from Luke, with a few messages and missed calls from

Cooper. One by one, she opened the messages from Luke, searching for an explanation as to how or why he could have just disappeared.

You're not even talking to me now?

Jess. I mean it, call me RIGHT NOW.

I swear, if you're with Cooper, I'll kill him.

I'm sorry, I didn't mean that.

Jess?

Jess, please. I love you, you know how much I love you.

I can't stand this. Please, at least just text me to let me know you're OK.

They all seemed to say the same thing in a slightly different way, but there were no clues about where Luke might have gone. The last text was time-stamped 00:25, the last call at 00:31.

Jess pocketed the phone in her dressing gown and raced back downstairs to where Michael and Hannah were waiting in the hall. 'He called me just after midnight,' she said. 'When did you last hear from him?'

Hannah glanced at Michael. 'Around the same time. He said he needed to talk to you, that you weren't answering his calls.'

'My phone was off.'

'He said he thought you were with Cooper?' There was a look in Hannah's eyes that Jess didn't like.

'Cooper was working then. I was asleep.'

Hannah's eyes widened. 'Does Cooper still work at that petrol station out east?'

'Yeah, why?'

'There was a fire there last night.'

'What?'

'Yeah,' said Hannah, her eyes shifting. 'I went driving around, looking for Luke. The roads were all closed off. It was pretty bad.'

Another fire? 'What time was it?' Jess asked, her voice very quiet.

'Must have been just after one,' Hannah said. 'But Jess, I don't think you're—'

Jess pulled the phone from her pocket and found the messages from Cooper. She scrolled through them, until she found what she was looking for.

Hey, I'm worried about you. I'm on shift until 2, but you can text me. I'll call you when I'm done, OK?

The nausea she had felt when she first tried to get out of bed returned, washing over her in strong waves.

'Jess?' Michael said. 'What is it?'

Trying to swallow away the bile that was rising in her throat, Jess went back to Luke's texts.

I swear, if you're with Cooper, I'll kill him.

COOPER

Cooper blinked at the beam of sunlight streaming through the gap in his curtains.

For a moment there was nothing but the acknowledgement of a new day; then the memories of yesterday hit him like a punch to the face.

He groaned.

He felt like he'd run a marathon. Or been run over. Every muscle in his body screamed in protest as he rolled on to his side and glanced at the phone on his bedside table. No messages, no missed calls.

He clicked on the internet icon and pulled up the search engine, typing in *news fire east end london*, before hitting enter.

A number of news stories appeared and Cooper's stomach turned as he read the first headline.

'PETROL STATION OWNER DEAD IN EAST END FIRE.'

Unable to bring himself to read the story, Cooper tossed the phone on to the bed beside him and lay back on his pillow. He breathed deeply as he tried to blink away the tears.

He needed to speak to Jess.

He told himself it was just to check that she was OK, but seeing her had awoken something inside him, a need that was fuelled by the pain, terror and guilt that was about to consume him.

He picked up the phone again and called her mobile. It went straight to voicemail, just as it had done the night before. Why wasn't she answering?

Somewhere in the back of his mind was an unpleasant voice, a quiet nagging that Jess may have taken too much, or had a bad reaction to the pills.

The same voice that said he should have gone to her house, told her father the truth and just faced the consequences.

But Cooper didn't like that thought, so he pushed it away and instead found comfort in the part of his brain that told him everything would be OK. The same part of his brain he'd been trying to quieten in recent weeks, as it seemed to be able to convince him that he could get away with anything.

Looking at the backpack beside his bed, stuffed with drugs and stolen money, he felt a burning regret that he'd not managed to do a better job of suppressing that part of his brain.

He pulled the cover away from his bruised and battered body, wincing as he sat himself on the edge of his bed.

How had he managed to screw up so badly in such a short space of time? It was almost laughable, especially given the fact that on New Year's Eve he'd promised himself that he was done with getting into trouble. Now, only two days in, he was in more trouble than he'd ever known.

He needed coffee.

Pulling himself up, he walked through to the kitchen to see Amy sitting at the table, texting. She looked up as Cooper walked in. 'Wow. You look terrible.'

Without a word, Cooper sat heavily in the chair opposite and tossed his own phone on to the table. He grabbed her mug of half drunk coffee and took a swig, grimacing. 'That's cold,' he said, placing it back on the table.

'It's how I like it,' she said, picking it up and taking a sip. 'What time did you get in last night? I didn't hear you.'

'No idea,' Cooper said, massaging his temple.

'What? What's happened?'

He looked at her.

'Come on, Sam. Twin thing? I can always tell.'

'Twin thing,' he repeated. 'Right.'

'Seriously, Sam. What's going on?' Amy lay her phone on the table beside the coffee mug and leaned towards him, her heart pendant swinging from her throat.

'There was a fire,' he said, unable to look her in the eye. 'At the Fill 'n' Save.'

'What? A fire? At a pump?'

'The whole damn thing,' Cooper said. 'It's gone, Amy. It's all gone.'

'I . . .' Amy shook her head. 'I don't understand. How can it all be gone? Are you OK? Is Phil—' She stopped as Cooper covered his eyes.

'He's dead,' Cooper said. 'He didn't make it out.' He wiped away the tears with the heel of his hand and shook his head. 'It should have been me, Amy. It was my shift.' He finally looked at her. 'I got fired last night,' he said. 'Phil found the pills in my bag and sacked me.'

'Jesus, Sam. Did he call the police?'

Cooper shrugged. 'I don't know. I don't think so. We'd know by now, wouldn't we?'

'So what now? Did he take the pills? What about Leon? Sam, I think it's time to call the police. If you don't have the money, then—'

'I got the money. I stole it from Phil right before he died.' He stopped, unable to believe the words that had just come out of his mouth. 'What the hell is wrong with me?'

Amy stared. 'You got it? How much?'

'I don't even know.' He got up and walked through to his bedroom. He grabbed the backpack by one of the padded straps and carried it back through to the kitchen and dumped it on the chair he had been sitting on. The fabric bag was at the bottom and Cooper reached down past the bags of pills to pull it out. He upturned it on to the kitchen table and three bound wads of notes slid out. Each was wrapped in a paper band and labelled in black marker pen with £1k.

'Three grand?' Amy picked up one of the bundles and flicked through the notes. 'You really think there's three grand here?'

Cooper dropped his backpack on to the floor and sat down. 'Looks like it,' he said, running his hand across his cropped hair. 'There's no way I'd have got away with taking that much. Phil would've figured it was me soon enough, especially after finding all those pills.' He looked at his sister. 'I'm basically turning into Dad, aren't I?'

Amy reached across the table and grabbed Cooper's hand. 'Dad tried his best with us, Sam. No matter what happened, he loved us and wanted us to be happy.'

Cooper pulled his hand away. He knew better than to get into this argument with Amy, always and forever a daddy's girl, but he couldn't help himself. 'There's never an excuse, Amy. He hurt people.'

'Only to protect us.'

Cooper looked at his sister, her eyes fierce, a hand clutched to her chest. 'You know he'd do anything for us. Mum would too.'

'And where did that land them? And us, for that matter?' Cooper stood up and began shoving the bundles of cash back into the fabric bag. 'We're alone, fending for ourselves, because he couldn't handle a nine-to-five like everyone else?' He snorted, an angry laugh. 'Jesus, Amy. When are you going to stop defending him?'

He heard her sniff, but refused to look her in the eye. He'd made her cry, and while that made him feel bad, he knew it was what she needed to hear. 'I'm not going to be like him,' he snapped, jamming the bag of money into his backpack. 'I'm not a drug dealer.'

'Oh really?' Amy said through her tears. 'Then why do you have a bag full of drugs and stolen money, Sam? You say you can't think of anything worse than being like him, yet here you are.'

'I don't have a choice.'

Amy tossed her phone on to the kitchen table. 'Yes you do,' she snapped. 'You could call the police right now and end all this.'

'It's too late for that and you know it. How am I going to explain all this money to the police?'

'You don't have to explain the money. They don't need to know about that.'

But there was the video footage Leon had of the drug deal. Even if that were a lie, there was something else holding him back from going to the police.

He looked at Amy, suddenly unable to think of anything but the threats Leon had made against her. Was he really stupid enough to think that shopping Leon to the police would be the end of it?

They would never be safe.

No, the only thing he could do was to get Leon the money he owed him.

He had three grand already and Leon only needed a

third of that by midnight. That would leave him another two grand, plus the three hundred he'd made in the previous night's deal. A nice buffer, should Leon decide he wanted to impose another time frame, and a bit of time for Cooper to figure out his next move.

Whatever that might be.

Cooper's phone buzzed. Something inside him jumped as he saw Jess's name appear on the screen. He snatched it up and pressed the answer button. 'Jess? Is that you?'

'Yeah.'

'Are you OK? I've been trying to call. I was so worried when you didn't answer last night.'

'I'm fine.' Her voice wavered, telling Cooper she was far from it. 'Are you OK? I thought . . .'

The line went quiet for a moment and Cooper heard her breathing, shaky and slow.

'I thought something might have happened to you. I heard about the fire at the Fill 'n' Save.'

Leaning back in his chair, Cooper covered his eyes. 'Yeah. Yeah, it's pretty bad. But I wasn't there when it happened. I— My shift finished early.'

'I have to ask you something,' Jess said, though there was hesitation in her voice.

'Sure. What is it?'

'Have you seen Luke? I mean, did he come by while you were working?'

'No. Why?'

Jess paused. 'He's disappeared. Nobody's seen him since

he was at the hospital last night. And he said— I mean, I got a text from him saying that he thought you and I were together and . . .' Her voice trailed off.

'And what? Jess?' Cooper sat upright in his chair. 'What did he say?'

Another pause.

'I think I need to come over.'

JESS

Hannah glared at Jess. 'It wasn't Luke. He didn't burn down the garage.'

'I didn't say it was,' Jess snapped. 'I'm just telling you what his text said.'

Hannah turned to where Cooper and Jag stood in the kitchen doorway. 'It wasn't Luke,' she repeated. Her eyes were red and heavy, with dark circles. 'He wouldn't do something like that.'

'We know he wouldn't,' Cooper said. 'Look, I'm not gonna lie, I'm not his biggest fan, for . . .' He waved his hand and glanced at Jess. 'Whatever reason. But the idea that he'd hurt someone?'

Jess looked away, determined not to let Cooper see her reaction to his words. She could feel them all looking at her; Amy from her position on the chair opposite where she sat, Hannah leaning against the counter, and the two boys in the doorway. It had been over a year since they'd all been in the same room together, and it was as awkward as she'd imagined it would be.

'Jess?'

Too late. She looked back at Cooper, holding his gaze. 'What?'

For a moment, Cooper stared. He'd always had a way of being able to see beyond whatever barrier she tried to put up and it annoyed her more than anything. His jaw clenched. '*Did* he hurt you?'

'It's not . . .' Jess swallowed and she could feel Hannah's eyes boring into her. 'I mean, he didn't . . .'

Cooper's lips thinned. 'I swear,' he said, 'if he touched one hair on your head, I'll—'

'You'll what?' Hannah snapped, stepping away from the counter. Her eyes flicked from Cooper back to Jess. 'He didn't mean it, did he?' She pointed at Cooper. 'Tell him,' she cried, taking another step towards Jess, her purple hair swishing as she turned to Cooper. 'You don't know anything about him, Sam. It's not like Luke was even in our little gang, was he? So don't go judging someone you don't know.'

'He's the reason our *gang* broke up in the first place,' Amy muttered.

Hannah glared. 'I think you'll find that your brother screwed it up way before Luke and Jess got together.' She rose to her feet, jabbing a finger at Amy. 'And if you have anything else to say about someone who's not even here to defend himself—'

'Hey,' Jag soothed, 'just calm down, all right?'

Hannah spun to face him. 'Don't tell me to calm down,' she spat. 'Not when my brother is missing and people are accusing him of, what?' She turned again, this time to face Jess. 'What exactly are you saying, Jess? That he burned down the petrol station? You're calling your own boyfriend a murderer?' She blinked quickly, trying to hold back the tears. 'Look, none of us are perfect, OK? We've all done things we regret and Luke's no exception. But it doesn't mean he's a cold-blooded killer.' Throwing her hands up, she began to walk towards the door. 'I have to go. I can't be here listening to this crap when I could be out looking for him.'

'Hey.' Cooper reached for her arm but she pulled away.

'Don't touch me, Sam. I know how much you hate him, but you know what? He never did anything to you. You and Jess were already broken up, he had nothing to do with it. I know you're still in love with her,' Jess could feel Cooper's eyes on her, but she could only seem to stare at her feet, 'but that's not his problem, and it's not mine.'

She pushed past, her shoulder colliding with Cooper's as she strode out of the kitchen.

There was a moment of silence before the front door slammed and Jag let out a low whistle. 'Wow,' he said, his eyebrows shooting up. 'She's not happy, huh?' He smiled, but it quickly melted away in the stony silence.

Amy reached across the table and grabbed Jess's hand. 'I'm so sorry, hun.'

Jess looked up in surprise. 'For what?'

'I know we stopped talking so much after . . .' She glanced at Cooper. 'You know, after you guys broke up and everything. But that's no excuse. Especially given everything that's happened.'

Squeezing Amy's hand back, Jess smiled gratefully.

'What she said,' Cooper muttered. He kicked at the floor. 'I mean, what Hannah said about me.' He looked at Jess. 'And you.'

'It's OK,' Jess said. 'She was upset. She didn't know what she was talking about.' Or did she? Was Cooper still in love with her? And, more importantly, why did Jess care?

Cooper nodded and, though he quickly looked away, Jess could see the redness creeping up from his jawline. 'Seriously though, Jess. If Luke hurt you . . .'

'I don't want to talk about it.'

Nodding again, Cooper excused himself from the kitchen. A beat later, his bedroom door slammed shut.

'What's that about?' Jag asked.

Jess looked from Amy to Jag. 'I'll go,' she said, standing up. As she left the kitchen, Jag quickly took the newly empty seat opposite Amy.

The hallway was cold, much colder than the rest of the flat, mostly due to the gap around the front door that allowed the cold air to seep in. Jess stood outside Cooper's bedroom door and pressed her ear against it, hearing the tinny beat of music coming from his phone. For a moment her mind flashed back to Scarlett's house, to the conversation she'd overheard by doing the very same thing. She quickly pulled back, as though a similar fate might befall her if she listened in on Cooper, and instead gently rapped her knuckles against the peeling paintwork.

'Who is it?'

The music stopped.

'It's me. Jess.'

There was a moment of silence and the door handle turned. Cooper leaned against the doorframe, his eyes downcast. 'I'm sorry,' he said. 'It's not my place to say anything. It's your relationship, your decision.'

Jess chewed her lip, reaching out to touch the cut on his cheek. He winced and she pulled her hand back. 'Sorry. It's just . . . I've never seen you like this. It's not like you to get into fights.'

'Yeah, well I didn't fight so much as get the crap kicked out of me.' He smiled, though it was a little lopsided due to the swelling.

'It's not funny, Sam.'

'Sometimes you just have to laugh, though.' He looked her dead in the eye. 'Right?'

Jess smiled. 'That was always your motto. I guess you haven't changed at all.' She looked past him into the bedroom, at where his duvet lay crumpled in a heap on the bed. 'Can we talk? In private, I mean?'

'Sure.' He stepped to one side and Jess entered the room, the smell of boys' shower gel and deodorant hitting her and instantly igniting memories she had never realized were missing.

Her breathing seemed to slow, her heart quickening as she recalled the first time she had stepped into this very room, well over a year and a half ago.

The door clicked behind her and she turned to see Cooper leaning against it, just as he had done that night.

She realized she could easily revisit that night if she wanted to. Now that she had her own supply of Nostalgex.

'You OK?' he asked. 'You look like you've seen a ghost.'

'I'm fine.' Jess pushed the pair of jeans that lay across Cooper's bed to the floor and sat down on the empty space, trying to push away the intrusive thoughts of the memory she might recapture with a couple of pills. 'It's just that it looks exactly the same.'

'Yeah,' Cooper agreed, scratching the back of his head. 'My interior designers have been pretty busy, so I have to wait a little longer before it's decorated.'

'You're an idiot.' Jess smiled, instantly feeling more at ease. What was she so worried about? This was Sam Cooper, after all. He wasn't bad, or mean. He was just a bit of an idiot.

He sat on the bed beside her, one knee tucked up in front of his chest, as he waited for her to speak.

'I think you know what I'm going to tell you,' she said. 'You've probably connected the dots already.'

Cooper nodded. 'I'm not going to make you tell me anything you don't want to, but you have to know that if

208

it's what I'm thinking, I'm afraid I can't get too worked up over the fact that he might be in trouble.'

Though his voice was calm, Cooper's fists were balled against his knees, his knuckles white.

'I'm not asking you to be worked up,' Jess said. 'What I want to ask you is how much trouble he might be in. With that Leon guy.' She took in his face, battered and bruised, and tried not to think about whether something similar might be happening to Luke at that very moment.

'I would say he's probably in more trouble than he's ever known.'

Jess's stomach rolled. No matter what Luke had done to her, she couldn't stand the thought of anything happening to him. She may not love him any more, but the love she had felt had left a scar, one that would tie him to her forever. 'You said you know Leon – the guy who did this to you?'

'We grew up together.' Cooper's eyes shifted. 'Our dads kind of worked together.'

'In the army?'

Cooper paused, his throat bobbing as he swallowed. His eyes locked with hers. 'My dad wasn't in the army. I lied.'

She stared, somehow unsurprised that, yet again, Cooper had lied to her. 'Then what does he do? I thought your mum and dad were abroad. That's why you live here with your uncle. Not that I've ever met him, either—'

'My parents are in prison,' Cooper blurted out. His eyes fell away and his shoulders sagged. 'Dad was a drug dealer and Mum went down with him. He'll probably spend the rest of his life behind bars and we won't see her for years.'

Jess paused. Her initial surge of anger was replaced with a gut-wrenching sense of pity. He looked so defeated. 'Why didn't you tell me? Why lie, Sam?'

'You really don't know why I'd lie about something like that?'

'Of course, but I was your *girlfriend*. That didn't count for anything?'

'It counted for more than you'll ever know.' He shook his head. 'Look, I know I should have told you the truth, but I was ashamed. Starting college seemed like the perfect fresh start, a place where nobody knew me and I didn't have to be the son of Jimmy Cooper, East End drug lord.'

'Does anyone know?'

'Only Jag. He's the only person I still know from my past life.' He looked at her confused face and smiled. 'Sorry. That's what I call the time before Mum and Dad were arrested and I ended up here. My past life.'

Jess stared at him. She knew every angle of his face, thought she had known every angle of *him*. But had she ever really known him at all? 'Was it that bad? That you had to lie?'

'Look, I know how much of an idiot I was, and probably still am, and it kills me to think that people would associate me with the crap he did. I know I'm not the most straight-laced guy out there, but I'm not my father.' He looked at her, his eyes fierce. 'I am not my father and I never will be.' He lowered his head into his hands.

'OK,' Jess whispered. 'OK.'

She had been wrong, she realized that now. People do change. Cooper had opened up to her more in the last few minutes than he'd ever done when they were together. Though maybe change was the wrong word. An unpleasant sinking sensation in her chest told her that maybe he'd always been this person, but she'd just been too wrapped up in her own wants and needs to see that. She'd been chasing perfection, studying for the grades that would get her into medical school and looking for a love like the ones she'd seen in the movies. Like the relationship she'd thought her parents had had.

And what had she found?

The silence was filled with a sudden burst of music, making her jump.

Cooper reached into his pocket and pulled out his mobile. She saw him frown at the phone before lifting it to his ear. 'Hello?'

There was a brief pause before his eyes widened, locking with Jess's.

'Yeah, I have the money.'

Jess frowned.

'Docklands, right? Of course I remember. I have the scars to remind me, thanks very much.' He smirked. 'How's the nose?' His face dropped as he listened to whatever the caller was saying. 'Yeah, no. Sorry, man.' He touched his

211

jaw. 'Hey, listen, Leon. I have to ask you something. You know anything about a kid called Luke Vaughan? My age?'

Jess scooted across the bed, leaning in as she tried to hear what the caller was saying, but it was too late. Cooper lowered the phone.

'What did he say?'

'He said he didn't know anything.'

'Do you believe him?'

Cooper paused.

'No.'

JESS

This time, the chemical tide was significantly more pleasant.

As Jess turned on her pillow, she was able to feel each individual fibre of the cotton that brushed against her cheek. Spots of colour burst in front of her eyes as she blinked, colours that she'd never even seen before.

As the drug began to pull her into the fog of memories, her breathing slowed and the sensation of cool air rushing into her lungs was like nothing she'd ever experienced.

This time, she understood the part of Nostalgex that made people come back for more. It wasn't just for the memories.

Jess closed her eyes and Cooper was there, on the stupid skateboard he'd ridden for the entire previous summer. It was hot, the sun beating down from the spotless sky above, and the concrete was hot beneath Jess's bare thighs. She

213

was leaning against the park's fountain, her chemistry revision guide open on her lap.

'It's too hot to revise,' Cooper groaned, the wheels of his board clacking sharply against the ground as he tried yet another flip.

'You've always got an excuse,' Jess snapped, not taking her eyes from the chemical equation she was attempting to decipher. She was taken aback at the tone in her voice, sure that she couldn't have ever spoken to Cooper in that way.

And yet, here was the evidence.

She felt her eyes narrowing as she glared at him. 'Just because you can knock out an essay in an hour and get an A for it, doesn't mean we all can.'

Cooper skated up to the fountain and peered over the edge. 'Why does it matter how long it takes?' he asked. 'Just so long as it's done. What's the big deal, Jess?'

Without a word, Jess turned back to her revision. Moments later, a splash of water hit the back of her neck and she looked up to see Cooper laughing. When he saw her expression, his face fell. 'Oh, come on. I was only messing around.'

Before Jess stood up and walked away with her book, she stopped the memory and took a moment to look at the image she'd freeze-framed in her mind.

The look on Cooper's face was one of confusion and hurt. What had he actually done wrong? She couldn't understand that herself, even though she remembered this day.

At least, she'd thought she'd remembered it.

Maybe it hadn't all been his fault.

The scene folded in on itself, the edges blurring and fading with the busy noises of the London park, until new sounds and images began to come into focus.

She was walking through a street, the houses on either side of her adorned with Christmas lights that flashed and twinkled in the darkness. A man staggered along the pavement opposite and raised his beer bottle as he passed, shouting something incoherent in a cheery voice.

'Jess, just wait a second, will you?' Scarlett caught up to Jess and linked arms.

'I swear Scarlett, if he's doing what I think he's doing . . .'

'And what exactly do you think he's doing? Come on, let's just get back to the party.' She tried to stop, but Jess barrelled forwards, dragging Scarlett with her.

'You'll see,' Jess said. She stopped outside one of the terraced houses and pointed at the two bikes propped up against the low brick wall. Jag's and Cooper's. A few drunk students smoked in the small front garden, laughing loudly while music blared inside. 'You ever heard Sam and Jag talking about these stupid crash and dash things?'

'Crash and dash?' Scarlett started to laugh, but her face fell when the shouting started. A group of people bundled out of the front door, with two familiar faces among the crowd. One of the partygoers had Cooper in a headlock, while Jag was wrestling over a backpack. A beer bottle fell from the bag and smashed on the ground, just enough of a momentary distraction for Jag to break away and grab his bike.

'Jag!' Jess shouted.

Jag looked up, his eyes wide as he pulled his bike away from the wall. 'Jess? What are you doing here?'

'Looking for you and Sam!' She started forwards, just as Cooper was thrown to the ground. 'What the hell are you two doing?'

'Get out of here,' Jag yelled. 'Cooper'll be fine.'

'He's about to get his head kicked in!' Jess reached into her jacket pocket, pulled out her phone and started dialling. 'I'm calling the police!'

As if by magic, a sudden calm fell over the crowd. There were now eight or nine students outside the house, all of whom were surrounding Cooper. He looked up at Jess from his position on the ground. 'Put the phone away,' he shouted. 'Are you nuts? You'll get me arrested!'

'Should've thought about that before you broke into our house,' one of the students said, before delivering a swift kick to Cooper's ribs. He doubled over, disappearing behind the feet of the crowd who were once again gathering around him.

Scarlett screamed and covered her mouth.

'I'm calling the police,' Jess yelled. With a shaking hand, she lifted the phone to her ear as Jag ran towards the shouting crowd, launching himself into the throng and yelling Cooper's name.

The scene collapsed in on itself once more and now

Cooper was in handcuffs, being led to a waiting police car while the police officer in front of Jess scribbled in his notebook.

'I'm sorry,' she mouthed, hugging herself to force some warmth back into her freezing body.

But Cooper only shook his head and looked away.

He didn't look at her again for a very long time.

COOPER

The night sky was clearer than it had been on New Year's Eve, though the lack of a cloud blanket made it far, far colder.

Cooper stamped his feet, which were quickly turning numb.

'You shouldn't have come,' he muttered, turning to where Jess stood in the shadow of one of the looming warehouses, arms folded over her chest as she suppressed a shiver.

Jess thrust her hands deeply into the pockets of her thick coat. The fur-trimmed hood framed her face, which was barely visible in the shadows, though her eyes were obviously bloodshot and lined with heavy bags. She looked ill. 'Don't be ridiculous. You're an idiot for thinking it was a good idea to come out here on your own.'

'You followed me, Jess.'

'You came out here *alone*,' she repeated.

'Yeah, well.' Cooper sniffed. 'After what happened to me last time, and given what happened to Phil, I pretty much assumed it was best to keep the people I like out of it.'

'And what about the people who like you?' Jess shot back. 'They don't get a say as to whether they want to get involved? You know, when Jag finds out you came here without him . . .'

Cooper's hand instinctively touched the phone in his coat pocket. Jag had been texting and calling all night, knowing that the meeting was due to take place but without knowing when or where. And Cooper hadn't replied to a single message.

She was right. Jag would be mad as hell when Cooper next saw him, but it seemed a small price to pay for keeping him safe. Knowing that Phil was dead, possibly because of him, was bad enough. He would never be able to live with himself if something else happened. Jag would understand that, surely?

A car engine sounded in the distance.

'Get back,' Cooper snapped, reaching out an arm in an attempt to herd Jess further into the shadows.

She pushed his arm away. 'I want to see,' she hissed. 'He might have Luke with him.'

He spun to face her. 'And you think it's going to help the situation if he sees you here? If he sees you, he's going to think there are more people. And if things get nasty, I'm telling you, he won't hesitate to—'

Gravel crunched beneath tyre as a pair of headlights swung into view.

'Fine,' Jess whispered, her voice faltering as she stepped backwards into the darkness.

Cooper followed Jess into the shadows as the car stopped in the centre of the courtyard, surrounded on all sides by abandoned brick warehouses. Most of the warehouses were fronted with metal rolling doors, though some were missing to expose the darkness within. Almost all of the walls and metal grills were covered with graffiti and Cooper shuddered to think what atrocities might lie within. He'd heard the stories about the docklands; apparently gangland shootings had taken place here over the years, though he'd never actually seen anything in the news.

He knew of one guy who'd sold some dodgy pills to a mobster's son, resulting in the teen's death. The story went that the mobster had some of his chums find the pill pusher while he was dealing, bring him here and shoot him in the kneecaps, then dump him outside the morgue of the local hospital. A warning if ever there was one, Cooper thought. His stomach flipped as the car rolled to a halt.

Who was to say that Leon wasn't carrying a gun? Now that he thought about it, there was probably a good chance that Leon was carrying, given his childhood obsession with weapons.

The engine switched off and the headlights died, submerging the courtyard in inky blackness. The car door opened, causing the interior light to flick on and illuminate Leon's face in an orange glow.

Jess moved back, further into the shadows. 'Can you see Luke?' she whispered. 'It doesn't look like there's anyone else in the car.'

The front seat beside Leon certainly looked empty, but Cooper knew from personal experience that Leon didn't always carry his passengers that way. 'I can't see anyone,' he replied. 'Could he be in the back?'

He felt Jess move against him, her hand resting on his arm as she strained to take a closer look. 'I don't think so.'

Leon stepped out of the car. Instinctively, Cooper moved back, forcing Jess back into the shadows of the warehouse they were hiding behind.

'What are you doing?' Jess whispered. 'Aren't you going to go over there?'

'In a minute,' Cooper replied. 'I just want to watch him for a moment.'

It was true; in the way that one might approach a dangerous animal, Cooper wanted to watch Leon for a few seconds first. Get a feel for his attitude, his body language. He also wanted to take a moment to check out any possible escape routes, to give himself as much of an advantage as possible if anything went wrong.

Leaning against the bonnet of his car, Leon fished in his coat pocket and retrieved a packet of cigarettes. A flame blossomed as he flicked a lighter with his other hand, before a jet of smoke trailed from his nose and mouth. The tinny beat of a ringtone broke the silence.

With the cigarette dangling from his lips, Leon pulled out his phone. He stared at the screen for a moment, hesitating as he took the cigarette from his lips and blew out another stream of smoke.

'Yeah?' he said into the mouthpiece.

He turned his back on where Cooper and Jess were hidden in the shadows.

'I'm dealing with it, OK? I told you, I went to the hospital last night but he wasn't there.'

Another pause. Jess squeezed Cooper's arm and he nodded in acknowledgement. Leon was talking about Luke.

'I dunno, probably ran off, didn't he? Maybe saw me coming.' He took another drag of his cigarette. 'Look, we made an agreement about how far this was going to go. I never agreed to—'

Whoever was on the other end of the phone must have interrupted Leon. He exhaled a plume of smoke and glanced around.

'No, he's not here yet. You sure he'll have the money?'

Leon turned, this time looking right to where Cooper and Jess were hiding. Cooper's breath caught in his throat and he felt Jess tighten against him, but knew there was no way Leon would be able to see them in the darkness.

'I dunno. I'm still not sure he was really—'

Leon had been cut off again and he was now kicking at the ground, looking almost nervous.

'OK, I hear you. Yeah, I'll talk to you later then.'

Leon pocketed the phone and took a final, deep drag on the cigarette before flicking it away. It bounced on the concrete before it came to a rest, the red tip glowing in the darkness.

'Wait here,' Cooper whispered, turning to Jess. She nodded.

He stepped out of the shadows, adjusting his backpack so the weight was spread more evenly across his shoulders.

Leon immediately glanced in his direction, his shoulders and back straightening as he raised himself up to his full height, like a cobra preparing to strike.

Cooper stopped three or four metres from where Leon stood, and nodded, suddenly aware of how he felt like a little boy trying to act like a big man. As Leon lifted his chin in response, Cooper realized they were both as nervous as each other. Leon's throat bobbed as he swallowed heavily, though his shoulders remained square.

'All right?' Leon asked in his familiar rasping tones. Much of the bravado he'd carried on New Year's Eve seemed to have dissipated and Cooper wondered if the anger and aggressiveness he'd seen that night had been borne out of something else. In all fairness, Cooper had had a fairly severe concussion at the time, so who knew what had really happened?

'Hey,' Cooper replied. 'How's the nose?'

Leon's lips twitched into the vaguest hint of a smile and Cooper was instantly transported back in time, to when they were seven or eight years old and running through

Leon's garden in the middle of summer. Their fathers sitting on the lawn chairs, Leon's dad Frank wearing those stupid sunglasses that he didn't even take off in the house. And, of course, the flash of gold every time he threw his head back and laughed at something that Cooper's father had said.

'I've had worse than a broken nose,' Leon said with a smirk. 'From people much tougher than you. And it ain't like you've got the prettiest face right now either, is it?'

Cooper let out a small laugh. 'Yeah, I'm pretty sure I've looked better.'

Leon glanced over his shoulder. 'Are we gonna do this, then? I've got places to be.'

'Yeah,' Cooper replied. 'Sure thing.' He shrugged his bag from his back and unzipped it. He'd already counted out the money Leon had asked for, deciding to leave the rest at home. The last thing he wanted was for Leon to see the extra cash.

Without hesitation, he grabbed the bundle of notes and held them out to Leon.

'Cheers.' Leon took the bundle and quickly flicked through the notes, his lips moving without sound as he counted the money. With a nod, he lifted his jacket and tucked the notes into the back pocket of his jeans. Then he looked at Cooper and, though the shadows danced across his face as he went to speak, Cooper was able to make out what could only be an expression of regret. 'Listen, Sam.'

Hearing Leon call him Sam was like a slap to the face.

Leon was one of the few people to have called him Sam, but not since they were kids. Not since everything changed.

'You need to know something,' Leon said. 'None of this was my idea.'

Cooper stared. 'What do you mean? What wasn't your idea?'

Glancing over his shoulder, Leon shifted nervously. 'This whole thing's a setup.' He leaned in closer and Cooper could smell the tobacco on his breath. 'There's this guy, I call him Whiteface. He's the one who told me to pick you up from the churchyard. You were followed that night, by Whiteface. He was the one who knocked you out.'

Cooper shook his head. None of it made any sense. 'What? What the hell are you talking about? Whiteface?' Why would Leon be telling him all this? Was it just a way of scaring him more, to make sure he did everything Leon asked of him? Because it was working.

'I've only ever seen him a few times, to pick up drugs or drop off money. But he always wears a white mask. And on the phone, he uses some kind of voice distortion, so I don't even know what the guy sounds like. He's never spoken to me in person, only by text or with that weird voice thing.'

'I literally have no idea what you're talking about, Leon.' Cooper's heart was racing as quickly as his mind. Maybe this Whiteface had been involved with his dad. Or maybe he was a rival of Cooper's father, someone who wanted to get revenge, or—

Leon sucked his teeth impatiently, pulling Cooper's

attention back to the conversation. 'Listen, this guy told me if I helped set you up, I could walk away.' His eyes shifted. 'He knows something about me, something that could get me put away for a very long time.'

'But why me? What have *I* done?' The revelation that Cooper had been targeted, that it wasn't a case of him being in the wrong place at the wrong time, was terrifying. Someone wanted something from Cooper.

Somebody dangerous.

But who?

Leon shrugged. 'I've learned not to ask questions. This guy isn't someone to mess with.'

He should never have let Jess come. This mess was even bigger than he'd realized and there was no way he was going to let her get caught up in it any more than she already was. 'So why are you telling me this? Why not just do what he wants and walk away?'

The expression on Leon's face began to change and for the first time in his life, Cooper saw him looking truly afraid. And that made Cooper's fear mutate into pure terror. 'Because he keeps changing the goalposts, doesn't he? He wants me to do something else now, something I never signed up for.' He reached into his pocket and pulled out his cigarettes. His hands shook, the flame trembling as he lifted it to the cigarette. 'You know that fire? The one in Bow on New Year's?' He blew out a stream of smoke as Cooper nodded. 'That was him. Whiteface wanted one of his dealers dead. To send a message. But the kid got out and now he wants me to finish the job.'

'Luke Vaughan. That fire was supposed to kill him?' Cooper's stomach plummeted. This person was also an attempted murderer.

Leon nodded. 'And if I don't do what he wants, you think I'm not going to be his next target?' He took another drag of his cigarette. 'I'm telling you this because you've always been smarter than me, Cooper. There's got to be a way out, right?'

'How the hell am I supposed to know?' Cooper snapped. 'What does this guy want from me? And how did he figure out that you knew me?' He paused. 'This has to be someone from our past. Someone who knows our dads. It's the only explanation.'

Before Leon was able to answer, his phone beeped. He glanced at the screen, then lifted his chin, squaring his jaw.

'I gotta go,' he said, turning away from Cooper. 'And I'm gonna need another grand, this time next week.'

'What? What about everything you just told me?'

'I don't know,' Leon said, already halfway back to his car. He flicked his cigarette to the ground. 'Just try and figure something out, OK? Because I've got nothing.'

Cooper exhaled, grateful for the money that was sitting at home. And the fact that he had another seven days to think of a way out.

As Leon's car pulled away, Jess stepped out from the shadows.

'You heard that?' Cooper asked.

'All of it,' Jess said, her voice wavering.

'You think he was telling the truth?'

'Yeah. I'd totally forgotten about it, but in the message on Luke's phone, the one from Leon? It said that Whiteface wanted his money.'

'Who the hell is this Whiteface?'

Jess stared back, her face filled with horror. 'I don't know,' she said. 'But I think I saw him, Cooper. I think I saw the person who tried to kill Luke.'

JESS

Jess wrapped her coat tightly around her body, trying to keep the warmth in and the dampness out. A blanket of cloud now covered what had been a spotless night sky and a heavy drizzle had started to fall, the tiny droplets sparkling in the orange glow of the street lights. 'Do you think this Whiteface person's already got Luke?'

A terrible ache pulsed in her guts, a nauseating mixture of worry, guilt and a sense of foreboding that she couldn't think too much about, because if she let it, it would no doubt eat her alive from the inside out. But she wasn't quite sure who she was most worried about: Cooper or Luke?

'I don't know,' Cooper said. Even in the darkness, Jess could feel Cooper staring at her as they walked. 'But I'd say it was unlikely, especially if this Whiteface person wants Leon to . . .' He paused, and Jess could hear the fear in his own voice. 'To take care of him. Luke's probably scared.

He's probably in hiding somewhere. I know I would be. He's probably fine.'

Probably.

All the possibilities that came with that word seemed to explode inside Jess's head and her stomach twisted, threatening to spill its contents all over the gum-strewn street they were walking on.

They turned into Jess's street in silence. Narrower than the main road they had been walking on, the pavement was flanked by a row of cars, like soldiers on guard as they marched past.

'Luke's a big guy,' Cooper continued, though his voice was uncertain, like he was clutching at something to say to make Jess feel better. 'And smart, too. I'm pretty sure he—'

Jess stopped, abruptly enough for Cooper to pause and follow her gaze.

Fifty metres ahead of them, a lone figure stood beneath a street light directly outside Jess's front door. The same street light that lit her room at night if she didn't have her curtains pulled tightly enough across her window.

'Who is that?' Cooper took a step forward, squinting through the drizzle.

Without even taking a moment to answer, and spurred on by the sudden burst of heat coursing through her veins, Jess started to run. Her feet pounded against the pavement, sending water flying up and soaking into her socks, but she didn't care.

The figure turned towards her, his features sharpening

under the street light.

By the time she reached him, the fire in her veins had reached her throat and she let out a strangled sob before launching herself at him and throwing her arms around his neck.

One of Luke's arms wrapped around her, pulling her against him for just a second or two before she pulled back and smashed her fists against his chest.

'Where did you go?' she screamed, wet hair clinging to her face. She noticed the way his injured arm was still strapped to his body with a sling and it was enough to make her pause, before the heat resurfaced and she lunged for him again, this time grabbing at his coat. 'Where were you, Luke?'

'Jess . . .' Luke started, reaching to take hold of one of her arms. 'Just wait, listen to me.'

'Hey!' Cooper called from somewhere behind. 'Let go of her!'

Jess turned to see Cooper jogging towards them. When she looked back at Luke, she saw a familiar expression; one he had sworn she would never have to see again.

'You've been with him?' he spat, his fingers tightening around Jess's wrist. '*Again?*' He twisted her arm and Jess yelped, releasing her grip on his jacket.

'You're hurting me!' She turned her body in an attempt to counteract the way he was forcing her arm. Pain shot from her elbow into her shoulder and she cried out again, certain that he was about to snap her arm.

'Get off her,' Cooper growled. 'Now.'

Luke's fingers loosened and he shoved her away.

She stumbled back and the world turned upside down before white pain exploded in the back of her head. For a brief moment she thought she was lying on the ground, but as the lights around her pulsed in and out of focus, the shouting between Luke and Cooper fading and rising in volume, she realized she was actually slumped against a low brick wall.

With a hand that felt detached from her body, she touched the back of her head and it came away sticky and warm.

'– doing with my girlfriend, anyway?'

Jess looked up to see Luke take a step towards Cooper, his shoulders square and his one good arm clenched at his side.

'Seriously,' Cooper was saying, his hands palm up in front of his body. 'I'm not going to fight you, man.'

Luke's arm shot forwards, grabbing a fistful of Cooper's top in his hand. 'Did I ask for your permission?'

Cooper shook his head. 'I'm telling you, this is not going to end well.'

'Stop it,' Jess mumbled, trying to get to her feet. The pavement tilted beneath her and she sat heavily on the ground again. 'Stop it!' she shouted, this time managing to form the words a little more clearly. Her head throbbed, but she was pretty sure she hadn't actually lost consciousness. The edges of her vision were blurred, but she couldn't tell if it was because of the blow to her head, or the after effects of the Nostalgex she'd taken earlier.

'Can't you see what you've done?' Cooper was yelling now, pointing at Jess. 'Look, look at what you did to her. And all you can think about is blaming me? For what exactly?' He barked out a laugh, shaking his head in disbelief. 'You've got some issues, dude.'

From her position on the ground, Jess was once again able to see the switch in expression on Luke's face. The way that darkness came over him so quickly was terrifying, though she had never really understood that until now.

How could she not have seen it before? How could she not have realized, that night under the stars in the car park?

And as quickly as the shadows deepened the lines on his face, Luke pulled his fist back and swung at Cooper's jaw. It connected with a sickening thud and Cooper stumbled back, colliding with the lamppost.

Nausea swirled in Jess's belly again, just as it had done when the group of students had attacked Cooper a year ago. 'Stop it!' she screamed. 'Just stop!'

'What the *hell* is going on?' Hannah was marching towards them from the house next door to Jess's.

'Luke? Jesus.' She grabbed her brother, pulling him into a hug. 'Jesus,' she repeated, pushing him away and slapping him hard on the shoulder. Then, noticing Jess, she crouched down beside her. 'Shit, Jess. Are you OK?'

Still clutching the back of her head, Jess nodded, but her chin crumpled and she started to cry.

'Did you do this?' Hannah turned to Luke, her voice low.

Luke only looked on, his eyes flicking from Jess, to Hannah, to where Cooper stood leaning against the lamppost, his fingers resting lightly against his jaw.

The darkness that had twisted Luke's features only moments before had now melted away, leaving him with the wide-eyed look of a sleepwalker who had awoken to find himself standing naked outside his house.

'No,' he said, grabbing his hair and shaking his head as he stared at Jess. 'I mean— I didn't mean to.'

'What's the matter with you?' Hannah spat, rising up to look her brother square in the eye. 'And where have you been? You know how worried we've been? Do you have any idea what Mum and Dad are going through? They're out right now, driving around looking for you.'

'I had to,' Luke mumbled. 'There was someone, I mean, there was—'

'Leon?' Jess asked. 'Is that who you're running from? Or is it Whiteface?'

Luke turned to Cooper. 'What did you tell her?' He stepped towards him, voice rising once more. 'What have you said?'

'Does it matter?' Jess asked. 'Does it change anything you've done?'

'I told you,' Luke said. 'Everything I've done has been for you.'

'You were dealing drugs for me? How does that serve

234

anyone but yourself?'

Balling his fists at his temples, Luke sunk to his knees. 'None of this was supposed to happen,' he said, though Jess wasn't sure who he was addressing any more. 'It was supposed to solve everything.'

'What are you talking about?' Hannah snapped. 'What could it possibly solve?'

'You really think I was going to get into med school without help?' he asked, turning to look at his sister. 'You know how smart Jess is – what chance would I have to get into the same uni as her?'

For a moment nobody spoke.

'You were taking Nostalgex?' Jess asked. 'You were using it to cheat in the exams?' Her head was spinning and she was finding it hard to process everything he was telling her. Then she gasped. 'Is that what you were talking about with Scarlett at the party? That kind of cheating?'

Jess felt sick. She'd got it so, so wrong. And if she'd been wrong about that, what else had she been wrong about? She clutched her head, pressing hard against her temples. This was what Luke always did – made her question everything.

Luke knelt beside Jess and took her hand. 'You really think I could be with anyone but you?' He kissed her hand, but she pulled it away. 'Please, Jess.'

'No. You may not have cheated in the way I thought, but you still lied to me. And Scarlett? She knew?'

Luke nodded. 'She was taking them too. Once she found

out I had them, she made me sell them to her.'

Hannah was shaking her head, looking at her brother like she was seeing him for the first time. 'Jesus, Luke. What the hell were you thinking? How could you even afford those things?'

'He was dealing them,' Cooper said. 'It's how a lot of junkies afford their habit.'

Luke rose to his feet, his eyes dark. 'Call me a junky again,' he snarled. 'I dare you.'

Cooper raised his hands. 'Hey, take it easy.'

'You were dealing?' Hannah asked. 'This just gets worse.'

'Just stay out of it,' Luke yelled. 'You don't have a clue.' He turned to Jess. 'Do you still have them? The pills? Please, I need them, you have no idea how much trouble I'm in if I don't get money to Leon. You don't know what happens to people who don't pay what he owes them.'

Jess stared, her head throbbing. She didn't recognize him any more. The Luke she knew never existed, she realized that now. 'The fire,' she said. 'At Scarlett's house. Did you know that was because of you? People could have died because of *your* selfishness. Scarlett could have died!'

Luke said nothing.

'I have money,' Cooper said. He glanced at Jess before turning back to Luke. 'I can give you a loan for a couple of days. How much do you need?'

'I don't need anything from you,' Luke spat.

'Listen to yourself,' Hannah said. 'Are you really that much of an idiot?'

236

'I think he is,' Cooper replied.

With a roar, Luke lunged towards Cooper. Hannah grabbed him, but Luke shrugged her off, reaching for Cooper once more. This time Cooper was too quick. He ducked beneath Luke's punch, then quickly spun and grabbed his injured arm, sling and all.

Bellowing in pain, Luke grabbed at Cooper's face with his uninjured hand, clawing at his eyes as he tried to pull himself from Cooper's grip.

'Enough!'

Jess hadn't even heard her own front door opening, but Michael was already on the street, pulling Cooper away from Luke.

'You,' he said, pointing first towards Luke, then Hannah, then to the open front door of their house. 'And you. Get inside, now.'

With his jaw set, Luke moved towards Michael and, for a moment, Jess thought he might just take a swing at her father.

Michael took Luke by the shoulders before pulling him into a hug. 'Do you know how worried we've all been?' He grabbed the back of Luke's head, then stepped back to look him in the eye. 'I'll call your parents and tell them you're home. Now get inside while I'm still pleased to see you.' He looked at where Jess sat crumpled on the pavement. 'Because,' he said, his voice remaining surprisingly calm, 'I can guarantee you that within the next five seconds, any relief I might be feeling will be replaced with all the rage of a father who sees his only daughter injured at the feet of her boyfriend.'

His shoulders deflating, Luke took one last glance at Jess before walking back into his house.

Michael looked at Hannah. 'You too,' he said, though his voice was significantly more gentle. 'Your brother needs you.'

Hannah nodded and followed after Luke. The front door closed behind her and then there was nothing but silence and the rain.

'Here,' Michael said, reaching out to Jess. As he helped her to her feet, Jess looked to where Cooper stood, soaking wet and holding his bruised jaw.

'Are you OK?' she asked, almost in a whisper.

'I've had worse.'

Michael turned, as though noticing Cooper for the first time. Wrapping an arm around Jess, he started to lead her to the front door. Once they were inside, he turned to where Cooper still stood, alone in the rain. With a hand on the doorframe, Michael nodded at Cooper.

'Well? Are you coming in, or are you just going to stand there?'

Cooper glanced over his shoulder, then stepped through the front gate and into the house.

COOPER

Cooper winced, holding the tea-towel-wrapped frozen peas to his jaw as gently as he could. In the corner of the room, an old cathode-ray television set was showing a black and white film set inside a submarine.

He looked at Jess, who was sitting directly opposite him and holding a similar makeshift ice pack to the back of her head. She was staring straight back, her eyes red raw and somehow empty, as though she were looking through him rather than at him.

Like she was looking at something very far away.

The lounge was as warm and as comforting as Cooper remembered. A number of lamps threw a soft golden light on comfy looking armchairs and a large sofa covered with colourful scatter cushions and a tartan throw. The sofa upon which Cooper now sat. The furniture was huddled around a fireplace that was filled with glowing coals and he was grateful for the warmth that radiated from it, taking the chill from his bones.

A cup of tea was placed with a soft clunk on the wooden coffee table in front of him. Cooper looked up to see Michael placing another mug in front of Jess, who was still staring through him.

Michael picked up a remote from the pine coffee table and pointed it at the TV set, the picture reducing to a pinpoint with a crackle of static. The screen turned black and the room was silent apart from the pop of the fire and the ticking of a clock on top of the mantel.

'Now,' Michael said. 'Who's going to tell me what's going on?'

Though the question was directed at both of them, Michael was looking directly at Cooper. He waited for Jess to answer, but when she only continued to stare back at him, he realized she wasn't going to be particularly forthcoming.

It was like being at a job interview, Cooper thought. Both of them just looking at him, waiting for whatever answers they were searching for. Very different answers, he suspected.

Cooper lowered the ice pack. 'Luke pushed Jess over,' Cooper said, choosing his words as carefully as he could. 'Though I don't think he meant to hurt her.'

Michael nodded and he settled into the large armchair, placing his hands together in a prayer position and touching his forefingers to his lips. 'And why would he do something like that, Sam?'

'I . . .' Cooper looked at Jess, but she was now looking at the floor, her mouth down-turned and her eyes filled with tears.

She was ashamed.

'You know what?' Michael said, holding up a hand to stop Cooper from speaking. 'Before you answer that, I need to tell you something.'

Jess glanced at her father.

'I saw what happened,' he continued. 'I know that you didn't hit him back.' Michael studied Cooper's face. 'I've known you for a while now Sam, and I've never known you to get into a fight. Yet here you are, your face a mess from what I can only assume are injuries acquired before tonight?'

'Yes, Mr Gordon.' Cooper twisted his fingers together, annoyed at how small he felt. Like a child in the head teacher's office. He could feel Michael staring at him, trying to work him out.

'I'm assuming that whoever did that to you,' Michael said, gesturing towards the wounds on Cooper's face, 'got away with minimal injury? That you only did what you had to do, like you did tonight?'

Cooper nodded.

'You're a good kid, Sam. And sometimes good kids get caught up in bad situations.' He turned to Jess, leaning to reposition the ice pack on the back of her head. 'Sometimes even the best kids can get caught up in a mess they never saw coming.'

Shame burned in Cooper's chest. Jess had never told her father about his arrest last year and for that he'd only ever been grateful.

With her free hand, the other still on the ice pack, Jess reached up to wipe away her tears. 'I'm sorry,' she whispered. 'I'm so sorry.'

Michael kissed her on the forehead. 'You have nothing to be sorry about. Luke's very charming. I've watched that boy grow up and would never have imagined he was capable of what I saw tonight. He's obviously a very troubled young man.' Michael's voice grew firm, yet he still spoke to Jess with nothing but love. 'And someone you should probably reconsider being involved with.'

Jess hacked out a laugh. 'Don't worry about that. It's over.'

'Good,' Michael said with a nod. 'Now, can we talk about what happened tonight?'

Cooper glanced at Jess. The far-away gaze had been replaced with one of panic, and she looked back at Cooper with wide eyes. 'OK,' he said. 'But I just . . .'

'I'm assuming Luke was unhappy about you two spending time together?'

'Pretty much,' Cooper agreed.

'Look,' Michael said, taking the ice pack from Jess and getting to his feet. 'Let me give you both some advice, OK? You have the right to be friends with anyone you want, but the key is to be open and honest about your intentions.' He looked at Cooper, the corner of his mouth twitching. 'From both sides. You get what I'm saying?'

'I get you,' Cooper said. 'You're saying that I shouldn't try to be friends with someone in a relationship . . .' He swallowed, looking down at his hands. 'If I still have feelings for them.' He nodded. 'You're right. But what if she's being treated badly? You can't walk away from someone you care about if you know that's the case, can you?'

'As I said,' Michael said, trying in vain to catch the drips from the makeshift ice pack. 'You're a good kid. But right now, I need to go and see if we have any more frozen peas.' He walked out, leaving Jess staring at Cooper.

'Thanks.'

'What for?'

'For coming up with a story so quickly.'

'Who said it was a story?' Leaning back against the sofa, Cooper replaced his own melting ice pack against his jaw and closed his eyes, not wanting to see the look on Jess's face. He was too tired to see her response, just like he'd been too tired to lie to Michael, or come up with some crazy story about how they might have got into the fight.

'Cooper—'

'Don't,' Cooper said, not opening his eyes. 'I can't talk about it. Not now.' He paused. 'Even though I meant every word.'

The fire crackled, the clock continued to tick and for just a second Cooper thought that maybe everything would work out, one way or another. He'd been such an idiot.

How could he have blamed her for what had happened last year? It was his own fault that he'd been arrested. All Jess had done was try to help him be the best he could be.

Then an almighty crash made Cooper's eyes fly open and he looked up to see Michael barrel through the lounge door, not saying a word as he grabbed the cordless phone from the coffee table and started dialling.

'Dad?' Jess was on her feet.

'Wait here,' Michael snapped, his eyes wide and wild as he marched from the room. 'Yes,' he barked. 'Fire brigade, please.'

The front door opened and Michael's voice, filled with urgency, faded as he disappeared into the night.

Jess looked at Cooper. 'Do you smell that?' Her voice rising, she started to move towards the door.

Cooper did smell something.

He jumped to his feet, chasing Jess outside into the hallway, which was already half filled with smoke. He looked back, but it wasn't coming from anywhere inside the house. It was coming from outside, where he could now hear Jess screaming, could hear Michael shouting over a number of other voices. Lifting his jacket to cover his nose and mouth, he pushed through the cloud of smoke, trying not to breathe. It grew denser as he went through the front door, then almost disappeared once he stepped out into the night air. He turned back to look, then stumbled as if someone had just landed another punch on his jaw.

Smoke spewed from the front door of Luke and Hannah's house, a menacing red and orange glow flickering behind the thick plumes.

Cooper ran on to the street, joining the gathering crowd. He saw Michael at the bay window of the lounge, throwing his elbow at the glass, once, twice, only to have it bounce back with the same force.

'Is there anyone in there?' someone was shouting from nearby. 'Has anyone called the fire brigade?'

Michael searched the small front garden in which he stood, surrounded by spiked metal railings, then bent down to pick up a loose brick. He pulled his sleeve over his hand and turned back to the window. This time it caved in on the first blow and the same black smoke that was pouring out of the front door now began to billow through the smashed glass.

He smashed at the window again and again, knocking out the rest of the glass from within one of the wooden frames, then he dropped the brick and without a moment's hesitation, hooked a leg inside and disappeared into the house.

'Dad, wait!' Jess ran forwards, but Cooper grabbed her.

Upstairs, one of the sash windows thudded open. Cooper looked up to see Hannah hanging out of the window, coughing and crying.

'Hannah,' Cooper shouted. 'Can you jump?'

'No,' she called back. 'The railings. Where's Luke? Has he got out yet? The stairs are blocked, I can't get down.'

The railings at the front of the property were less than a metre from the house. If Hannah were to jump, there was a good chance she could impale herself on the spikes. 'You need to lower yourself,' Cooper called. 'Climb out on to the sill and turn around.'

'Is Luke out?' she shouted again. 'I'm not leaving without him.'

'He's out,' Cooper shouted back. He could feel Jess's eyes on him, but he continued, 'He's fine, he's waiting for you.'

Hannah's legs swung out on to the window sill. 'It's too high,' she cried. 'I can't do it.'

Cooper let go of Jess and rushed forwards.

Sirens wailed in the distance, but the smoke pouring out of the front windows told him they wouldn't arrive in time. 'You have to, Hannah.'

Hannah twisted her body and started to lower herself from the sill. Her torso moved steadily downwards until she was only a couple of metres from the ground.

'Just let go,' Cooper shouted. 'It's not that far.'

She did. Her body dropped and she landed in a heap on the concrete floor not far from where Cooper stood. She was coughing, engulfed in the smoke that continued to billow from the front windows.

Cooper pulled her up, wrapping one arm around her waist as he helped her out on to the street. She was limping badly, but Cooper figured that even a broken ankle was a small price to pay.

'Where's Luke?' she asked. 'I want to see him.'

There was now a large crowd surrounding the house and Hannah scanned the group before turning to look at Cooper. 'Where is he?'

A voice shouted from within the crowd. 'Someone's coming, look.'

Cooper turned back to see a lone figure, hunched and hacking, climbing out through the broken lounge window.

'Is that him?' Hannah cried. 'Is that Luke?'

'Dad!' Jess ran to meet Michael as he staggered out on to the street, before collapsing to his hands and knees, coughing.

'Where is he?' Hannah screamed, trying to pull away from Cooper. 'Is he still inside?'

As flames began to lick from every window, Cooper could only nod.

JESS

A skin had formed on Jess's coffee, but she didn't care.

The same numbness she'd felt in the hospital had returned, but this time she was grateful for the empty feeling, like her stomach had been scooped out with a giant spoon, because the alternative was something much, much worse.

Oh, it was there. She knew it was there, lurking somewhere over her shoulder like the black dog in the bereavement leaflet, biding its time. Soon enough, the beast that was going to be her acceptance of Luke's death would pounce and maul her to within an inch of her life, tearing her to pieces until she wished for death to come for her, too.

But for now, grief could wait in the shadows. It was denial's turn today.

'You not going to drink that?' Cooper asked, sliding the

coffee mug a few centimetres towards Jess.

She looked at him, really looked at him, like she was seeing him through new eyes. He really did still care about her. After all this time. 'No.' She forced a smile, to try to appear less ungrateful. 'No thanks.'

'OK.' He nodded, his eyes shifting to the doorway where Amy stood, arms folded as she leaned against the doorframe.

'So what did the police say?' Amy asked. 'Do they know what happened?'

'It was definitely arson,' Jess replied. It was strange, to hear herself talking as though nothing had happened. It was as if she'd retreated to a tiny corner of her own brain, watching on as the rest of her body continued on auto-pilot. Like she was watching herself acting in some terrible soap opera. 'Scarlett's party and Luke's place. Both arson.'

'You were at the station for hours.'

Jess glared at Amy. 'They had a lot of questions.' She pushed the coffee mug back towards Cooper. She didn't want to see that skin floating on the top. It was making her feel sick. All she wanted was to go home, curl up in her bed and take another hit of Nostalgex. To revisit a time before her life imploded. 'I was present at two fires, two cases of *arson*, within a few days. I'm surprised it wasn't longer.'

Amy glanced at Cooper.

'I didn't say anything about you,' Jess said. 'But I told them everything about Leon. And Whiteface, though they'd never heard of him and looked at me like I was crazy.'

'Who the hell is Whiteface?' Amy asked.

'The guy who Leon works for,' said Cooper. 'At least that's what he told me. Who knows if he's telling the truth – the guy's obviously nuts.'

Jess's phone vibrated in her pocket, but she ignored it. It was probably her father, calling again to ask when she was coming home. But she wasn't going back there any time soon, not when she knew she'd have to look at the burned out shell of Luke's house again. She wasn't ready, not yet. 'I'm sorry,' she said, lowering her head into her hands. 'I know this could all come back to you. But I didn't know what else to do. I can't let them get away with it, I just can't. Luke was messed up, I know that, but he didn't deserve to die.'

Cooper frowned. 'You did what you had to do.'

'So what now?' Amy asked. 'What happens when they find Leon? And he tells them about you?'

'People are dying, Amy,' Cooper snapped. 'I'm not going to worry about myself right now. Not when it could be you next.'

'Nothing's going to happen to me, Sam.'

'I'm sure Scarlett and Luke thought the same thing.' He caught Jess's eye and she stared back, still comfortably numb in that cosy little corner of her brain.

A loud knock came from the front door. Cooper tapped the last two *shave-and-a-haircut* beats out on the table in front of him.

'You asked Jag over?' Amy asked with a groan.

'No,' replied Cooper. 'But you know what he's like. The

all-seeing-eye of East London. If it's happened, Jag knows about it.' He glanced at Jess and his voice softened. 'You OK if he comes in?'

Jess shrugged a shoulder as Amy went to answer the door. Though she'd never admit it to him, she was actually kind of glad to see Jag's face appear in the doorway. He didn't mean any harm, he never had. And you could always count on Jag to say something to lift the mood.

Not today, though. He covered the distance between Jess and the doorway in two strides and leaned down to hug her. For a moment she was startled, her arms hanging uselessly at her sides while she looked at Cooper. He was watching on with a mixture of mild amusement and, what was that? Jealousy? Jess patted Jag on the back and he pulled back, before running his hands through his hair.

'I'm really sorry,' he said. 'About Luke and everything.'

Jess nodded. 'Yeah. Me too.'

Cooper's phone danced on the table as it began to ring and vibrate at the same time. He scooped it up and held it to his ear, the look on his face immediately giving away who he was talking to. 'Tonight?' he asked, his brow furrowing. 'But I only just paid you last night.'

'Who is it?' Amy hissed from her position in the doorway. 'Is that Leon? What does he want?'

Cooper held up a hand and he turned away. 'Yeah, I can meet you. Docklands? Same time.'

Amy stepped forwards, craning to listen to the conversation.

'Yeah. Sure thing,' Cooper continued, though he didn't sound entirely convinced by the words he was speaking. Then he looked at his phone, frowning. 'He hung up.'

'What did he say?' Amy asked.

'He wants to meet. To talk.'

'About what?' Jag asked. 'The weather? Coop, the guy's a psycho, I wouldn't trust him as far as I could throw him.'

Cooper only nodded. He was chewing on the corner of his lip. 'There's something I'm missing,' he said to no one in particular. 'Something that links all of this together.'

He stood up and walked from the room.

After a beat, Jag spoke. 'What was that about?'

Jess stared at the empty doorway. There was something about the expression on Cooper's face before he left, something about the way his eyes weren't exactly focussing. Like he was looking into the past, searching for a memory he wasn't even sure existed.

Though Jess knew there were ways of finding out.

She jumped up and marched from the room, ignoring the questions from Amy and Jag. Cooper's door was closed, but she didn't bother knocking. Pushing it open, she strode in to see him sitting on his bed, his backpack open on the floor and a bag of Nostalgex on the duvet beside him, the contents partly spilling on to the cotton sheet. In one hand were four or five of the pills, in the other was a glass of water.

'Cooper—'

'You took this many, right?' He wouldn't even look at

her; his eyes remained focussed on the pills.

'Yes, but—'

'Look,' he said. 'If there's a way of figuring out what happened, how we got into this mess, maybe we'll be able to figure out a way to fix it. Maybe we can help Leon, if he's really telling the truth.' He looked at her, the icy blue of his eyes somehow softer than she'd remembered. 'I know it's too late for Luke and I'm sorry about that, I really am. If I could go back in time, I would, Jess. I really would.'

Jess closed her eyes. 'I know.' When she next opened them, Cooper's hand was empty and his throat bobbed as he chugged the glass of water.

He placed the glass on his bedside table and stuck his tongue out. 'Man, they're bitter.'

Jess turned and slid the bolt to lock Cooper's door. 'I can't believe you took them.'

'Why? You did,' he said simply, looking straight at her. Their eyes locked for a moment before Cooper broke her gaze. 'I can't see how else we can fix this. Not if we don't understand why any of this has happened. Maybe there's nothing I can do to help, but if there is, if there's something in my memories . . . I just can't help but think that I've missed something.'

Jess nodded.

'What did you see?' Cooper looked up again. 'When you took them?'

'I saw a lot. And not always what I wanted to see, either.'

'What do you mean?'

She paused. 'I wanted to forget everything that had happened,' she said. 'Even just for an hour or two. But the memories weren't the same. You can't relive something in the same way when you feel differently about it.'

'And what is it that you feel differently about?'

'A lot of things.' She looked at Cooper. 'You know when I first took the pills, you told me to think of something that made me happy?'

'Yeah.'

'To start with, I was thinking about Luke. But it wasn't a happy feeling any more. Even the good times. They looked the same, but I just didn't feel the same way about it.'

'So what did make you happy?'

Jess tucked a strand of hair behind her ear, her fingers brushing against the back of her neck. If she closed her eyes, she knew she'd be able to feel the warmth of the sun from that summer's day. 'Something else,' she said quietly. 'Something from a different time.'

Cooper blinked, his eyes shifting as though he was looking at the room for the first time. 'Whoa.' He grabbed hold of the duvet, like his bed might tip and throw him off at any moment.

'It's OK,' Jess said, taking his hand. 'It's a bit weird to start with, but you'll get used to it.'

'Is this it?' he asked, holding his other hand out in front of him and staring at it before turning to look at Jess. 'It's like I'm having flashbacks.'

'That's just the start,' she said. 'You took a lot, like I did, so it'll be more like a really vivid dream. It feels like you're actually there, experiencing it all over again. Just remember, think of something happy to start with.'

'Happy.' Closing his eyes, Cooper let his head sink back into the pillow. 'Hey. Remember that one day?' he said, a smile spreading across his face as he closed his eyes. 'At Festival X? You were wearing that yellow sundress. I always loved how you looked in yellow.'

Jess stared, almost able to feel the warm glow of sun on the back of her neck. 'Of course I remember.'

'That's good,' he murmured. 'Hey, why did you break up with me again?'

'I thought you broke up with me?'

He squeezed her hand. 'Why would I have broken up with you? You were the best thing to ever happen to me.'

She frowned.

They'd never had a break up conversation. Cooper never called after his arrest, but then again, she'd never called him.

They'd both been too stubborn.

For a moment, Jess thought her heart might just collapse in on itself.

'Hey, remember that night? In the tent?' Cooper smiled again and the imaginary warmth on Jess's neck turned to a burning heat, one that quickly spread to her cheeks.

'Stop it,' she said, slapping his arm. 'Don't think about that!'

Cooper opened one eye, his smile widening. 'Sorry,' he

said. 'Can't help it.' He laughed, but his words were beginning to slur, like he was drunk.

The images of that evening instantly filled Jess's head, as vivid as if it had been yesterday.

But of course the memories were fresh in her mind.

She'd only just relived it all herself.

COOPER

He knew he hadn't taken the pills for this, but he couldn't think of anything else.

The very moment Jess had taken his hand in hers, his mind had been transported back in time to that summer's day, eighteen months ago. Just like Jess had described, it was as if he were there, reliving it all over again. As if he could reach out and touch her, the yellow material of her dress bright against her smooth, dark skin. But try as he might, all he could do was watch on from somewhere inside his own body, as a past version of himself stepped towards her, his hands reaching out to snake around her waist, his fingers lacing together across her tummy as he leaned down to kiss a spot on the back of her neck that had been warmed by the sun.

Then her hands were across his and she turned to face him, and she was even more beautiful than he'd remembered.

'The band's going to start soon,' she said, turning her face as he leaned to kiss her again. His lips connected with the smooth skin of her cheek and he felt a shift as she smiled. 'You want to go and watch from the top of the hill?'

Cooper looked up at the hill, already covered with people on picnic blankets. Like ants on the hillside. Then he looked back towards the stage, where steam was rising from the crowd who were already pushing and shoving in an effort to get closer to the front.

'Nah,' he heard himself say. 'I'd rather go and mosh. You want to come?'

Jess shook her head. 'Too many people. I got a black eye the last time I went in one of those with you. Remember?' She took his hand in hers and pressed her body against his, a smile playing across her lips. 'Come and sit with me.'

Cooper leaned down and planted a kiss on the top of Jess's head. 'I'll meet you up there later,' he said, already walking away. He didn't even look to see the disappointment he now knew would have been in her eyes.

What an idiot he'd been.

Why hadn't he just gone with her?

If he could do it all over again, he'd turn around at that very moment and walk with her to that hill. He'd sit and talk with her, paying no attention to the band that he'd grow bored of within six months and never listen to again. Maybe if he'd done that the first time, things would be different now.

Cooper cursed himself as he walked away from Jess,

unable to control his body as he moved closer to the stage. How he wished he could stop himself and turn around, but he knew it was impossible. This was a memory, nothing more. There was no way of changing something that had already happened.

The air around him began to shimmer, the sounds of the crowds and the distant music playing from the other stages growing denser, as though coming through water. The light faded and he was falling through nothing, until he blinked and found himself in front of a small fire, surrounded by tents. The sky was black and peppered with starlight, while bass thumped somewhere in the distance. Nearby, someone was shouting incoherently while raucous laughter rang out.

Jess was beside Cooper, her hand on his knee as they both watched Jag, animatedly telling a story on the other side of the fire.

'And I'm telling you, man,' Jag was saying. 'The bus driver must have chased me for at least another half a mile.' He burst out laughing again, shaking his head as tears streamed from his eyes.

Cooper was also roaring with laughter.

'Hey,' Jess said, trailing a finger down Cooper's arm.

He turned to look at her and she smiled at him, the shadows on her face flickering as the fire danced in front of where they sat. 'Hey,' he replied, leaning in to kiss her nose, then her lips.

'Right,' Jag said, tossing his beer can to one side before

letting out a huge belch. 'If you two are going to start doing that, then I'm off to bed.'

But Cooper wasn't paying attention. His hand was on Jess's thigh, his fingers at the hem of her skirt, and she was kissing him, her hand on the back of his head as she pulled him closer towards her.

'Get a room!' a voice called out from somewhere nearby.

Cooper laughed, but Jess was already on her feet, walking towards her tent. She turned back to him as she started to unzip the canvas. 'You coming?' she asked.

There was a moment where Cooper had paused, unsure if she was asking him what he thought she was asking him, but it lasted less than a heartbeat. He got up and followed her towards the tent.

Where had it gone so wrong?

How had he messed up something that could have been so perfect?

He knew the answer of course, had seen it for himself when he'd walked away from Jess earlier that day. Now that he thought about it, it was something he did a lot back then. Always looking for a good time, regardless of how it might affect the people he cared about. The saddest part was that he wanted to change but, if anything, he was now in the biggest mess of his life.

A festival-goer stumbled past, almost tripping over one of the guy ropes. A rubber demon mask covered his face, while his torso was bare, his trousers hanging low to reveal the waistband of his boxers. 'Watch it!' he shouted at no one in particular, though his voice was muffled by the mask he was wearing.

Stop.

Everything around Cooper froze. Though he couldn't move, he could see everything clearly, illuminated in the soft orange glow cast by the fire that was somewhere behind him.

The guy in the mask was mid stumble, his body in a gravity-defying position as his foot pulled against the guy rope that was threatening to trip him over.

Cooper stared at the mask. He'd taken those pills for a reason, and it wasn't to come and relive this night with Jess.

Then, as if someone had pressed a switch that turned off the starlight, the blackness returned. The next time Cooper opened his eyes, he was back on the path in St Steven's churchyard, straddling his bike while he stared at the figure in front of him. It was dark, just like it had been in his previous memory, but now it was cold. His breath hung in pockets of mist before his face as he turned to look behind him for the way out he knew wasn't there. His instinct told him to turn around, to face his attacker, but of course he knew he couldn't do that.

Still, the blow to the head was almost as much of a shock as it had been the first time. He tumbled to the ground, the night sky flipping as he fell. While the pain was there, as sharp and as brutal as it had been before, this time he was actually lucid and able to focus. Apparently a concussion only hid one's memories because what he was experiencing now was as lucid as anything he'd ever experienced.

If not more so.

He could smell the night air, crisp and cool.

He could feel the metal frame of his bike tangled beneath his legs, the way the chain was digging into his calf and the handlebar only a few inches from ruining his chances of ever having children.

He could see his attacker, standing over him with that bottle, looking at him in that almost quizzical way. And then Cooper's hand was reaching up to take a pathetic swipe at the figure's face.

But it wasn't a face at all.

It was a white mask, featureless apart from two black eye-holes.

Whiteface.

Cooper's fingers connected with smooth plastic and it shifted beneath his touch, the mask slipping from his attacker's face as they whispered two words, two words whose memory had been smothered by the thick blanket of concussion.

'I'm sorry.'

And in that instant, as the figure raised the bottle up and brought it crashing down over his head to return him to the darkness, he saw the face of the person who had done this to him.

Amy.

JESS

It was like watching someone having a nightmare in a movie.

Cooper's head moved from side to side, his face creasing as he grimaced, a thin film of sweat beading on his forehead. His lips were moving, as though he were trying to speak. Jess knew exactly how helpless he was feeling, watching his memories unfold while being totally unable to do anything about them.

'It's OK,' she said, squeezing his hand. 'It's not real, not any more.' She was sure that he couldn't hear her, but then his eyes flew open.

'A mask,' he said, his chest heaving.

'What?'

He looked right at her, eyes wide. 'Whiteface. The person who attacked me. They were wearing a mask. A white mask.' Then his eyes rolled back into his head and he

263

fell back against the pillow again, his breathing slowing. 'Amy,' he whispered. 'Amy.'

Jess dropped his hand. She ran through to the kitchen where Jag was sitting at the table, typing on his phone. Amy was leaning against the counter, clutching a fresh cup of coffee.

'It's all connected,' she blurted out. 'What happened on New Year's Eve at Scarlett's house, the person who attacked Cooper. They were both wearing masks and I bet you,' she said, ignoring the look on Jag's face that said he was listening to the ravings of a madwoman, 'I bet you that the fire at the Fill 'n' Save is connected too.' She knew her eyes were wide and that her voice was coming out too fast and too high pitched, but she didn't care. 'Cooper was supposed to be working that night. He must have been the original target.'

Jag looked past her shoulder, out into the empty hallway. 'Where is Cooper?'

'Sam?' Amy called. She turned and disappeared into the hallway. 'Sam? Can you come out here so we can—'

Jess chased after her, but it was too late. Amy stood in the doorway to Cooper's bedroom. She turned to face Jess, eyes cold. 'What did he take? Those stupid red pills?'

Behind Amy, Cooper was still sprawled on the bed, his mouth moving as he whispered something incoherent, his eyelids fluttering as the whites of his eyes shifted beneath.

'What the hell?' Jag stood behind Jess, staring at Cooper.

Jess followed Amy into the bedroom. 'I couldn't have stopped him even if I wanted to.'

Leaning over her brother, Amy gently slapped his face. 'Sam?' Her voice was loud, firm. 'Sam, it's Amy. How many did you take?'

'Five,' Jess said. She knew that Cooper was in no fit state to answer.

'Shit.' Amy clutched the side of her head. 'Shit, shit, *shit.*'

'It'll be fine,' Jess said, reaching out to touch Amy's arm. 'I took some myself, so I—'

'You took them?' Pulling away from Jess, Amy laughed, though her lips were thin, her teeth bared. 'So, what? You and my brother are druggies now? Are you the one who gave them to him?'

'Amy . . .' Jess stepped back. 'You know I'd never—'

'Never what?'

Jess shook her head. 'We did it for a reason.'

'There's always a reason,' Amy snapped, pushing past Jess and Jag into the hallway. 'Just like Dad had his reasons.' She grabbed a bag that was hanging from the kitchen door handle and slung it over her shoulder. 'I can't deal with this now,' she said, reaching for the front door. 'Not when he's like that.'

'But don't you think you should just—' Jag started.

'Just what?'

'I don't think you should leave,' Jess said. 'He was saying your name. Maybe he saw something you need to know about.'

'It can wait. I need to get out of here.' Amy glared at Jess. 'And you'd better hope that nothing happens to him, otherwise you won't just have Luke's death on your conscience.' She stepped out of the front door and slammed it behind her.

Letting out a low whistle, Jag turned to Jess. 'You know she doesn't mean that, right? Nobody thinks any of this is your—'

And then it hit her, all at once. The black dog she'd seen in that leaflet was no longer behind her, it was on her, sinking its teeth into her heart.

The first sob came with such force, she thought she might actually be sick. Jess reached up to cover her mouth as the tears rolled, thick and fast. All at once, she was filled with the grief that had been hiding beneath the surface, ready to strike when she was least ready.

'Hey,' Jag said, grabbing her by the shoulders and pulling her against him. 'It's going to be OK. We're going to work it out.'

'I didn't want him to die, Jag. I never wanted him to die.'

'I know.'

She wiped her eyes. 'Do you really think Amy's mad at me for letting Cooper take the pills?'

'No, she knows it's not your fault.' Then he grabbed his coat from the peg. 'But I can't let her go alone,' he said. 'Not after everything that's been going on. Cooper would never forgive me if something happened to her.' He turned to Jess. 'Stay here and keep an eye on Coop. You'll be OK, right?'

Jess nodded and Jag closed the front door behind him.

COOPER

Leon.

A familiar voice carried to him, as light as the summer's breeze that had played with the hem of Jess's yellow sundress.

Leon ran past him, his hair slick with water and plastered to his forehead. Cooper was wet too, but the coolness of the water was pleasant, welcome on his skin. The garden sprinklers were on, watering the expansive lawns that surrounded the huge house behind them, while the barbecue pit smouldered nearby, ready to cook Frank's favourite hog roast.

He remembered that summer; it had been one of the hottest on record. At least that's what all the grown-ups kept saying.

'Pew, pew!' Leon aimed two fingers at Cooper, pretending to fire a gun. Before darting behind one of the huge, ornate plant pots that were scattered around the garden, Leon grinned, his teeth white and whole.

Gold now.

On the patio sat Cooper's father, discussing something Very Important with Leon's dad Frank. It was always something Very Important, something that wasn't for kids' ears, according to Frank. The boys knew better than to interrupt their dads when they were having Very Important discussions, and had learned quickly to keep out of their way during these times. Cooper's mother clucked around the men, filling the tall glasses on the table in front of them with drinks, ice clinking as she poured.

On that hot summer's day ten years ago, with Amy reading nearby under the shade of an apple tree, Leon had smiled at Cooper, asked if he wanted to 'see something cool'.

Cooper nodded, then followed Leon towards the house.

'Where are you going?' Amy called out from under her tree, the same spot she would always sit in when they were at Leon's. Always facing the patio, where she could see their father.

'Nowhere,' Leon had shouted back. 'Boys only.'

And Amy had scowled, lifting the book back up to cover her face.

Cooper followed Leon inside and up the stairs to one of the spare bedrooms. The white walls were covered in art; canvases splashed with all the colours of the rainbow. The house itself was modern and minimalist, the dark grey carpet and glass and chrome surfaces giving the property a cold, clinical feel.

They had walked together along the narrow hallway, the carpet rough beneath Cooper's bare feet.

In the back room, Leon led Cooper to the built-in wardrobe, fronted by mirrored doors. He'd slid one of the panels back, revealing his mother's winter wardrobe, each dress covered with a plastic slip.

Leon pulled a chair from the corner of the room, climbed up and reached to grab one of the many shoeboxes stacked on the wardrobe's shelf. He brought it down and placed it on the bed with care, as though it might contain something explosive.

'Promise not to tell?' Leon had asked in a dramatic whisper, his eyes wide.

Cooper had only nodded, his eyes twice as wide as Leon's.

Leon's voice dropped further. 'Pinky swear? No returns?'

'Pinky swear,' Cooper had confirmed, linking his own little finger with Leon's. 'No returns.'

Then, looking at Cooper again with that little half-smile, a look that said he was about to reveal the most amazing thing in the world, Leon lifted the lid of the box.

Inside the box was a gun.

Cooper had never seen a real gun before and his horror at the discovery was almost immediately over-ridden by his fascination.

'You can hold it,' Leon had said. 'I do, sometimes.'

With a hand that didn't feel like his own, Cooper had reached into the box, lifting the weapon and marvelling at its weight.

'It's not loaded.' Leon grabbed the gun from Cooper's hand, placing his finger over the trigger as he pointed it at the mirror. 'Bang, bang.' His half-smile turned into a grin and he lifted the gun, this time pointing it directly at Cooper's face. 'BANG!'

Cooper had stumbled back. 'Don't, I don't like it.'

'Don't be a wimp. Dad keeps all the bullets in a different box. It's not loaded.' His finger began to tighten on the trigger. 'Watch.'

Before he had the chance to squeeze the trigger home, Frank barrelled into the room, covering the distance between the door and where Leon stood in two massive steps. He snatched the gun and roared at Leon, bad words that Cooper had only ever heard grown-ups say to each other, but here Frank was, screaming in his son's face as he pushed him to the floor, straddling his chest with his knees.

Cooper hadn't remembered this part.

Why didn't he remember this part? It was like watching a familiar movie, yet this was a deleted scene. One that he was sure he'd never seen before.

'I've told you how many times?' Frank had yelled, grabbing Leon's jaw with his left hand.

Leon had started to cry, a terrified wail that made Cooper's stomach twist.

'How many times?' Frank repeated, squeezing Leon's jaw hard enough to make him yelp out in pain. In one swift motion, Frank shoved the gun into his son's open mouth.

Stop it! Cooper yelled from somewhere inside his own head. He could feel his heart racing, yet it wasn't the heart inside the child's body he was now occupying.

Why, why didn't he remember this?

Leon continued to sob, though the sound was now muffled against the barrel. Tears rolled down his face, mixing with snot and the saliva that was being forced from the corners of his lips. With wide eyes, he looked at Cooper, his breath coming in quick bursts through his streaming nose.

'Guns are not toys, Leon,' Frank snarled, his fingers tightening around his son's jaw, his knuckles white with the effort. 'And what's the golden rule?' He slowly withdrew the gun from Leon's mouth, strings of saliva hanging from the barrel as he relocated it to point at Leon's eye. 'The golden rule?' he repeated.

Leon took a deep, shuddering breath. 'All . . . it's always . . .' He let out another wail, squeezing his eyes tightly shut. 'A gun is always loaded.'

'And if it's not loaded?' Frank pressed the barrel against Leon's closed eye.

'It's still loaded.'

With a satisfied nod, Frank withdrew the gun and got to his feet. Without another word, or even a glance in the direction of his crying, shaking son, he lay the gun back in

271

the box, then replaced the box on the shelf. He slid the wardrobe door closed, turned, ruffled Cooper's hair and walked from the room.

Leon wiped his streaming nose on his T-shirt, then looked at Cooper with eyes as dark as the carpet he was sitting on. 'Why didn't you say anything?' he sobbed. 'You didn't *do* anything.'

And Cooper just stared, only just noticing the telltale dark patch that had appeared on the crotch of Leon's shorts.

Leon lurched to his feet. 'You didn't do *anything*,' he'd screamed again, running from the room. In the doorway stood Amy. She stared at Cooper for a moment before chasing after Leon. She must have followed them up, seen everything.

Don't just stand there. Go after them!

But he didn't. Not for a long time. He simply stood, staring at the half-closed wardrobe door. What had he been thinking at the time? Why had he remembered the part where Leon pointed the gun at him, but not the rest?

Then he was walking again, out through the door, down the hallway and out into the garden. Frank was sipping from a tall glass, nodding at something Cooper's father was saying. Frank looked at Cooper and smiled, exposing a row of gold teeth.

Under the apple tree, Leon was sitting with Amy, his head resting against her shoulder as he sniffled, wiping his nose with the back of his hand. She stroked his head and said something in his ear, something that Cooper couldn't hear from his position on the patio.

It wouldn't be the first time they'd sit together under the apple tree in that way. What had she said to him that day? Had it been enough to change their relationship?

Had it been enough for them to—

The image began to shimmer like a heat haze, the picture collapsing in on itself until a new image started to emerge.

Sitting in Leon's vast lounge, flicking through the channels on the huge TV while a young boy screamed and cried nearby, the noise punctuated with the sound of slapping and what could only be knuckles against flesh. Cooper felt himself frown as he lifted the remote and turned up the volume.

The picture changed again and Cooper was still in the lounge, but this was years later. New Year's Eve, four years earlier. This time, Leon was on the floor, blood pouring from his mouth while Amy knelt beside him, her hand on his shoulder. Music blared from invisible speakers mounted somewhere in the mouldings that lined the high ceilings and the crowd that had gathered around Leon stared at the teenager as he spat his two broken front teeth into his hand.

Cooper also watched on as Amy helped Leon up and led him from the room. Leon was saying something to her and Cooper could see he was trying his hardest not to cry, even as they walked past Frank. Frank didn't even look at his son, but instead laughed at something one of his party guests was saying as he lifted his glass of scotch, his knuckles red with blood.

It had been the last time he'd seen Frank, before Leon's dad took off and the police started nosing around, investigating his so-called disappearance. The same investigation that had led a trail of drugs and money to Cooper's front door and to his own parents.

Something buzzed beside Cooper's ear and he sprung forwards, gulping in deep breaths. He fell back, his head landing with a soft clump on the pillow.

He was in his bedroom, though it was now dark. On his bedside table, his phone was lit up, the source of the loud vibrating that had pulled him from his dream. If he could even call it that. A thin strip of light filtered through the crack in the door from the hallway. His head pounded, like he'd just woken up with the worst hangover. He licked his dry lips with an even drier tongue and sat up, the room swimming as he did so. Closing his eyes, he could still see Leon, blood dripping from his mouth. When he opened his eyes again, it took a while for the image to disappear, like he was looking at two images, one overlying the other. Then the image of Leon began to melt away again, his bedroom coming into sharper focus once more. Exhaling slowly, he swung his legs over the side of the bed and sat for a moment as a wave of nausea washed over him. Once it had subsided, he reached for his phone and opened the text message that had woken him.

When I said to come alone, I meant it.

There was a single attachment, one that made his stomach drop.

A photo of Amy in front of one of the dockland warehouses, a piece of gaffer tape covering her mouth, her nostrils flared and her eyes wide with fear.

JESS

Jess stared at the photo on the screen of Cooper's phone. 'We need to call the police.'

Cooper snatched his phone back. 'Not yet.'

'But this is serious. Amy's in trouble.'

'I think she's in a lot more trouble than either of us know,' he said, grabbing his coat. 'And somehow I don't think the police are going to be much good.'

'What are you talking about?'

Cooper stepped towards the front door but Jess grabbed his sleeve. 'Sam? Talk to me.'

He turned to look at her, his eyes wide and wild. 'It was Amy,' he said. 'She was the one who attacked me in the churchyard. It was her in the white mask.' He clutched his hands to his head, squeezing his eyes closed. 'Jeez, how long does it take for this stuff to wear off?'

Jess's hand fell from Cooper's jacket and her stomach

lurched. For a moment she thought she might be sick. 'It was Amy?' she whispered. 'That's impossible. There's no way.'

'It was her,' he said. 'I saw it, Jess. Unless the memories these pills show aren't real, then it was her.'

'Black hoodie? White mask?' Jess asked, her voice rising in pitch.

Cooper nodded.

'That's who I saw at the party. Just before the fire.' She shook her head. 'Is there any way she could have got from Scarlett's house to the churchyard in time?'

'I don't know,' Cooper said. 'But you have to know that it wasn't her. I mean, it was Amy, but someone made her do it. Leon must have made her do it. She said she was sorry and I know she wouldn't hurt me unless someone forced her.'

Jess nodded, but something didn't quite add up in her mind. It was like she was staring at a puzzle and there was no way of telling what the picture was without the last few pieces. 'I really think we should call the police,' she said gently.

'But what if she's been made to do something? She might have been forced into it, like I was. They've got me dealing on film, so who knows what they might have on Amy? It's bad enough that I've lost my parents, Jess. I can't lose Amy, too.'

'I'm sure the police will understand that—'

'No!' Cooper snapped, cutting her off mid-sentence.

'They won't even bother trying to understand, can't you see that?'

He pressed his hands against his temples again, wincing.

'Are you OK?'

'Yeah, it's just that I keep getting flashbacks. The memories keep coming, whether I want them to or not.' He blinked again, then started towards the front door.

'Sam, you can't go out like that!'

'I don't have much choice, do I? Amy's obviously in trouble and it's not like anyone else is going to help her. I need to get to the docklands.'

'I'm coming with you then.'

Cooper hesitated, but Jess grabbed her coat.

'I'm coming,' she said. 'Whether you like it or not.'

COOPER

'Leon!'

Cooper marched into the space between the warehouses. A thin film of mist clung to the tarmac and the chill of the night air permeated his bones. Combined with the adrenaline that was coursing through his blood vessels, it was a potent cocktail that made him feel more awake than he had done in days.

Just as well, considering the effects of the Nostalgex were still ravaging his body.

'Amy?' he shouted from behind cupped hands. 'Where are you?' The echo of his footsteps bounced from building to building, making it sound like he wasn't alone.

But of course, he wasn't. Jess was watching on from behind one of the warehouses, her phone ready to dial the police at a moment's notice. They'd agreed that she would call at the first sign of trouble, no matter what.

Cooper knew the risks involved, knew that he and Amy could both find themselves at the mercy of the law, but surely prison was better than death?

The air was thick with the stench of diesel, bonfire and barbecue. Not hugely typical for the time of year, but this was London, after all. In London, nothing could really be considered typical.

Still, who barbecued in January?

Cooper pulled out his phone and checked the time. He wasn't supposed to be meeting Leon for another twenty minutes, but Cooper knew he was here, somewhere.

Watching.

He sniffed the air again. The wind had changed direction, the thick mist rolling from the concreted forecourt to the cobbled walkways behind the warehouse he was standing next to. Black painted bollards stood sentinel between where Cooper stood and where the sharp drop reached down to meet the Thames, the fog drifting past and tumbling like a waterfall to meet the river. The barbecue smell seemed to grow in intensity, a sweet, almost sickly stench that reminded him a little of the marinated pork chops he'd slapped on the grill the previous summer, when his uncle was still around and there was something even vaguely resembling a food budget.

It was familiar, but it wasn't pork. Not quite.

Feeling a little more agitated, Cooper reached for his phone again, this time with the intention of actually calling Leon, or, at the very least, sending him a text to ask for an ETA.

But as he pulled the phone from his pocket, he saw what was making the mist so thick. Smoke was rolling out from one of the warehouses.

One of the metal shutters that was usually pulled down and padlocked on the warehouse opposite was rolled up; only a metre or so, but enough to show that someone may have recently set foot inside.

The smoke curled out from beneath the shutter like tendrils of ivy, mixing with the mist. As Cooper walked towards it, he was just about able to make out a flickering orange glow from within.

Something was on fire inside.

Not only that, but whatever was burning inside was creating that sickly barbecue smell, the one that smelled not quite enough like pork, threatening to spill the contents of his stomach all over the tarmac.

Cooper walked a little faster. 'Amy?' he shouted, breaking into a run.

Cooper crouched down, manoeuvring his body under the shutter and into the warehouse. His shoulders were heaving from the effort of breathing, his throat constricting in reaction to the smoke and another surge of adrenaline.

Banks of leaded windows lined each wall, though most were broken, and the occasional gust of wind shook the flames of the only two light sources. In the middle of the warehouse, only a few metres from where Cooper stood, was an old oil drum, fire licking over the top and bathing the area immediately around it in an orange glow. It did little, however, to penetrate the inky darkness.

'Amy?' he called again. The only answer was the echo of his own voice.

A breath of wind passed by Cooper, bringing with it more of the sickly barbecue stench. But the smell wasn't coming from the oil drum.

In the far corner was what looked like a smouldering pile of rags, the source of the majority of the smoke and the smell. But rags didn't have the very specific shape of what was, or rather what had been, burning in the corner of the warehouse.

'Jesus,' he whispered, an iron grip tightening around his heart. 'Jesus, no.'

He stumbled towards the burned remains. With each step, it became clearer that he was looking at a body. The arms were twisted up in front of the torso, the legs bent in a similar way, so the body was curled almost in a foetal position.

Falling to his knees, Cooper reached out to touch a charred shoulder. The body shifted under his touch, its shoulders twisting as it turned towards him, the crisp skin crackling as bones moved beneath soft, cooked flesh.

Cooper scurried back, looking away from the empty eye sockets that were now staring directly at him. His breath was coming in quick, shallow bursts and his thundering heart now seemed to be beating in his throat.

It wasn't Amy, he told himself. It couldn't be.

He had to look. If he looked, he'd see that there was no

282

necklace hanging beneath the blackened jaw. Because it wasn't Amy, it *wasn't*.

Inhaling a shaky breath, Cooper forced himself to focus on the body. The oil drum fire flickered, creating long shadows that danced on the walls behind the charred corpse.

The skull grinned at Cooper, as though mocking his terror.

Cooper's breath caught in his throat.

The victim's lips had peeled back from the heat of the fire, exposing the teeth beneath.

Gold teeth.

'Leon,' Cooper whispered. He sat heavily on the cold concrete floor, staring at the remains of his childhood friend.

Behind Cooper, something moved.

He jumped to his feet, turning to squint into the shadows, but there was nothing, only the crackle of the fire. Something popped inside the oil drum, sending a shower of sparks into the air.

For a moment he thought he'd been mistaken, or that perhaps it had been an urban fox, maybe even a large rat. But then a figure stepped out of the shadows, into the glow of flickering orange firelight.

Instinct drove Cooper to take a step back towards the shutter. He glanced back over his shoulder, certain that it was about to drop down and trap him in here with whoever was standing beside the oil drum. But the shutter didn't move.

'Amy? Is that you?'

The figure didn't say anything, only took another step forwards, closer to the fire. The flames flickered, then rose up again, throwing just enough light to illuminate the person's face.

It was Amy, but her mouth was covered with the same piece of tape from the photo he'd been sent. Her face was sooty and tracked with tears, her eyes wide and wild. Her arms were pulled back, her hands behind her back, probably bound with the same tape that covered her mouth.

'Jesus Amy, who—' He stepped towards her, but stopped when she began to shake her head furiously, her voice muffled behind the tape.

There was another figure behind Amy, but this person was wearing a white mask, the same featureless face-covering that his attacker had been wearing.

But that had been Amy. So who was in the mask now?

Cooper reached up to cover the large bruised lump on his forehead. His head was throbbing and his heart felt like it was about to burst through his ribcage.

'Who are you?' he asked. 'And what do you want?'

Without a word, the figure tossed a bag towards Cooper. A canvas holdall landed with a clump on the concrete floor, sending up a little cloud of dust that looked like smoke in the half-light.

The figure made no other move, just stared at Cooper through the black eye-holes of that white mask. Amy was shaking, moaning quietly behind the tape.

'What?' Cooper asked the masked figure. 'What do you want me to do with that?' Another gust of wind carried the diesel smell and what he now knew was burned flesh to where he stood. His stomach turned.

Why was he asking so many questions? There was a dead body only metres away and the murder weapon, the fire in the oil drum, was even closer. He reached for the bag, not taking his eyes from the masked figure in front of him. It was heavier than it looked and something shifted inside. Cooper pulled the zip back and yanked the canvas apart.

It was filled with money.

'What the—?'

He reached inside and pulled out a wad of cash. There must have been a grand, if not two, in the pile. He placed it on the floor beside him and pulled out another. This one was bound with a familiar paper strip, with £1k marked on it in black pen.

It was the same money he had given Leon, stolen from the Fill 'n' Save. Cooper shook his head. 'I don't understand.' He looked up at the masked figure again. This was the person who Leon called Whiteface. And he knew that Leon had never spoken to him, other than by text or distorted phone call. Cooper looked into the bag again. He pulled out another couple of wads of money to reveal a number of bags of pills beneath; far more than Cooper had been given to sell. This must have been Leon's stash.

'You want me to take Leon's place. Is that what this is about?'

Amy turned to look at Whiteface and he nodded. She turned back to Cooper, fresh tears tracking white lines down her dirty face.

'Please, just tell me why. Why me? I'm not—'

The figure in the mask shook their head. It was the smallest gesture, but enough for Cooper to pause, just long enough to notice that the person in the mask was doing more than just shaking their head.

They were also tapping their foot. It was so subtle, he could easily have missed it. In fact, for a moment he thought he might have imagined it, but then, once more, the figure's toes raised up before silently tapping out another rhythm.

Shave-and-a-haircut.

Jag.

No. It was impossible.

Bile rose in Cooper's throat.

Jag? He was the one who had killed Leon and was now holding his sister as hostage?

But . . . why? And why wasn't he saying anything? He obviously wanted Cooper to know it was him, so why not just take off the mask?

He looked up at Jag. Something was wrong. Something was very, very wrong.

Someone had made him do this. The same person who'd made Amy attack him in the churchyard.

And if that was true, it meant that the real Whiteface must be close by.

'OK,' Cooper said, zipping up the bag and taking a step back towards the grill, his hands empty as his eyes searched the shadows behind Jag, certain that they were being watched. 'How about I just finish selling what I've got and then—'

Jag shook his head again, this time in a more obvious fashion. He pointed at the bag, but his hand was shaking violently.

Cooper swallowed. His senses were on fire, his heart racing.

'You want me to take it?' he asked, unable to keep the fear from shaking his voice. The air was thick with the smell of diesel and the ripe aroma of Leon's cooked flesh.

Jag nodded, a little too hard. Like someone who was desperate to win a round of charades.

'OK.' Cooper zipped the bag and grabbed the handles. 'OK,' he repeated, his eyes darting from one corner of the warehouse to the other. He didn't want to leave Jag here, with Leon's remains and whatever or whoever was orchestrating this. He cleared his throat, trying but failing to inject a calm, yet authoritative tone to his voice. 'But you need to let Amy go first.'

Jag didn't move. His shoulders were rising and falling, his breathing much too fast. Just like Cooper's. He shook his head again.

'No!' Cooper cried. 'I'm not leaving without her!' His lips thinned against his teeth as anger began to override the terror coursing through his veins.

He stepped towards the oil drum, lifting the holdall as he did so.

'You hear me?' he shouted into the shadows. 'I'm not going anywhere without my sister.'

Jag didn't move. It didn't make any sense. None of it made any sense.

'Take the mask off,' he pleaded. 'I know it's you, Jag. Please, just take it off!'

Jag shook his head again, this time with more urgency.

'Fine,' Cooper roared. 'If no one's going to tell me what's going on, this can all burn.' He turned to the oil drum, lowering the bag into the flames.

'Wait.'

Cooper stopped. He turned to see Amy, the tape from her mouth gone. Her arms were no longer behind her back. In one hand she held the piece of tape that had been covering her mouth and in the other was a gun.

'Please,' Amy said, her voice way too calm. 'Just take the bag and go home, Sam.'

Cooper's eyes were fixed on the gun in his sister's hand. He couldn't seem to think or focus on anything else.

There had to be some mistake. Some explanation.

Cooper's fingers tightened around the handle and he pulled it back from the flames. 'Amy? What's going on?'

A clatter from the opposite corner of the warehouse broke the silence. Cooper turned. Jess? She was supposed to be waiting outside. When he looked back at his sister, his breath caught in his throat.

Amy was pointing the gun into the dark corner.

'Who's there?' She stepped forwards, tossing her blonde hair from her face as she peered into the shadows.

'Amy? What are—'

Spinning to face him, Amy started to shout. 'Shut up, Sam. Just shut the hell up. Jesus Christ, how stupid *are* you?'

Another clatter made Amy turn back to the corner of the warehouse. This time she fired off two rounds, her slim arms jerking expertly with each recoil as the shots rang out, deafening in the confines of the warehouse. Once the echoes had dispersed, Amy pointed the gun at Jag. 'I'm going to count to five,' she said with a sigh, as though the whole situation were boring her. 'And then I'm going to fire a bullet into his head. I suggest you come out and show your face, Jess.' She looked at Cooper. 'You just had to bring her, didn't you? It was bad enough when *he* was always hanging around like a bad smell,' she said, jerking her head to where Jag stood, his head shaking from side to side while a low moan escaped from beneath his mask. 'But now I have to put up with her as well?'

Cooper started to answer, but he was immediately cut off.

'And don't even think about running,' Amy snapped at Jag. 'Just like I told you before, if you even so much as fart without my permission, you get a bullet in the leg and a match to keep you warm.'

She levelled the gun. 'One,' she shouted, turning her

attention back to the corner of the warehouse and levelling the gun with Jag's eye. His shoulders began to hitch faster in time with his breathing.

'Amy.' Cooper dropped the bag. 'What the hell are you doing?'

'Shut up, Sam. Two.

'Three.' Her finger moved towards the trigger.

'Stop!' Jess emerged from the shadows, her hands held up in front of her body. 'Please, don't.'

Amy tucked the gun into the waistband of her jeans and held out her hand. 'Phone,' she snapped, clicking her fingers impatiently.

Glancing at Cooper, Jess reached into her pocket and pulled out her mobile. Amy snatched it from her fingers and dropped it to the ground, stamping on it and smashing the glass screen.

'Over there,' she said, waving the gun to where Jag stood by the oil drum. 'Go and get yourself warmed up by the fire.' She turned to Cooper. 'You couldn't just take the bag and go, could you?'

'I thought you were in trouble,' he said. He looked at where Jag stood with his arms now wrapped around Jess. 'But I guess I was wrong, huh?'

'I guess you were.' Amy grabbed the holdall and reached inside. She pulled out one of the bags filled with Nostalgex. 'These are all we need,' she whispered. 'You have no idea how many of these I have, Sam. We're going to be rich.'

'What are you talking about? Seriously Amy, I've got no

idea what's going on here. Did Leon make you do all this?'

'Seriously?' Amy laughed. 'That guy? Give me some credit, Sam. Leon's always been a loser, you know that.'

Cooper took the bag of pills. 'So where did you get these from?'

Snatching at the bag, Amy cursed as it split and a few of the pills scattered on the floor around them. She wrapped the plastic as best she could and shoved it back into the holdall. 'Well, I guess that is something I really should thank Leon for. Or maybe Frank.'

'Frank? He's back?'

'Unless you can come back from the dead,' Amy laughed, pulling the zipper of the holdall closed, 'then I'd say not.'

'Frank's dead?' Cooper's head was swimming, suddenly filled with images of Frank. Holding the gun to Leon's mouth. Drinking that glass of scotch, while blood dripped from his knuckles. 'How do you know?' Even as he asked the question, he started to feel sick.

'Well, Leon did the job with this,' she said, holding up the gun. 'And his barbecue pit did the rest.'

Nausea boiled and bubbled in Cooper's stomach. 'You burned him?'

'Nope, but I did make sure the fire stayed hot enough to get rid of any evidence. There's not much point in blackmailing someone if the police get there first, is there?'

'Shit.' Cooper shook his head. 'Shit.'

'Frank was a piece of shit,' Amy said. 'You saw what he did to Leon. He knocked his own son's teeth out for god's sake. You really think Leon wasn't going to snap eventually?'

'So he shot his own father?'

'Wouldn't you?'

'Of course not.' Cooper couldn't take his eyes from his sister. Who was this person? There had to be something else, someone else, making her do this.

But he could see the coldness in her eyes, the total lack of fear and empathy.

Amy shrugged. 'Then I guess being twins doesn't make us all that alike after all. Maybe you got Mum's genes and I got Dad's. That would make sense, given that I'm the one with the entrepreneurial skills.'

'Entrepreneurial skills? What?'

'Who do you think set this all up? You think Leon was smart enough to run something like this?' Amy pointed at the bag. 'This is only the beginning, Sam. I've got drugs and money stashed all over the East End. I've got fifty guys working for me. Leon's just the puppet.' She smiled regretfully. 'Or should I say he *was* the puppet. I mean come on, who's going to think a nine stone blonde girl is going to be able to handle a drugs ring?'

'What happened to Leon?' Cooper asked, his voice starting to sound slightly detached, like he was watching on from far away. This couldn't be happening. Not again. He couldn't be losing the last person on Earth he could truly call his family.

'Leon couldn't stand the heat,' Amy said, covering her mouth and giggling. 'Get it? Couldn't stand the heat.' When

292

Cooper only stared back, she sighed. 'Some of our dealers were getting slack,' she said. 'So we had to handle them. My choice of, shall we say, disposal, wasn't something that Leon was comfortable with.'

Cooper glanced at Leon's charred body and his stomach rolled. 'Your choice of disposal being fire?'

Amy shrugged. 'Shooting just seems so clichéd, don't you think? Besides, fire is the best way to destroy any evidence that might link back to the top. Anyway, Leon wanted out and I needed a new dealer. A new leader.'

'And you thought I would be the one to replace him?' It sounded like a question, but really it was a statement to himself. A way for him to try to understand what was happening.

'Why not? It's not like you've been a saint, Sam. Making a New Year's resolution to be a bit more sensible doesn't mean anything. You're a Cooper, it's in your blood. Just like it's in mine.'

'No,' Cooper spat. 'You know what I think about Dad. I'm not like him, Amy. And I thought you were different, too.'

Amy shrugged. 'Well, I'm sorry to disappoint, dear brother.'

'So it was you?' Jess cried. 'You were the one in the white mask at Scarlett's party? You set the fire?'

'Luke owed me money,' Amy snapped. 'It's not my fault that he was in someone else's house when his deadline came around. He knew the score. Anyway, we got him in the end, didn't we? Sends out a nice little message to any of my other dealers who think they can hold out on me.'

'And the Fill 'n' Save?' Cooper asked. 'Why? What did Phil ever do?'

'Collateral damage,' Amy replied. 'You don't think I was watching you that night? The night of your first big deal? I had to see if you had what it took. I saw everything, Sam. Couldn't have that fat git turning you in to the police when he found your bag of pills, could we? It would have ruined everything. Besides, it turned out for the best, didn't it? No evidence to tie you to the money you took.'

'You're crazy.' Jess was now sobbing. 'You're a murderer.'

Amy rolled her eyes. 'Seriously, Sam. You do pick the melodramatic ones, don't you?'

'None of this makes any sense,' Cooper said. 'Why me? Why get me involved with all this?'

'Because it's all for us, can't you see that? And I knew there'd be no way you'd join me without a little persuasion. I knew once you realized how much money we could make, you'd know it made sense.'

'So you persuaded me by smashing a bottle over my head? You set me up?'

'I really am sorry about that,' Amy said. 'But I had to make it realistic. Would you have started dealing if I'd just asked you pretty please with sugar on top? I knew it would take a while, but once you'd got a taste of the money, you'd see it was all worth it. Then we could be a team and things could go back to how they were when we—'

'What do you mean, things could go back to how they were? What the hell is wrong with you, Amy?'

'Oh please, like you don't miss it? The nice house, the nice clothes? Being able to *eat* when we wanted?' She grabbed the heart pendant that Cooper had bought her for Christmas. 'You think I can go through the rest of my life putting up with cheap crap that makes my skin turn green?'

'So you just decided the best course of action was to become a drug dealer?' Cooper whispered.

Amy lifted her chin in defiance. 'It was good enough for Dad.'

'Dad's in prison,' Cooper roared, grabbing the holdall. He reached inside and pulled out a bundle of cash. 'You want to know what I think of it all?' He turned and hurled the money at the oil can. It bounced once on the rim, span up into the air, then tumbled down into the flames.

'Are you a moron?' Amy screamed, grabbing for the bag handle, but missing.

Cooper pulled back and grabbed another bundle, tossing it into the flames. Then he lifted the whole bag and stepped towards the drum. 'Let them go,' he said, nodding to where Jag still stood with his arms around Jess. 'Let them both leave, or I'll dump the lot in the fire.'

Amy laughed. 'You think that's all I've got? There's more where that came from, Sam.' Her eyes narrowed. 'Put the bag down.'

'Let them go first.'

'I'm doing this for us,' she said, her voice softening.

'Can't you understand that? All of this has been for us, so we can be happy.'

'Don't listen to her,' Jess said. 'Don't fall for it.'

'You shut up,' Amy said, pointing the gun at Jess.

'Let them go,' Cooper repeated.

With a sigh, Amy turned to point the gun at Cooper. 'You're my brother and I love you, but don't for a second think I'm about to go to prison for you.'

Cooper started to lower the bag, flames licking at the base of the holdall. 'Let. Them. Go.'

'No.'

The shot rang out, as loud as an explosion. Jess screamed and covered her ears, while Jag pulled up his mask, revealing an ashen face and a mouth that, sure enough, was covered with gaffer tape.

Amy's shoulders were rising and falling, her hands still tightly clutching the gun that was still pointing at Cooper. Her eyes were wide, but she said nothing.

And Cooper looked down to see a black spot on his T-shirt that hadn't been there before. Lowering the bag to the ground he watched, mesmerized, as the spot grew.

The handles slipped from his fingers and the bag fell to the ground.

Moments later, he fell beside it.

JESS

With her scream still ringing in her ears, Jess rushed forwards to where Cooper lay on the ground, one hand on his belly, the other groping blindly at the ground around him, as though he couldn't quite work out why he was on the floor.

'Leave him,' Amy said, but her voice was weak.

Ignoring the gun that was still pointing in her direction, Jess lifted Cooper's shirt. Blood gushed from a hole an inch to the left of his belly button. He groaned, his eyes rolling. 'Quick,' Jess cried, turning to Jag. 'Bring me something to stop the bleeding.'

Ripping the gaffer tape from his mouth, Jag pulled the black hoodie over his head.

Amy had lowered the gun and it now dangled at her side as she watched on. 'I told him to put the bag down,' she murmured. 'I told him.'

Jess took the black fabric from Jag and bundled it tightly against the wound in Cooper's belly. He made no sound and Jess realized he had stopped moving. Rivulets of blood still streamed from all directions, but she couldn't push any harder. 'Help me,' she sobbed. Jag fell to his knees beside her and placed his hands over the top of hers. The additional pressure went some way to stemming the flow of blood, but it wasn't enough.

'He needs an ambulance,' Jag said. 'Please, Amy. He's your brother.'

Without taking her eyes from Cooper, Amy tucked the gun into her waistband then reached into her pocket and pulled out her phone. She moved slowly, awkwardly.

'I can't,' she said, as though in a daze. 'They'll send the police.'

'You think the police aren't already on their way?' Jess yelled. 'You don't think I called them from outside when I first saw the smoke?'

Amy paused. 'You're lying.'

'Listen,' Jess said. Somewhere in the distance, sirens wailed. 'Can you hear that? They're coming anyway, Amy. It's over. But you've still got the chance to do the right thing.'

Staring at the phone in her hand, Amy only shook her head. 'He'll be fine,' she said, though it sounded more like she was trying to convince herself. 'He'll be OK and then we can go home. To our real home.'

'He's going to die,' Jag snapped. 'I know you have very

little regard for human life, we've all seen that, but this is your *brother*. Are you really going to let him die over a bag of money and drugs?'

Amy's head snapped up and her eyes focussed once more. It was like Jag had spoken the magic words that had brought her back to life. 'It's not just money,' she spat. 'It's everything that was taken from us.' She stepped forwards and scooped up the bag, before walking towards the open shutter.

'You can't just leave,' Jess screamed. 'What's wrong with you? You're really just going to leave him here to die?'

'No,' Amy said. She turned to look back at them, and the reflection of the oil drum fire danced in her eyes. 'Not just him.'

Before she'd even pulled the gun from her waistband, Jag was on his feet and running towards her. Amy's eyes widened in surprise and she raised her empty hands to defend herself just as Jag threw himself forwards, his body colliding with hers in something resembling a rugby tackle. Jag's arms wrapped around her waist as his body propelled hers backwards and her tiny frame thudded heavily against the ground, the air shooting from her lungs with a whoosh.

She groaned, but Jag wasn't done. He was on his feet before she'd managed to regain her breath, dragging her up by her hair and pulling her back into the warehouse as she kicked and screamed.

'You're not going anywhere,' he snarled, his hand tangling tighter in her long blonde hair. She reached for her gun once more, but it had been knocked from her waistband in the struggle and lay on the concrete, glinting in the firelight.

'I'll kill you,' she shrieked, clawing at Jag's face. 'I'll kill all of you!' Her nails dug at his flesh and she dragged them down, gouging deep trenches into his cheek which filled quickly with blood.

Jess glanced back down at Cooper. His stomach was now entirely covered in blood and she could no longer see how much he was losing. Judging by the dark pool that was expanding beneath his body and moving towards her knees, she guessed it was too much.

'Don't die,' she whispered. 'Please, Sam. Don't die.' Taking one hand from the diesel- and blood-soaked hoodie, she touched his cheek. His eyelids fluttered and his mouth twitched.

She leaned down and touched her lips to his.

She barely felt it, but Jess was sure that Sam Cooper kissed her back.

Then he stopped moving altogether.

COOPER

The hem of her yellow dress lifted in the breeze as he followed her across the field. The colours were like nothing he'd ever witnessed before; the sky was the most incredible blue and there wasn't a cloud to be seen.

The sun was warm and the music was softer than he remembered, but perhaps that was because now he was only focussed on her. Just as he should have been then.

He wrapped his arms around her waist, his hands coming to rest on her stomach and he smiled as her hands covered his. Leaning down, he placed a kiss on her neck, her skin warm from the sun. Every nerve in his body was on fire, every sense and synapse seemed to be alive as she turned to face him and she was beautiful, the most beautiful thing he had ever seen.

'The band's going to start soon,' she said, though it was like her voice was coming from very far away. Not quite in time with the movement of her lips.

He leaned in to kiss her, his lips connecting with her cheek, the skin there so smooth he thought he could just sink right in and drown in her.

'You want to go and watch from the top of the hill?'

Cooper looked up at the hill, already covered with people on picnic blankets. Like ants covering the hillside. Then he looked back towards the stage, where steam was rising from the crowd, who were already pushing and shoving in an effort to get closer to the front.

'I'd like nothing more than to sit with you,' he said. 'For as long as you want.'

And she smiled as she leaned in to kiss him.

Her lips brushed against his and everything was white light and he was falling, falling.

And everything was perfect.

And then it was nothing.

JESS

Pulsing blue light filled the empty space of the warehouse, but Jess didn't move.

She barely noticed when they took Amy away, or when Jag sank to the ground beside her, resting his own head on Cooper's chest as he sobbed heavily. She said nothing when Jag was led away.

Even when the nice female officer came and placed a blanket around her shoulders, telling her it was time to go, she didn't move. She didn't hear what the officer said to her, because by then the Nostalgex she had found on the floor was coursing through her bloodstream.

She'd only taken two, just enough to escape for a while. Just until she was ready.

She was comfortable there, even though her legs were asleep from kneeling on the concrete and her back ached from where she had crouched over Cooper for so long, in an attempt to stop the blood that had eventually stopped on its own, when Cooper's heart had ceased trying to pump it around his body.

And though Cooper's hand was now cold in her own, she continued to lay her head on his body, her ear pressed against his still chest, listening to the sound of nothing.

She knew she would have to move eventually and she knew that the big black dog was somewhere nearby, just as he had been so often over the last few days. But he would have to wait.

Right now, she was lying in the park with Cooper while clouds drifted overhead, laughing as he insisted the huge white cumulus directly above them was shaped like a penguin.

'I should go,' she sighed, looking at her watch. 'I have to get an essay finished for tomorrow. And you do, too.'

He turned to lie on his side, one of his legs wrapping around hers and his hand coming to rest gently on her stomach. 'Just a while longer. Please?'

'I'm sorry,' she said, smiling as he pouted at her.

He leaned in to kiss her. 'Whatever you want,' he said. 'But I think I'll just lie here a little longer.'

Jess opened her eyes, to see the pulsing blue lights and the policewoman waiting patiently beside her.

'You take as long as you need,' she whispered.

Then she was done and the big black dog came in for its attack.

304

JESS

Jag wiped away the tears with the sleeve of his black suit.

'And then,' he said, dissolving into another fit of laughter, 'he got that bike of his up on the wall around the fountain. You remember, when someone put all that Fairy Liquid into it?'

Jess nodded, also unable to contain her laughter. Jag had kept her smiling all afternoon and, apart from the funeral itself, she was happier than she'd felt in a while. On the sofa beside her, Scarlett giggled along, her shoulders bouncing as she laughed. Though still fragile from her hospital stay, she had put on a little weight in recent days, so her bones no longer jutted quite as alarmingly as when she was first discharged.

'Anyway,' Jag continued, 'there's all these girls there, sunbathing on blankets and watching this guy who's been doing wheelies and whatever else it was he was trying to impress them with, and they all watch him get up on the wall of the fountain. But the thing is, whoever put the washing-up liquid in the fountain had spilled it on the wall, too. So he goes to do a wheelie and the back wheel slips in the washing-up liquid, and he goes arse over tit into the fountain.'

Jag collapsed back against the couch, shaking with laughter once more. 'I'm telling you, Jess, it was the funniest thing I've ever seen.'

Now crying herself, Jess could barely contain the fit of giggles that was almost stopping her from breathing.

'Did he get wet?' Scarlett asked.

'Did he get wet?' Jag roared. 'He came out of that thing soaked head to toe and covered in bubbles like some kind of mutant from a comic book.'

'Bubble boy,' Jess laughed.

'That's it. Proper superhero.' Jag's laughter began to fade and for the first time since they'd left the church, he looked truly sad. 'He was my hero, though. You know what I mean?'

Jess nodded, forcing a smile as Scarlett gave her hand a little squeeze. 'Yeah. I know.'

'Like, he didn't have an easy ride of it, what with his mum and dad being locked up. But he did the best with what he had.' He looked at Jess. 'And I know he never told you about that, but he was embarrassed, you know? He thought so much of you and it killed him to think you might judge him for what they did.'

'And maybe he had a point,' Jess said. 'Maybe I would have done, back then.'

'Yeah,' said Scarlett. 'But you know what? I think we've all changed over the last couple of years.'

'So,' Jag said, clutching his mug as he leaned forwards in his seat. 'What do you think Coop would have done? You know, if none of this stuff had happened. You think he'd have kept straight?'

Jess smiled. 'I think so. He loved Amy so much. I think he'd have done it for her.'

'It's crazy,' Jag said, slowly exhaling. 'Still can't get my head around it. I know she was never my greatest fan, but I really thought she loved Cooper.'

'Who knows what really goes on in people's minds? Look at Luke. I thought I knew him, but he was a total stranger.'

'Have you seen Hannah?' Jag asked.

Jess shook her head. 'They went to stay with her grandparents in Wales until the house gets sorted. I don't even know if she's coming back.'

There was a moment of silence, then Jag cleared his throat and got to his feet. 'I should get off,' he said. 'But hey, are you guys around later? I was thinking of taking a walk through the park. You know, round by the fountain?'

Jess glanced at Scarlett, who was nodding enthusiastically. 'I don't know,' she said. 'It sounds great, but . . .' Her voice tailed off.

'It's no big deal,' Jag said with a shrug. 'Just text me if

you want to come.' He leaned forwards and planted kisses on Jess and Scarlett's cheeks.

'Thanks, Jag.'

'Actually, I should be going as well.' Scarlett went to stand up and Jag reached out a hand to help her to her feet. She turned to Jess. 'Text me later, OK?'

Jess nodded and followed them to the front door. When they were gone and she was finally alone, she walked through the empty hallway and up to her bedroom. It was only mid-afternoon, but it felt like the middle of the night.

She was exhausted.

She sat at her dressing table and reached for a wipe to remove her makeup. Everything on her body was a reminder of the funeral and she wanted it all gone, to strip herself of the day.

As she pulled one of the wipes across her eye, she paused.

In the mirror, she could see the reflection of Cooper's jacket hanging on the back of her door. Jess turned in her seat and for a moment only stared. She stood up and took the jacket from the hook, pulling it tightly around herself. His scent was already fading, but still she lifted the material to her face and breathed deeply.

He'd never once asked for it back.

And now there was nobody left to give it to.

Jess placed her hands into the pockets and her fingers brushed against something. She scooped up the objects and pulled them out.

Three Nostalgex pills.

Jess stared at the drugs, bright red against the palm of her hand. On the dressing table, her phone beeped, but she didn't bother to look at it. Instead, she grabbed the phone and walked to the bathroom, clutching the pills tightly.

An empty glass stood on the shelf above the sink. She placed her phone on the shelf, filled the glass with water, then glanced at her reflection in the mirror.

This would be the last time, she told herself.

One last visit to see Cooper. She would study his face, the way he moved, the sound of his voice – she'd memorize it all and then she could begin to move on.

Just one more time.

She lifted the pills to her lips, and her phone beeped again, stopping her from tossing the pills into her mouth.

She glanced down to see a message from Jag. Then she lowered her hand.

What was she *really* trying to achieve by taking the drugs? However she tried to justify it, the truth was that the Nostalgex was nothing but a temporary fix. It wasn't real, and she would never move on if she kept trying to grasp on to the past. No matter how many pills she took, time would continue to slip through her fingers like sand and she would never, ever be able to return to a time when Cooper was alive.

Jess tried to swallow, but there was a lump in her throat and her reflection was blurred by the tears she thought she'd already cried dry.

Cooper was gone, but she was still alive and she wasn't going to spend her life chasing after a happiness that was already behind her.

There would be more happiness.

New memories.

She picked up her phone and opened Jag's text.

Going to the park now, before it gets too dark. Let us know if u want to come.

Jess exhaled, took one last look at the pills, then dropped them into the toilet and flushed them away. Then she zipped up Cooper's jacket and typed a quick reply.

Sounds great. I'm on my way.

Acknowledgements

As always, I must thank my wonderful agent Stephanie Thwaites, for listening to me rambling about anything and everything, book related or not! My incredible, enthusiastic and very lovely editor, Naomi Greenwood, who is always ready to meet for coffee, chats and diabolical plotting sessions. I'm so very, very lucky to have you! Also to all the people at Hodder who have helped shape *The Memory Hit* into what it is today. Big shout out to 'Team Hodder': Sarah Mussi and Taran Matharu, two fantastic, inspiring authors. It's been a pleasure, guys. Also thank you to the fab PJ and all at AuthorProfile for helping to make me slightly less of a luddite. I'm sorry for laughing during the voice coaching sessions. (Not sorry at all. It was hilarious!)

Sophy, my wonderful, patient, inspiring friend. Where would I be today if it weren't for you? I love you.

To my three amigos, Jo, Clare and Amanda. I love you all and, my god, are we going to celebrate in style very very soon! I don't know what I would do without you. Also to Kenny, Andy and Nick, for your patience and understanding when it's time for us to do our thang!

Mads, you complete and utter beauty – thank you for always being at the end of the phone. It's meant the world to me. Love you, gorgeous girl!

To Noah 'Shitbag' Kelly . . . No insult is big enough, you complete and utter toolbag. I'd say how awesome you are, but you'd only tell me to piss off, so I'll just say nothing. To the talented Nick Bradley – one day soon it'll be my turn to say お疲れ様でした! Until then, keep putting pen to paper. You've got this, Bradders! And thank you for the support in battling against the night babies, the day babies and the doubt babies. One day we'll win the war.

Kelly Quirke, you've been amazing. Thank you for all the support with absolutely everything! You're a star.

Vicky and Billy Willcock – I'm most definitely going to write the book we discussed, though I'll deny that Billy had anything to do with it. I'll give him credit for the front cover, though! Oh, and Vics . . . Black vodka, baby!

Naomi Doran and Steph Corley, my wonderful Cav girls. No matter how much time passes, it's always like yesterday. Love you both.

Chas, your support has, and always will be appreciated.

Mum and Dad, Matt and Sophia (and little Mr Bump!) . . . I love you all. Mum and Dad, there isn't enough ink in the world for me to say what I need to, so instead I'll just do my best to show you my gratitude, every single day. I love you, I love you, I love you.

And finally, to my pal Foot Foot . . . Thank you for everything.

I've landed.